The Buffalo Scout

STEPHEN MCDONALD

Published by Richter Publishing LLC www.richterpublishing.com

Book Cover Design: Richter Publishing & images from Shutterstock

Editors: Haley Morton, Margarita Martinez & Monica San Nicolas

Book Formatting: Monica San Nicolas

ISBN: 978-1-954094-10-9

DISCLAIMER

DEDICATION

To Earl McDonald, the best cowboy I have ever known, and Mattie McDonald, the mother who raised me to be all that I am.

CONTENTS

PREFACE

Just outside the three Indians' camp, I was kneeling with three arrows in place for speed shooting. I sited in just left of the far Indian's heart, and with the swiftness of a well-trained warrior, within ten seconds, all three Indians were in great pain as I approached to take my vengeance for the murder of my friend Sleeping Bird.

INTRODUCTION

This book is a work of historical fiction following a character's life starting in his homeland of Africa in the mid-1800s. His journey to America was not of his choice. The hardships he endured in his efforts to survive and always be a noble warrior are not intended to represent historical facts or any character ever portrayed in any literary form.

Today, it is hard to imagine how difficult life was in the 1800s, in what was then still the unsettled American West. There were those coming to seek fortune, fame, or a new start. Many had a lot to forget, while others wanted to remember their homeland.

Slavery was the American way back in those days, and although the importation of slaves had been banned in the 1700s, some slave traders continued to smuggle African people into the United States. The slave trade market was a very lucrative business for those with the resources and audacity to steal people, chain them up, and bring them to America to be sold for a profit.

During that era, many slaves overcame adversity and found a new way, a better way to live in the America they were forced to call home. American history gives accounts of many of these people's accomplishments, but we can only assume that most have never been recorded.

This story follows the success of one man who escaped slavery, made his way west, and became a legend. I introduce you to the fictional character: "the Buffalo Scout."

CHAPTER 1: CALL TO DUTY

I'm known out here in New Mexico as the Buffalo Scout. I have been scouting and bringing in criminals for the U.S. government for more than ten years, and I have been very successful at doing both. I had lived through many tragic and painful events to get there. The general gave me a mission to find some gun runners that had been selling to the Apaches for several years. Three groups of army patrols had attempted to capture them, but all came back empty-handed.

I knew I needed to succeed on this mission because, as immigrants arrived on the East Coast and migrated west as settlers, they depended on the army for safe passage through the unsettled parts of the country. The army took great pride in ensuring that those settlers made it to their chosen destination. Stopping the source of guns being sold to Indians would help the army protect the settlers.

The general told me that he had confidence that I could capture the gun runners. He wanted them alive, if possible. I didn't like killing criminals, so I had no issue with him wanting them captured. I had left the fort about three weeks before, picked up their trail over a week ago, and had been following it ever since while keeping a keen eye on the surrounding area because it was Apache territory. At times, the trail just seemed to disappear. I knew this territory well, so I was able to make a very educated guess as to where the gun runners were headed.

My trusted black stallion, Ole Lightning, had been with me on many assignments, and he had saved my life a time or two. There were not many horses who possessed his special training. I had used the knowledge I learned about horses on the plantation in Mississippi to breed fine horses until I lucked out on this magnificent stallion. Together, my best friend Jose and I had taught Ole Lightning many tricks and that training had proven to be very helpful throughout the years.

Indians adored my horse and had made several attempts to steal him. But there was one thing I knew for sure: they would never take him from me. I pitied the foolish Indian that tried to take Ole Lightning or attempted to ride him. I had seen the remains of several braves that had tried.

Me and Ole Lightning were patient and very deliberate in how we pursued these gun runners. Even so, they had tested our abilities. I had even thought about giving up, but that was not what a warrior did. We just keep tracking, knowing that the further that we got into the Apache territory, the greater the chance that we might not make it home. If a lone rider was spotted by Apaches out in the open, he was probably going to die a terrible death. I always traveled a path close to the rocks so that I would have a defendable position if I got attacked by the Apaches. This made the trip longer, but my staying alive was much more important.

There was not much of interest to look at in this desert like area, so staying alert was hard. I was sitting up straight, adjusting my posture, cracking my neck to try to keep my muscles sharp. I couldn't afford to lose focus, so I forced these negative thoughts out of my mind. With the rocks blurring on for what seemed like forever in front of me, I found my mind wandering to the adventures that got me here.

Me and Ole Lightning had been tested by the meanest Indians and criminals in this territory, and we had left them dead, wishing for death or just thanking God they were still alive. I thought of some of the battles I survived. After one such battle, I was riding along rocks like these with an Indian chief who told me that I had gifts that western Indians admired. Indians believed that the white man would never know how to get one over on me because of those gifts. Gifts like tracking the way Indians did, the keen survival instincts that brought me from Mississippi all the way out west with the white man hunting me, and a supernatural ability to read the land. Some Indians said they thought I was a sort of god, but I knew that was certainly not true.

I am black, with black, curly hair. Indians call black soldiers "buffalo soldiers" because of how our curly hair resembled the hair on the necks of buffalos. This hair might have been something special to them, but it had done little to help us as a people, forced to come to America and then abandoned when slavery was abolished. All of us were forced to find a way to survive or die here.

The Lakota Indians had given me the nickname that I was so proud of, "Buffalo Scout." That nickname is the only part of the little fame I've acquired that becomes me. Being a western legend can strike fear into your enemies, but to me, it's better to be unknown. I liked the solitude of the open trail, having the sky as my roof and the stars as my nighttime companions. It was the best environment for me and Ole Lightning to take care of each other.

Mostly, the excitement of tracking the scoundrels that I brought to justice gave me that warm feeling within my heart that I had so longed for. I needed to forget, even just for a few moments, the life I was once forced to live in slavery. And tracking keeps my mind busy; keeps me focused on what's right in front of me, rather than the bloody remnants of my past.

I came to America as a boy of about sixteen years old. I still had nightmares about being captured, chained, and brought to America in that death-pit that they called a ship. So many of the captives did not survive the trip. I shuddered in my saddle thinking about how ashamed I felt when I thought of how the stronger African tribes would capture and sell the weaker tribes to the slave traders. Ole Lightning felt me squirm and huffed a little. A smile crept into the corners of my mouth again at the thought of this horse knowing me so well.

I took great pride in knowing that I freed myself from slavery. By the grace of God, I had made my way out west while the majority of runaway slaves fled north. The Underground Railroad was a great organization, yet I felt I stood a better chance being alone in the West rather than trying to survive the journey north and then having to survive in cold Canada country.

I've always been a survivor, from my boyhood in Africa, when I was a skilled hunter, and my warrior skills were advanced for a boy of my age. As a slave, I was chained and beaten, but I never let my thoughts be imprisoned. In the end, I showed them how determined I was to be free. Those thoughts are still with me now, out working for the U.S. Army with my freedom.

I was a survivor, and I had no fear of anything that walked the earth. The overseers would do anything to break a slave's spirit and gain control of him. I behaved as they asked to keep them from killing me or beating other slaves that I had come to somewhat accept as family.

For most slaves, the many years of slavery came to an end during the Civil War. Man, did those southern states fight to maintain the lifestyle they had become accustomed to, much of which depended on having slaves do their work while they profited. The abuse ensured that slaves could not become educated, comfortable, or proud enough to make an attempt to change the situation they were in. The Civil War was proof that Southerners felt justified in this treatment.

It had always been odd to me that they thought of the slaves as animals and less than human, yet the masters and male overseers were all too comfortable with having slave women as bed wenches. How selfish they were. It served them right that some of the white women fancied being serviced by the black bucks (as slave men were called).

White women were shunned, beaten, and some killed for being with a black buck; this included any babies they birthed. Yet, the babies born to the slave women were kept alive and enslaved. If it weren't so horrifying, I would have laughed at the hypocrisy of it all.

I could feel Ole Lightning getting agitated beneath me and realized I had completely tensed up from being so deep in my own tragic past. I rolled my neck again and patted his neck "Sorry, Lightning, I was back in Mississippi. I'm here now." He whinnied in return. "God, this horse is special." I focused back in on the task at hand, repeating the general's words in my head: "Bring them back *alive*. These men will pay for their crimes. I want to see the whites of their eyes. You hear me?" I heard him loud and clear.

I had ridden about ten miles so far today and had not seen much that would help me find the trail of the gun runners. There were fewer rocks in the area, but they were large enough to provide some protection if I got attacked. I felt that I was within a few miles of a known Apache camp so if I didn't find something soon, I would be taking a big risk in moving too much further ahead. As if he were listening to my thoughts, a moment later, Ole Lightning moved ahead without me urging him, so I knew he sensed something that I couldn't. As we approached a small rocky area, I noticed some interesting tracks. There were six sets of shod horse tracks entering and leaving a campsite, the remains of a fire, and evidence that someone had eaten in the area. Two sets of the horse tracks appeared to have made a slightly deeper impression in the soft sand than the other four sets of tracks. This all added up to it being the gun runners. As I stopped Ole Lightning to check the signs, I said to myself as I pulled back on the reins, "These old boys we be tracking are very smart. They're good at covering their trails, they wouldn't just leave a camp so obviously used, so I have to be very diligent in checking everything that's out of place or disturbed."

This was Apache country, so I took the time to scan the landscape to make sure it was safe to dismount.

As I walked around the campsite, I said, "Oh, would you look at this? They be some smart ones, but I'm smarter. These signs indicate that they camped here last night, yet there are no signs of a man peeing or taking a crap, and there are no signs of horses doing the same. Ole partner, looks as if they want us to believe that they camped here. If they did, they also did something else here that they don't want us to know about.

"I think I'll just spend a little more time here to make sure I'm not missing anything important. Could be the difference between me living or dying. Besides, once the sun is shining from a different angle, we may just discover what those scoundrels are up to. It is close enough to dinner hour anyway, and that ole sun is showing out today. It doesn't help any that this desert area seems to just swallow up any breeze that tries to cross it."

An hour or more later, I was feeling better after eating and feeding Ole Lightning. Our water was running low, so I didn't drink much of it. Ole Lightning needed it more than I did, and he nickered as if he agreed. I smiled and kept checking our surroundings, looking for signs of trouble. Nothing happened, so I thought, *we cannot catch them guys if we don't get back to chasing them, so I'll take one more look at these tracks and study this campsite a bit more before we leave*. Something was off, I needed to figure out what it was before too long.

Once I started walking around the camp again, Ole Lightning was smelling the sand near the horse tracks and I noticed his ears flicker as he stamped and pawed the sand near the tracks. I saw what he was pawing at, but I was too focused on what I was doing to see anything. As I refocused on what I was doing I saw the tumbleweed. I couldn't believe I had overlooked it earlier. Talking to myself, I said "well, well, what do you know? One lone tumbleweed bush out here in the middle of all of these rocks and this sea of desert sand doesn't make sense because there isn't a tree or water hole within ten miles of this place."

I looked at Ole Lightning and said, "Now we have some serious sign-reading to do because this tumbleweed being here is very odd and hard to figure." He looked at me and his ears flickered as if he was telling me that I was onto something now.

Sometimes your ole eyes will play tricks on you, causing you to not see something that is right there in front of them. I resolved to move around it in a circle to view the shadow from different angles. I learned this trick from the Cherokee Indians and their good mountain-man friend that they called Moose Fighter. With a little luck, the answer will become visible from one angle or another. I circled the tumbleweed slowly, being sure to not miss anything.

"Well look at what just came to view. Those ole rascals sure are good at covering their tracks. This ole tumbleweed seems to be fixed in place by something. Appears that it is a marker of some sort." I started to dig around it, looking for the answer.

I said, "Ole Lightning, you best keep a keen watch for us because I'm mighty busy figuring this one out."

Ole Lightning nickered as if to respond to me, so all I could think to say was, "What a horse," as the grin on my face got bigger.

My hands moved through the sand quickly until they hit a piece of rough, thick twine that was taut when pulled. I tugged a little harder on it, still no budge. It had to be attaching this tumbleweed to something pretty heavy buried here. I couldn't pull it up, so it had to be something of considerable size. That was when I noticed that the soils had been disturbed in a sizeable area around the tumbleweed. "Oh gosh, that is what Ole Lightning was trying to point out to me by pawing the soil". I didn't have the words to praise this horse, so I just said, "Thank you, Lord."

I stood, wiped my hands on my pants, and took the two steps to Ole Lightning to get my military shovel. I pulled it out and got to work digging around the string. This digging was not something I liked, but at least this time I was not planting no damn cotton seeds or dead bodies. I was certain that there was something buried here that would help me capture the gun runners.

As I dug, I could tell that the soil had been disturbed in a sizable area around the string. I could tell that it had been disturbed recently, because it was coming up much easier than I anticipated.

After removing a foot or so of soil, the shovel hit something solid. I looked at Ole Lightning and said, "Looks like we hit pay dirt this time. This ole shovel just struck something solid, and that tells me that the digging is almost over." It only took a few minutes to uncover the anchor-point for the string.

The string was tied to the top of a crate labeled "Winchesters" in faded letters. "My, my, those ole rascals went and buried the crates of guns." I stood up to check our surroundings again and have a sip of water. As I looked at the horse tracks leaving the campsite, I could tell that two sets of the tracks were deeper than the rest, but not quite as deep as the ones entering the campsite. On horseback, a rider probable couldn't see that slight difference. I was thinking, I couldn't have come up with a plan this deceptive if I had a year to think about it. These ole boys had buried the rifles right here, covered their tracks, and disappeared. I snapped my fingers as I said, "That was how they'd been outfoxing the army all of these years."

Had I not discovered this, even if I were to catch them, there would be no evidence that they were the gun runners, since all their guns were buried in the ground miles away. No evidence, no way to bring them to justice.

Sadly, I realized I had a lot more digging to do. I kept digging until I had uncovered four crates of guns plus several boxes of rifle cartridges. I opened one crate to verify that it contained the repeating rifles as the crate was labeled. The guns were new and still wrapped in the protective paper. This was what I was looking for so now I needed to find and capture the men that buried them here. I stood up, wiped the sweat off my forehead and began to hatch a plan. I needed to do some serious thinking to get these ole scoundrels. They were too good for me to call them rascals anymore. They were some smart scoundrels. I took a good drink from the canteen, allowing myself the luxury despite us running low as a victory for finding the guns. All the while scanning the surrounding area for any signs of danger. I didn't see anything and Ole Lightning didn't sense anything, so he was standing alert while I was thinking.

I thought, *if I was them and I had buried the guns, I would be planning on coming back to get them, or maybe the Apaches knew the location and that the tumbleweed was the location of the guns.* No, that part didn't work. If the Apaches knew of the location, they could watch the gun runners ride off and then ride in and dig up the guns. Those scoundrels would be back, and we were going to nail them this time. With some luck, we would get a few of those renegade Apaches as well.

After about five minutes of thinking I resolved to open all the crates and remove the firing pins from the rifles so they could not be fired, then load all the cartridges into my saddle bags. The crates with guns were too heavy to move alone, but I couldn't let the gun runners find them too easily even if they were pretty harmless without their firing pins. I removed the crate tops and set to work on the rifles, using nimble fingers to quickly remove the firing pins, my sweat picking up dust as it ran down my face. I had to keep wiping it away to keep it out of my eyes. I set the lone crate lid, tied to the tumbleweed aside to bury in a new hole I would dig, hoping that no one would know that it had been moved. I buried this crate lid near the hole where the guns were actually buried. I chose a location that was equal distance from the horse tracks as the tumbleweed was when I found it. I dug my hole about the same size as the one the guns are buried to help fool them. I use some of the protective paper as a makeshift lid for the one I buried in my hole and covered the gun crates. I spent some time stomping the soil to make it look as much like the natural soils around it. I walked and had Ole Lightning walk around on that area to make it harder for someone to know the soils had been disturbed. I made sure everything looked just like what I found when I discovered the tumbleweed marker, taking care to remove all of my tracks to make it look like no one has been here, except to ride through, check the signs they left for a pursuer to find and continue in pursuit of the gun runners. And, because I don't like to take any chances, I even planted some dynamite around the campsite in places that I was sure that I could hit from my defensive location with my old trusted Henry buffalo rifle.

While scanning my surroundings earlier, I had chosen some rocks just east of the campsite that would be a good defensive position. They were far enough away to keep the gun runners' horses from smelling Ole Lightning, so I took one last look to make sure everything was the way they left it. We left the campsite following their trail to convince them that their secret was still a secret. I would double back and make our way to the defensive position and wait to see what happens.

As I followed their false trail, I was thinking, planning the battle that was destined to happen. With a lot of bad luck, the Apaches will come for the guns, discover that they are not where the marker was, and they will go back to kill the gun runners. With a little good luck, we would capture the gun runners when they return for the guns. With a lot of good luck, the Apaches would come with the gun runners and I would be able to Kill some Apaches and capture at least one of the gun runners to take back. That way, the general could get some much-needed information from him. These scoundrels were just the delivery men, so the army needed to capture the leaders if we were to ever stop them.

By the time I doubled back and got settled down in the rocks, the sun was still hot and beating, but it would be setting in about an hour or so. There was no shade within miles so I staked Ole Lightning down close behind some larger rocks so at least when the sun got closer to the horizon his legs and torso might get some shade. It wasn't much, but it was the best that could be done. Ole Lightning was sensing that we would be waiting for a while so he let his eyes close for a little nap. His senses were much keener than a man's so if anyone approached the area, he would alert me.

I didn't expect anything to happen before morning, but these ole boys had pulled some fancy tricks and had done some very peculiar things. Those false trails, the confusing campsite, and burying the guns were unusual tactics for gun runners. I had their guns now, so as long as I played this hand right, it would be hard for me to lose.

The sun was close to setting and the few clouds streaked light across the sky in oranges and reds. I stood up on the tallest rock to check my surroundings and look for smoke signals. The desert looked like a dream today, like it was impossible that there was a single other soul out there. The quiet was comforting so I was sure nothing would happen until tomorrow morning. Now was my chance to rest so I had my edge when the fight came. I needed to take a nap while the sun was setting. I couldn't risk having a fire to help me stay alert during the night, and I couldn't afford to doze off during the night, because many men had died at the hands of night-crawling snakes and scorpions that crept close when there was no fire burning.

So, I lay down as the light faded under the horizon, watching it go, trying to calm my mind enough for sleep. But the gun runners kept coming back to the front of my mind. Some said they had eluded being captured because they were a group of ex-soldiers and a highly-decorated Lakota Indian scout. Judging by some of the tricks they had used, I could believe that they knew the army's tactics, so they had planned their deliveries to avoid the army patrols.

I got a little nap and with the sun fully set, the heat disappeared with the light so that woke me. The light from the moon was nearly unfiltered by clouds. It was nearly bright out even without a fire and I could see far into the horizon. It was a good night for a fire if there ever had to be one, but I couldn't take that chance in Apache territory.

I figured they hid the guns because they knew someone was on their trail. At least, I was certainly hoping that's why they buried them. If that wasn't the reason, they could have easily been spying on everything that I had done that day.

I discounted that thought since they had made no attempt to stop me or jump me. I felt that I still had the advantage. Those ole boys were used to the army sending soldiers or Indian scouts after them, but I wasn't a normal army scout. The gun runners might've known military protocol, but they didn't know me. I always got my man, and I did it my way. And my way worked. Worked so well that I was the best scout that the army had in this area. These gun runners didn't know I was after them, which is exactly the edge I needed. They were in for a big surprise, courtesy of Ole Lightning and me. Now all we had to do was wait to see what happened.

I ate my field rations, fed Ole Lightning and gave him some more water. The moon was shining very brightly so I chanced getting a little more sleep since Ole Lightning was within ten feet of my resting place and nothing was going to sneak up on him. I woke up about an hour later, still hungry, so I had some more hardtack, cheese, and crackers to quiet my growling stomach. I'd managed to get a rabbit yesterday, so the trail food that I had would do for a day or more.

Most man-hunters hated waiting, but not me. The waiting was like freedom. I didn't have to do anything, be anywhere, or care about anything except waiting. I had plenty of time to check my guns and sharpen my cavalry sword and my other knives. Too many men lose their lives because they don't take proper care of their weapons. I had been taught that as a boy back in Africa, and it was a lesson I learned the importance of early.

Long ago, I'd started carrying a minimum of four pistols, a standard rifle, and the Henry buffalo repeater rifle. Yes, it was extra weight for Ole Lightning, but he was used to carrying it for short periods of time like now. That was why I had him and why I took such great care of him.

We'd started out from the fort with a packhorse who had carried the extra weaponry for most of the trip. As we traveled, the packhorse's load was lessened as I hid food, water, and other supplies along the return trail, just as the Cherokee Indians had taught me. If I had to return on foot, the supplies would be a lifesaver.

That packhorse was relaxing in a box canyon that no other living man, including Indians, knew about. I hoped he was not too fat to do his work when we got back there. Thanks to him, though, Ole Lightning had only been carrying the extra guns and supplies the last couple of days, and he didn't mind at all.

I'd learned of that hidden canyon several years back when I'd needed a safe place to hide while on the run from Apaches. My ole trapper friend—the one the Indians called Tall Knives—had discovered it years before and kept it a secret. I rescued him from a band of Apaches, and he took us there to hide until they gave up looking for us.

Tall Knives survived many battles to die a happy old man of natural causes. I buried him there, in the canyon, and I went by a couple of times a year to tend to his grave.

When these Indian uprisings were over and I felt like giving up scouting for the army, I planned to build a home near the canyon and live out my later years there. I was in my thirties now, so I had lots of time to do all of that. Right now, I was going to wait for company.

I got up to make sure Ole Lightning was okay. As I patted him on the nose, I told him, "You are on watch, so stay alert." He flickered his ears and nudged me with his nose as if to let me know that he understood.

We seemed to still be alone, and I figured it was just past midnight. I would stay awake the rest of what turned out to be a peaceful night.

It was a beautiful sunrise, and was already warmer than I liked. I was hoping it would be a very hot day because Apaches were human and they tended to stay in the shade when it was very hot. That would mean that fewer of them would show up to get the guns, making the odds better for me.

I watered Ole Lightning and fed him some grain because I figured that we would be riding out of this place in a hurry. I was ready for the battle and waiting. Then, about an hour after sunrise, I could see smoke signals in the distant sky south of me. Since I had spent time with both the Cherokee and Lakota Indians, I could understand the smoke signals, and that was very helpful when one was scouting and fighting Apaches.

After reading the smoke signals, I told Ole Lightning, "We will be having company this morning, so keep quiet and rest. I just don't know how quickly we may have to ride out of this place to save our hides if things don't go as I hope they will." As I looked at my horse, I felt a little guilty for leaving him saddled all night, but it was the safest thing to do during a stake-out in Apache territory.

I climbed to the top of the largest rock to get a better view of the area. The Apaches could come from several directions and although I had a good defensive position, the last thing I wanted to do was get caught in a crossfire and have no way to escape. Once I saw the dust of the horses approaching from the south, I checked the other directions for more and saw none. By the time I could see the approaching horses I felt like I had waited all day, but it was still early morning, the sun only a short distance above the eastern horizon. Once they were within a mile of the campsite, I could see that it was several Apaches with extra horses, probably for carrying the guns. I could also see some additional riders approaching from another direction. I rubbed my eyes to make sure I wasn't imagining it. They were still there. How had I missed them? As they got closer, I noticed that they were walking their horses which causes much less dust and that they had appeared from over a ridge just southwest of the campsite. It was obvious that they were going to meet at the campsite. I took another quick look around to make sure they were the only groups of approaching riders.

The first part of my plan was in play and I was certain that they already knew that someone had visited the campsite because I'd made no attempt to hide the tracks I made on the way in and out of the campsite. I had followed the general path that the gun runners had taken when they left the camp. They left a false trail to lead a pursuer into a trap and once I knew that, I back-tracked until I could take an alternate route to get back to the campsite. Based on how the groups were not at all cautious as they approached the camp, my trick appeared to have worked.

As the second group of riders got within a half mile of the campsite, I could see that the second group was not all Apaches. There appeared to be four Apaches, three white men, and another Indian. I thought that was odd, so I focused more on him because there was something familiar about how he sat in the saddle. My mind put all of the pieces in the right places and I was sure that person was Many Trails, the Lakota Indian scout who I had ridden with on military campaigns. The army's suspicion that the gang included some of their own was now a reality. With the scout on their side, it was easy to understand how they had been able to elude all the teams that the army had sent to capture them. Additionally, with him being an Indian, it was easier for the gang to communicate with Apaches.

The scout knew all the army's tricks and tactics. If he was part of the gang, it was most likely that the army officer that had deserted more than a year ago was part of the gang as well, but none of the men look like the officer. He and the Indian scout were a team, so the general suspected foul play and had rewards posted for their capture. It was seldom that I wanted to see anyone get killed but, for those traitors, death was deserved, and I didn't care how it came to them.

Two of the gun runners continued to the campsite with some of the Apaches, while the other gun runner, the Indian Scout and three of the Apaches waited about one hundred yards away.

Being only about two hundred yards away from the campsite, I felt that I could easily shoot the three Apaches before they would understand that Ole Henry was sending lead their way. The Indian scout and gun runner would be easy targets as well if they elected to try riding off.

It was well documented that the man with his back to the sun had the edge, so I had purposely set up my ambush position on the east side of the campsite to have the sun behind me and in their faces, should they spot me and start shooting. My rifle barrels were coated with a substance that prevented glare caused by sunlight, so it would be hard for them to spot me in my rock fortress that way. But it was hard to coat field glasses, so I had to handle them in a way that minimized the reflection. But even so, by the time they spotted me, it would be too late because Ole Henry would already be knocking them straight to hell where they belonged.

I chanced looking through the glasses to see how armed the Apaches were. Some had rifles, but most had lances and bow and arrows. I noticed the gun runner's hands were tied to the saddle horn and his feet were tied in the stirrups and he had no guns. More importantly, I could tell that the gun runner who was tied to the horse was Major Roberts. He had grown so much facial hair that I couldn't recognize him at the further distance. Damn, this manhunt was getting more interesting than I expected. The general's suspicion was now verified, and that made me even more determined to capture the gun runners.

I moved the field glasses to view the campsite, lowering them to reduce the chance of the sunlight reflecting off them. I didn't recognize the other two gun runners. The Apaches and two gun runners were advancing toward the campsite, as the rage within me was rising in anticipation of the fight I faced. I was somewhat torn between what was right and what would keep me alive. I knew that army protocol required a soldier to give his opponent the opportunity to surrender, but I also was rather certain that the gun runners and Apaches would not surrender. There would be a gun battle, and if I was to come out of it alive, I knew I had to use the element of surprise as the second phase of my plan to capture or kill those distributing guns to the Apaches. The first phase of my plan was playing out just as I needed it to and now was not the time to be changing what I had planned.

The Apaches were fighting to keep their land, and the settlers were fighting to colonize the West. The two didn't complement each other, and protecting the settlers was my calling. I had no choice, I had to kill. I had to survive this battle between me: the good, and them: the evil. I had to help the army protect the settlers. I knew that if I failed, the Apaches would have more guns. I also knew that if I failed, I would probably die.

I knew I could never stop all the bloodshed, but if I could stop any of it, I saw it as my duty to do so. As much as I didn't like it, it wasn't safe for me to give the Apaches a chance to live today, so I put any thought of asking them to surrender out of my mind. I had prayed and asked for forgiveness for all my sins. I had called upon my Great Spirit Warrior god to grant me the victory, so now I had to get it done.

I said to myself, "Well, ole Running Dreamer (my Cherokee Indian given name), it is time to earn your pay and make a positive difference out here in the wide-open West."

There were too many of them to fight off if they decided to rush me, so I focused on steadying myself to have the best chance of making every shot count. I would have very little, if any chance of getting out of here alive if I didn't capture or kill every living soul in this camp area, excluding myself. So, I stared down the barrel of my gun, sweat beading through my brow, as the Apaches arrived at the campsite and dismounted. Once they hit that crate top digging, I would let Ole Henry's music fill the air and bring them scoundrels to dance, run, or die.

In times like this, I allowed the rage within me to take command of my body. The visions of my family and village people in Africa being murdered, the death scene on the boat as we sailed to America, the shame of being sold into slavery, the horrific life as a slave, and the senseless murder of Sleeping Bird had all created this rage. Killing was the only way that I knew to calm this sick side of me. I guess in some ways it gave this warrior the edge in a bloody battle.

I took a quick glance at Ole Lightning to make sure the rocks would protect him from bullets and I could tell that he knew we were about to fight. He remained quiet as he had been trained, but he was very attentive. Knowing that I could depend on him, I refocused and watched as the Apaches removed the tumbleweed and started digging with military shovels the gun runners must have provided. I held my breath, thinking, "What if the gun runners with them realized that the tumbleweed marker had been moved? What if they could tell something was up and started to run?" I let out my breath and sighed as they started digging without hesitation. And, once the Apaches got focused on digging up what they thought were guns, they paid little attention to anything else. I noticed that the other two gun runners were tied to their horses like Major Roberts.

The Indian scout was not tied like the other gun runners, and he had a pistol, but he didn't have a rifle or any other weapons that I could see. From the looks of things, I just might be saving the gun runners' bacon, just to see justice done the army way. The odds were evened in my favor, and a smile crept on my face. Just seconds later, the thud of the shovel hitting the wooden crate top was barely audible to me, but loud enough to encourage me to set the battle in motion. All eyes were on the hole as the Apaches were whooping and hollering in anticipation of having guns.

I knew it was time to take action. I aimed Ole Henry at the Apache with the most head feathers in the closer group, and I chose my second target as well. With a quick, smooth motion, I pulled the hammer back and heard the *click, click* as it locked. My finger itching at the trigger. I was focused on my target, but I knew I must repeat these motions over and over as quickly as possible until I knew I would be safe.

The morning silence was broken only by the Apaches' chatter as they worked to remove the dirt from the crate top until I let Ole Henry roar, once, twice, three times. The Apaches were so close together that I could see each of them fall as I sited in on and squeezed the trigger to kill the next one. Three Apaches were dead and I was sitting in on the next target as the other Apaches searched desperately to locate the shooter. That gave me time to get off three more shots and three more Apaches hit the dirt.

Confused, and fearing for his life, one of the Apaches took off running toward the Indian scout and Major Roberts. With a blood-curdling scream, that Apache aimed and fired at the scout. The impact of the rifle shot knocked him out of the saddle and he hit the ground, moaning in pain. One more player was out of the game. I hoped that he was not dead, but I feared he might have been. I would have to find that out later. The Apache who had gotten the shot off into the Indian scout was now trying to catch his horse and flee. He tripped on a rock and lost his footing as he lunged for the terrified horse's reins with no luck, still over a hundred yards from the end of my rifle range. I had some time to get him, and I could see Major Roberts was stunned, trying to get his horse to move, to no avail.

I wiped my brow and swung the rifle slightly to the side to focus on the other two Apaches at the further distance with Major Roberts. Just as one of them raised a tomahawk to end his life, I ended the Apache's life instead with a shot through his heart. I watched him fall to the ground as the roar of Ole Henry echoed in my ears.

The other Apache—the one that I took to be a chief had realized that everything had gone wrong, so he took the opportunity to turn his horse, with the intent of fleeing the scene. Knowing that I couldn't wait too long, I sighted in on the left side of the chief's back and, once the trigger had been squeezed, I watched as his body vaulted forward from the impact of the rifle slug. One of his legs caught in the stirrup and spooked the horse. As the horse dragged him toward the horizon, a part of me felt a little sorry for him.

I turned my focus back to the poor brave chasing his horse just as he was mounting to flee the scene. All had gone well so far, and I couldn't allow one of the Apaches to escape my trap and go tell the tribal leaders what had happened here. For some fool reason he had stopped and turned around, looking for me. Apparently, he thought he knew enough about guns, but his mistake was thinking he was out of rifle range. He was out of range for standard rifles, but not for Ole Henry.

I couldn't believe my eyes as he stopped and yelled back in my direction, as if taunting me. I returned his arrogance no mercy.

The first shot turned his horse's head into a bloody mess as he toppled. He untangled himself from the horse and attempted to flee, but he was a bit unstable. The second shot from Ole Henry shortened his body by separating his head from the rest of him. Needless to say, he died bravely but foolishly.

Major Roberts was still trying to urge his mount to take off by kicking and pounding the horse's sides. By then, the horse was moving, either out of fear from the shots or because of Roberts' frantic movements. I shot the horse, swiftly ending his life. I had just hoped to knock him off stride with a grazing shot, but he was gaining speed, making it hard to judge how far in front of him I needed to aim. There were plenty of horses available, so losing only two was a victory in many ways. I watched as the horse flopped over on top of him, pinning his leg. I hoped that leg wasn't broken, because I couldn't take the time to set it properly. There was a lot to do here and I had to get us away from this campsite as fast as possible.

Now I was left with three gun runners and the injured Indian scout. Two of which were tied together side by side, arm to arm and leg to leg, giving them almost no chance of running. Looking through my field glasses, I could see the fear in their eyes, and it appeared that one of them had pissed in his pants. I had to chuckle. I certainly was going to make him wear those pants until we got back to the fort.

Since the sound of gunfire travels a long distance, I took a few precious minutes to study the surrounding landscape to make sure that no other Apaches were coming to the campsite. Once I felt certain that no one was coming, I gathered up all my guns and mounted Ole Lightning to make my way to Major Roberts, whose leg was now stuck under the dead horse, and the Indian scout who had been shot by the frantic Apache at the beginning of the fight.

The Indian scout had a pistol, so I went to him first. He was not dead, but he was wounded badly enough to not be able to attempt to fight or escape. He looked at me through pain-stricken eyes, and he knew who I was and knew that I knew him as well. I watched as that look changed first to hate and then to scorn. We'd never really had any love for each other, so his reactions were consistent with what I anticipated.

He had attempted to lead me into an ambush several years back. Had it not been for Ole Lightning's keen senses, it would have worked. I would have been a dead man.

He was cursing me in an Indian dialect and attempting to spit in my face. I just smiled as I disarmed him, including the knife and pistol that I had taught him to carry in his boots. As I patted his body for more weapons he squirmed and spat and lunged. I avoided his aggressive actions and pressed the toe of my boot into his bleeding shoulder. That took the fight out of him. While disarming the Indian scout, I found the small knife that he had tucked away under his long, flowing black hair. It wasn't very big, but it didn't take a big knife to give such a skillful fighter the upper hand.

The blood coming from the wound was not substantial, definitely not enough to kill him and he had passed out from the pain, so I let him lie there while I turned to Major Roberts, trapped by the fallen horse. He was very much still alive. Alive enough to be cursing, veins popping from his neck, spittle landing all around him in the dust. He called me names that the lowest person in the depths of hell would be undeserving of.

Once I got close enough I squatted by his bulging red face and smirked. "You think the words of a deserting snake like you mean anything to me out here, ole boy? The only one who will hear your words is your executioner."

I removed his bandana and he could see the grin on my face as I rocked back up off my haunches and walked to the puddle of urine the horse had left when it died. I had my knife in hand and I guessed he thought I was going to kill him. The grin and knife were what finally shut up his cursing, the red in his face flushing to white as he began to beg.

"Please, please, no no. Have mercy! Oh, mother. I'm injured, I'm no threat to you. Your general will want to speak to me. I have information! Please!"

"Shut up, you whimpering coward," I said, "your injuries won't kill you and neither will I. You will face the general and get the execution you deserve".

I used my knife to cut off some of the long hair of the horse's tail to use in gagging him. The hair would discourage him from trying to chew through the bandana. I wrapped the bandana around the hair, walked right up to the major and gagged him with the gritty bandana. I could no longer understand a thing he was saying so I started humming "Yellow Rose of Texas".

The scene had me remembering how some of the slaves had been treated on the plantation, often just as entertainment for the whites. This thought made it hard for me to control my rage, but I knew the general would want this man alive. So, with a smirk on my face, I said, "I won't waste soap on such a filthy mouth. Maybe sucking on this bandana will teach you to eat your words."

He gave me the most hateful look. I added to his misery, enjoying myself by now, "Don't worry, once it loses its flavor, I'll soak it in piss again since you like the taste so much."

It was cruel, but that would be all the water he would be getting until we got back to a safe place along the trail to the fort.

We were only about three days from the fort, so, if necessary, they could make it without food, and maybe even without water. Besides, weak men are less likely to try an attack and even less likely to succeed. There were four of them and me all by myself, so I had to do everything that I could think of to better the odds of making it back to the fort with the prisoners.

I got the major untangled from the dead horse, put his saddle on the best of the Indian ponies, mounted him, tied him in the saddle, and tied his hat to his back to allow the sun to bake some of the evil out of his head. He would be going back to the fort alive, but if he was sunburnt, oh well. The general didn't say they had to be in great health; he just wanted them alive.

I had to laugh while I was planning how to get all of them back to the fort that was about sixty miles away, with thirty of those miles being desert land highly populated with hostile Apaches.

In a way, this scene was the reverse of the scene of the runaway slaves that were being returned to their masters by overseers. Me, a black man, taking three white men back to the general. The general was not a master of a plantation, but he was a powerful force out here in the western states.

My plan had contingencies for worst-case scenarios, including walking back the entire distance. The good news was that I'd found the gun runners and foiled the gun trade with the Apaches. I'd even killed some Apaches, including one I believed to be a high-ranking chief. In many ways, things were already going much better than I expected, so I felt that it was all right to feel pretty good about it all.

As I checked to make sure each of the Apaches was dead, I collected their guns and smashed them on the rocks to ensure that they would never fire again. There was no reason to take those old guns back to the fort, they would just be extra weight. When the chief fell from the horse, he dropped a pouch. It contained gold, so I took it, knowing that the general would need it for evidence against the gun runners. I took one more look around that part of the battleground so that the warrior in me could assess the success of this battle.

I tended to Many Trails' wound and bandaged it. I poured a little extra alcohol on the wound as I did it, just to watch him wince. It worked, so I had myself a little laugh about that. I gagged him, mounted him on his horse, tied him in the saddle, and headed down to the other two gun runners.

By the time I reached them, they were exhausted from fighting the rawhide strips that the Apaches had used to tie them up. Once I was close to them, I realized that one was a deserter named Alberts. He had grown his hair long and had a beard so that is why I didn't recognize him before. I had never seen the young man tied to him. Once the deserter recognized me, he pissed his pants again.

He hated me and the feeling was mutual. He was calling me a black ass bastard as I approached them. I didn't feel like cursing anymore, so I just smiled and told him the general was waiting to see him again. He called the general a bastard, so I hit him in the stomach to knock the wind out of him. He got the message and said nothing else to anger me. We had a lot of history, and it was not good. He had done everything in his power to get me kicked out of the fort after I exposed his friend Many Trails as a traitor. Little did he know that I had saved a major and the general during an Apache attack. The general and his most trusted officers knew of my bravery, dedication, and commitment to the army so his efforts got him a lot of latrine and barn stall cleaning duty.

With all of the gun runners in one group, I said, "Well, well, look at what the cat just caught! I just may make major myself for bringing you criminals in. Certainly will be a nice bonus to get the $3000 reward for your hides." Looking up to the sky, I said, "Lord, thank you for this day."

I gave the two men tied together a smile and told them, "The good news is you both now get to dig up the guns and load them on the pack animals. Alberts, you better get used to your pissed pants because you won't be getting any bathroom breaks from here on out."

I hobbled their horses, cut the rawhide straps securing their outside legs to their horses, pulled them off the horses and let them fall on the soft hot desert sand. I kept the men tied together at the adjoining legs and got them up on their feet. I told them, "More Apaches could be coming so it's best that you work fast." I directed them to where the guns were actually buried and told them to dig. Alberts said, "Why are we digging here". I said, "Because the guns are buried here, not over there." As I pointed to the marker, I said, "I moved the marker just in case I wasn't able to capture you criminals." Then I watched as they dug them up and loaded the crates on three horses instead of two, to lessen their load in case we had to run from the Apaches. I was good at packing animals, so I made sure that they did it correctly. I marched them over to where I had buried the firing pins, and they dug them up as instructed. I put the firing pins in an empty sack and tied it to Ole

Lightning's saddle. If anything bad happened to me, he would take off for the fort, so even if the Apaches got the guns they would be useless. I went back to the two gun runners as they were filling in the holes where the guns had been buried. The work went quick, so the guns were packed in less than an hour.

The major was outraged. His eyes widening and thinning to slits as he watched me direct the men to where the guns actually were. I knew his words would be hateful, but he was gagged so I couldn't hear them. I hated bad men who were greedy and would do anything to make quick money, and I had learned to let that hate motivate me when I needed to capture them.

"You all earned a bonus for your cooperation. You and your partner will be tied right leg to left leg all the way back to the fort." I looked them in the eye and told them, "You have Major Roberts to thank for the uncomfortable ride back to the fort." With the work all completed, I gagged them too. I didn't need anyone making noise as we crossed that first thirty miles of desert to get back to a reasonably safe area. Once I had their attention, I made sure to look them both in the eyes before I whispered, "If the Apaches jump us, you are going to be left behind for them to capture." I didn't want Major Roberts or Many Trails to hear because they were smarter and scrappier and might try to escape more if they thought I would sacrifice them in a pinch.

I also decided to blindfold all of them so they would not see how I had their horses tied off on the lead lines. The less Major Roberts and Many Trails knew, the lesser the chance they would try escaping.

As I hobbled the remaining apache horses so they would not get back to the Apache village too quickly, I hoped that the Chief's horse didn't either. I needed all the time that I could buy to get out of this hostile Apache territory.

Getting the last two prisoners mounted and tied in the saddle was a task after what I had whispered to them, but I knocked them out, got them mounted, tied in the saddle and we were ready to ride out. I gathered their horses' reins and tied them off behind the packhorses carrying the guns. I used a separate lead line that I could cut in order to leave them to be captured, while I kept riding with the guns, with Major Roberts and Many Trails on their separate lead lines.

The packhorses with the guns would be cut loose next if it was necessary. This would surely cause the Apaches to slow their pursuit of the remaining members of the gun runners and me. The guns didn't have any firing pins, but only I knew that. I certainly hoped that, if necessary, cutting the packhorses loose would work because I wanted that $3000 reward, and I wanted the general to get his men.

All of the tasks were done, and we were ready to leave, so I took one more look around with the field glasses in hopes of seeing nothing. I was relieved when nothing was there.

They were expecting me to take a normal route to the fort, but I wasn't. I didn't come that way, and I certainly was not going back that way. We headed west for the hidden canyon that I knew no one knew of. The Indian scout had been there several years back, but he was injured and struggling with a bad fever, so he didn't see how we got there or how we got from there to the fort. Yes, I had myself a shortcut thanks to Tall Knives and his Indian wife.

So, we headed out, making no attempt to hide our direction. With the number of horses trailing behind me, it would have taken too much time to lay false trails or try hiding our tracks. Making good time was the best plan, so I took the most direct route to get out of this Apache territory.

With a little luck we would get at least an hour's head start, and with that and my knowledge of this territory, the best Apache tracker would not be able to catch up with me. I knew that I would probably have much more time than that because, once the camp was discovered, the Apaches would have to gather a war party to take after us, and that would take several hours. I expected to be safe and resting by then.

Besides, the Apaches would be expecting me to take the route to the fort that the army used. That thought gave me an idea, so I decided that once we had traveled about ten miles, I would take to the rocks, where it would be extremely hard to see any hoof prints. This would add about five miles to our journey but would hopefully fool the Apaches into believing we were laying a false trail for them and would change our course to get back on the established army route.

The Apaches would know that they could gain time on us if they didn't fall for that false-trail trick, so they would take the more direct route. If I was right, they would never find another sign of our tracks in the flat, rocky terrain.

Like the Apaches, the gun runners were expecting us to be on the established army route as well. Even with them being blindfolded, by the time they were sure that we were not on that route, though, we would be safe. Many Trails was the one most likely to sense this, even with him being blindfolded. Hopefully his injury would keep him focused on staying alive. Besides, with him being gagged, he couldn't tell the others.

With the prisoners gagged, we rode in silence, with our backs to the late morning sun. I constantly checked our back-trail for signs of someone following us because you could never be too careful out here. I kept watching for smoke signals alerting the various tribes that the gun trade had gone bad and warning them to be on the lookout for riders heading toward the sanctuary of the fort. It was like I was riding all alone, so I caught myself thinking about how I had planned the morning attack and executed it flawlessly. I was so thankful that I was able to get that special Henry repeating rifle several years back. A single-shot rifle in that situation might not have been enough to keep me breathing long enough to escape, let alone take all my enemies down. It was amazing how much the seemingly insignificant moments of one's past could save you later. My love, Sophie, had me going to church on Sundays so I glanced up toward heaven and thank the man upstairs for saving me one more time. I still believed in the Great Spirit Warrior, so I thanked him as well.

The rest of the trip to the hidden canyon went without incident. After almost ten hours in the saddle, the entrance to the secret canyon was less than a mile ahead of us when I noticed smoke signals in the southeastern sky. The Apaches had found out about my handiwork and they would be mad as hell and searching for the gun runners and me. Based on the way things looked when I was watching the gun runners and Apaches interact, these ole gun runners probably didn't want to be seen by the apaches any more than I did. I was guessing that was why they were not fussing or trying to escape.

As I neared the secret canyon, the rocks seemed to stretch on for miles, so I let my mind wander to Tall Knives. I remembered how he used to tell me that someday I would have all that I desired because of what that special canyon had hidden away in those massive walls. I had been there on many occasions and had seen nothing that should make him think that. But still, I wondered what he meant.

We made it to the entrance of the hidden canyon. The large rocks hiding its entrance were massive. They looked ageless, endless, and formidable even. They made the canyon only accessible by the one entrance. There were dead-end, smaller canyons beyond the initial entrance, so you had to know how to navigate your way in order to get to the large oasis hidden within the walls.

Once we were on the winding path within the rocks, I stopped and checked the blindfolds of the gun runners to ensure that the secret canyon remained a secret. Then I led the caravan in. As usual, I paused to admire the beauty of the canyon, hidden behind such massive and natural rock walls. The sun always created shadows in the canyon, the light projecting magnificent colors on the layers of rock. There was this quiet that made you feel that you had to be the only person on earth. There was a little pool of water that was the highlight of the canyon floor. I always wanted to go to it first to get a drink of that crystal clear water. But that would have to wait until I got the prisoners dismounted and secured.

As we turned the last corner on the passage into the canyon, the pack horse I had left behind lifted his head. He was still in the little corral with the supplies neatly stacked just as I left them. They were a welcome sight, because I could lighten Ole Lightning's load and have some decent food for supper.

I dismounted, dismounted the gun runners and tied them in a circle, except for the young one. I had his legs tied together in a way to allow him to walk, but not be able to run. He unsaddled their horses and tended to them. He helped me unload the pack horses and then I tied him to the other gun runners. He was so helpful and polite that I wondered why and how he got mixed up with these army deserters. I would make sure to include that in my official report.

I would shackle them later. First thing I needed to do was take care of Ole Lightning and rub him down really good while he dined on a big helping of oats. It had been weeks since he could relax and he deserved some special treatment for the part he played in finding the gun runners' trail.

I cooked and ate at my leisure before I did an extra special job of tying the prisoners with rawhide straps. I wetted them so that they would shrink during the night, as the captives would most certainly be trying to free themselves. My Cherokee friends had taught me how to do it that way, and I had never lost a captive. I shackled their legs with chains that had bells on them, and that gave me a much better comfort level to go to sleep. If they moved very much, I would hear the bells. Even if I didn't, Ole Lightning would, and he would alert me that something unusual had happened.

The clouds in the sky blocked out most of the moonlight and stars, so it wasn't likely that the Apaches would be out tonight. Even if they were, the darkness would make it more difficult to track us or move around the rocks surrounding this canyon.

With the prisoners bedded down and Ole Lightning resting, I took the time to write down what had happened over the past few days. I would review the notes in detail once I was back home to make sure that I didn't leave out anything important in the official report the army required. I thought of the day's events and wondered if the Great Spirit Warrior would be proud of how I performed in the battle. The older village men and my Indian friends had taught me to read signs, track, be patient and not give up. I'd used those valuable skills to track the gun runners, plan the attack, and execute that plan. I thought of the Great Spirit Warrior daily, and in a way, it gave me added strength.

***

The gun runners didn't try anything during the night, so I guessed they were as tired as I was. I slept like a baby for the first time since leaving the canyon four days ago and woke up early, well-rested, and ready to complete the journey to the fort.

It was a beautiful sunny morning. After feeding Ole Lightning and watering all of the horses I had coffee and ate some field rations for breakfast. I didn't feed the prisoner nor their horses, because we would be back at the fort before suppertime. They were worn out and I could hear their stomachs growling as I checked their shackles and rawhide bracelets. They each struggled as I mounted them on their horses, so I had to get a little rough with Major Roberts and Alberts. Many Trails' wound prevented him from putting up much of a struggle and the young lad did exactly as I instructed him. With the prisoners ready for travel, we hit the trail. They were still blindfolded, and those gags saved me from listening to a lot of bitching and cursing, so I rode in peace.

We were out of hostile Apache country, and I had another special surprise for the prisoners. I had arranged for four soldiers to wait for me at a specific spot to help me escort the prisoners to the fort.

After riding more than seven hours, it was great to see Sergeant Williams and the soldiers. I had been on many missions with them and knew that they were good in battle and I was thankful that the general sent them and not some rookies. As I studied their faces, it was hard to tell if they were more happy or surprised to see me. I knew I was happy to see them. Sergeant Williams was the first to walk up to me and his face broke into a wide grin when we met.

"You might really be a legend now, Scout," Sergeant Williams said as he looked at who I had with me. When his eyes met Major Roberts and Many Trails his grin turned cold as he continued, "The general will be most happy to see those two."

I snickered as their veins began to pop again with the sound of their muffled yelling. "How long have you been camped here". He replied, "About two weeks. The general had fresh food and water delivered to us every other day. We took turns checking back up the trail about five miles daily in hopes of seeing you. Wasn't expecting you to come from the direction that you approached." I told him, "I detoured off the main route a ways back just in case the Apaches were braver than usual in chasing me. I prevented them from getting more guns and killed several of them and they are really mad."

The sergeant looked at the pack horses and said, "Thank God those rifles didn't get in the hands of the Apaches." I nodded. "You wouldn't believe the plan they had. These are some smart, evil boys. I'm glad they're tied up, shackled and on the way to the fort. I will tell you about it as we ride."

He nodded back grimly, I could see in his eyes that he had been worried about me, but he didn't say anything. Instead, he issued orders to the soldiers to get ready to head out and we left for the fort.

I was tired but still very alert, plus, being around people I could talk to again had woken me up. I was sitting tall in the saddle because I wanted them to know that I was all right. The sergeant wanted to know why I had the lead lines of the trailing horses as I did. I explained why, and he nodded to show his approval of the cleverness of my method.

The gun runners could hear us, so they knew that I would have help getting them to the fort. They strained, trying to free their shackled hands, and we could hear their muffled curses. Back in the Canyon, I had shackled their legs under the horses' bellies, so the bells were chiming as the horses took every step. I knew their efforts were a waste of energy, but if I was facing what they knew they would get for selling guns to the Apaches, I probably would have been doing the same thing.

After being shackled for years of my life, after sitting among dead and dying people from my country in the belly of a boat, I didn't have much pity for them.

This mission was about over, and, with the additional help, we were almost certain to reach the fort by the end of the day. Had it been just me and Ole Lightning, though, we would have ridden hard and reached the fort in about half the time that it took us to get there with the prisoners.

Ole Lightning was as spirited as ever and set a good pace. I rode beside the sergeant, with one soldier ahead of us, riding point, while the other two soldiers rode drag. We all were surveying our surroundings because you could not trust that the Apaches wouldn't attempt an attack to get their hands on the guns.

Me and the sergeant talked about what had been going on while I was away from the fort. As usual, not much excitement. I had been gone for several weeks, so the general was concerned about me.

The sergeant told me that he wasn't all that surprised that the Indian scout and the major had turned bad. He agreed that they'd probably had a hand in allowing the gun runners to elude the army for all these years. I felt bad for the Indian scout, because I knew he had a wife and three children. It was sad to think about what could happen to his family. They would be cast out from their tribe because the scout was a traitor to other Indians, and they would not be accepted by the white man because they were Indians. Only the thought of the many innocent people and soldiers that had died at the hands of the Apaches with the rifles these gun runners sold them made me feel better about the whole situation.

After riding for about two hours, the fort was in sight about a mile or so ahead of us. Those massive walls with the lookout towers were a sight to behold when you had been away for a while. The chimney smoke was visible as high up as the eye could see. The town was between us and the fort, and the people were probably gathering in the streets. I hated to take the prisoners through town because whites didn't like to see other whites in chains that had been put on them by a black man. It was always a nervous few minutes as I traveled down that street. It was only about a hundred yards long, but it always seemed to be much longer because of the hateful looks and words directed at me.

We stopped to check the prisoners' restraints before we got too close to the town and fort. I directed the soldiers to remove the horse-piss bandana from Major Roberts' mouth, as well as the gags and blindfolds of the other prisoners. I wanted them to be able to talk and even scream if they wanted to, for there was no way for any of them to escape now.

They all looked worried, and they had a good reason to be. I didn't think the general would waste any time setting their trial date, and they were most certainly going to be executed. The guns and the money that they'd expected to get from the Apaches would be all the evidence that the general needed to convict them. If they were smart, they would cooperate, and perhaps one of them would get prison time in lieu of the firing squad or the hanging gallows. I knew there was no hope for the deserters or the Indian scout, but maybe the young one had a chance to escape death.

Once we were within a quarter-mile of the fort, the soldier riding point fired the signal shots to alert the commanding officer that we were on our way in. The officer on duty had standing orders to dispatch soldiers to come meet me when I was returning with prisoners because people in this area had a great hate for the Apaches, and many of the white men would not like me, a black man, bringing in white men in chains.

The soldiers met us at the edge of the town and took up their positions on both sides of the prisoners. Their show of rifles was a clear signal for the townsfolk that the army was not going to tolerate any of them attempting to disrupt justice.

It was hard for me not to smirk as I rode through the town because I knew there were several white men that wanted to kill me for capturing white men. I just sat in the saddle, letting Ole Lightning lead us through the town and into the fort.

I had only one thing on my mind anytime I rode through the town: my Sophie, the love of my life. I had seen her for the first time on this street several years back. She had been my inspiration since then. As I passed the dry goods store where she worked, I could see her standing just inside the door. She was beautiful. Long hair, sparkling eyes and those inviting lips that I so love. She wasn't very tall, but her smile was my star of hope. Her smile told me that I was her inspiration and that always caused the rage that I used to survive missions to subside. Instantly, I was more of a man and less of a warrior. This man needed to finish this mission and go home to wait for the woman that inspires him.

Since news of my return had reached the fort before we did, the sentries had the gates open, and they came to attention until the sergeant saluted them. I had returned many times before with prisoners, but never had there been such a reception line, waiting to see the prisoners. The fort was buzzing like a beehive as we rode toward the headquarters.

Many of the soldiers had been subjected to harsh treatment by Major Roberts, so they were lining our path to get their chance at heckling him as he passed. A ranking officer barked out a command to put an end to all of that.

To my surprise, the general was standing on the porch of his quarters. While others just saw a smile on his face, showing his happiness for the capture of the gun runners, I saw much more. He was like a proud father greeting a son. The pride in his eyes cut only by a twinge of relief. The moment was almost overwhelming. Only the excitement of the soldiers and the barking orders of the officers kept me from getting misty-eyed.

We rode right up to him and I dismounted, stretched, and tried to get the kink out of my back. I used my bandana to wipe some of the sweat and grit off my face as I grinned, stepping up to his porch. He gave me a moment and then extended his arm to give me a pat on the shoulder. It was our way of embracing in public. He asked if I had any trouble capturing the gun runners, so I gave him a brief summary of the mission and said I would give a detailed account for the official report.

The general issued orders to the officers to take charge of the prisoners. As they pulled them off their horses, the general walked up to Major Roberts and Many Trails. I had seen that stern look on his face only once, so I knew he was one angry man. He was the general, though, so he didn't let his emotions get out of control. He just told them, "Welcome back."

He did the traditional army about-face and asked me to come to his office. It was times like this that I felt proud of what I could do, for the opportunities I had been given, so much of which I owed to people I had known earlier in my life. My friend Sleeping Bird had taught me to read, write, and do numbers when we were in the Cherokee camp in eastern Oklahoma Territory. Folks at the fort and in the town still didn't know that I had those skills, but the general did. So, when we got in his office, I would give him my report, and he would have his most trusted assistant rewrite it to preserve my secret.

***

As much as I cherished the moment with the general, I was ready to be home. I went to see my closest friend, Jose, who I left Ole Lightning with. Jose helped me care for my livestock, especially while I was gone on missions. Jose would reshod him as we always did after being out on a long mission. Ole Lightning was in good hands and I needed to refuel and refresh myself. I went to the mess hall to have a snack and then later that day, I went to the general's office again, and he confirmed that I would be getting the reward for the capture of Major Roberts and Many Trails, as well as a bonus for getting the job done. The general didn't have an immediate need for the $2000 that I took off the dead Apache chief and delivered to him in the privacy of his office, as our operation was well funded. He didn't see why the government needed to know about it, so he gave that to me, provided he never heard about it again. I was shocked, but all so happy! The gun runners didn't know that I had found it on the apaches, and even if they did, they would not be alive long enough to tell anyone. The general was keeping them locked up in seclusion with no visitors allowed. This mission had turned out to be a great one for me. I was stunned by how much money I was carrying out of his office. White men all around me, not knowing I had $5500 tucked under my clothes.

I had one more thing to do before I could relax, so I went to the army stable to get Ole Lightning. Jose had him fixed up with some new shoes, he had been washed and rubbed down, mane and tail had been trimmed and he was sporting a new halter that Jose had made for him. He looked great so with a stable hand carrying my saddle, I headed to my little house just outside of the fort to feed him some more and place some fresh hay in his stall, just the way he liked it. He seemed to know he was home. Sophie had given me that "I will see you later at your house" look, and I knew exactly what that meant. These days, I lived to see that woman.

CHAPTER 2: CHILDHOOD DAYS

I was always more compassionate after seeing Sophie. Earlier as I rode through town, I saw her face and was able to smile at others even though I knew the whites thought I was less of a person than them. I lived in a world controlled by them, but I was making a great life for myself, so one day what they thought would be of little or no concern to me. For now, I just had to grin and bear it.

The one constant in my life had been how rewarding it was to get back home. My little house just outside the fort wasn't much, but it was where I found true peace of mind. I had a barn for my horses and a small corral. The house was small and open, so when I stepped through the door, I could see the kitchen, my bed, and the dresser where I kept most of what I owned.

I checked the rug that covered my secret hiding place for valuables. The small pebble that I'd placed under one corner was just as I left it, so I knew it was undisturbed. I added the money to my valuables for safekeeping and replaced the pebble and rug. The money would probably be safer in the local bank, but I didn't trust the white men who ran it. A black man was not supposed to have that much money and I didn't want to explain how I happened to have it.

My books were visible on the little shelf on one wall. The Indian blanket that lay on my bed was a treasured possession from some of my first American friends. It wasn't fancy, but it was colorful, thick and made with loving hands. It was one of the first things that was given to me as I ran from slavery.

It didn't matter if I was only gone five minutes; when I crossed the threshold to enter my house, that feeling of being home warmed my heart. I was so blessed that the general had a house built for me just outside the fort but not in the adjacent town. You see, I was the only black government employee at this fort, and even though much had changed, it hadn't changed enough for a black man to be housed with white men. I was a government employee, not a soldier, so living in an army barracks was against protocol.

My home was not subject to being searched by army officers, so they didn't know what I had as possessions. I liked it better because I could do things that I wanted to keep secret from the whites. Things like reading and teaching Sophie to read, write, and do numbers.

As I relaxed at my little kitchen table, eating a snack, I took my field notes out of the saddle bags to review the notes I always made when I was on a mission. After being satisfied that I didn't leave any important details off my official report, relaxation was all that I wanted. Sitting in true silence, my thoughts not on keeping myself alive or planning my next attack for the first time in weeks, I was brought back to being a boy in Africa. Whenever I thought about that time, I cried and longed to be back there with my family, happy and enjoying a much simpler life. I guess in a way, remembering it kept me tied to my family and homeland.

The Africa that I remembered was a whole different world from America. I could go out into the jungle to play or hunt with no worries about anything but surviving. The elders of the village were on constant watch both for dangerous animals and the merciless hunters from neighboring hostile villages.

Day after day and night after night, they would take turns watching to protect us from the outside world. Here in America, the army did all the defending for the people. People didn't have to worry as much about being attacked, but they still had to worry about having enough to eat, having a place to lay their heads.

Back then, very few Africans knew anything of the outside world, but the elders spoke quietly about threats from other parts of the world, whole tribes disappearing overnight, and giant sea vessels taking them away where they were never seen again. In the months before I was captured, they'd seemed more concerned about being able to protect our village. They'd even started training us boys at an earlier age so we could help, should our village come under attack.

At the time, I was fourteen and thrilled to be learning the skills of the warriors. I wasn't thinking about the threats that started this training, I was just excited to be learning. We boys spent the mornings learning to be warriors and afternoons learning how to be hunters. We had to find our way through the jungle to get to rivers, other friendly villages, and our food sources. This took away from our playtime, but the elders turned some of our warrior training into games.

In recent years, each family had built a safe place for their women and children out in the jungle and away from the village. We, the young warriors, were assigned the responsibility of getting the women and smaller children to the safe places if the village was attacked.

I had two sisters and four brothers. The three older brothers were village warriors and spent most of their time on sentry duty. My younger brother was just eleven at the time, and he was between our two sisters.

I continued learning to track and hunt for food and to kill predators that would attack villagers. Yet, improving my warrior skills was my focus. I became a great spear maker and a good wrestler. I made knives and learned to throw them with great accuracy. One of my favorite skills was using my shield and weapon against an opponent. I was well on my way to mastering all the warrior skills in those two years. Just when I thought I knew it all, one of the elders would teach me something else that could make the difference in battle. I began to understand that each elder was exceptionally skilled.

My father would always tell me to watch, learn, and spend the time to become exceptional at what I had been taught, so I spent endless hours doing as he instructed. After a while, I could see the benefits as we boys competed in the warrior skills games, such as spear and knife throwing, blocking weapons with our shields and taking down an opponent in hand-to-hand combat. While the other boys spent their precious free time playing, I continued to work on my survival, hunting, and waring skills. The Great Spirit Warrior had touched my soul and I was determined to be the best warrior in the village.

As we junior warriors practiced our skills for the elders, I did what was necessary to beat my opponents, but I was careful to not dishonor them. This was a village, and honor was one of the most treasured things to have as a warrior or village elder.

Father spent a lot of time teaching us the history of our people and the importance of family and being an honorable member of the village. Girls were taught this as well, because they were expected to help raise the younger children, and they would have to teach their own children as they became mothers. Women were not warriors, but they were taught basic survival skills so they could provide and care for the family if the father died. The village boys were also taught about cooking, love, and compassion by the village mothers. This made the village a very peaceful place to live.

Day after day, the village elders seemed to talk more and more in secret. On occasion, one or two of our warriors went into the jungle and never returned to the village. Sometimes the elders would find evidence that some animal had killed them. Sometimes there would be no evidence of what happened. It had only gotten worse in the six months before I was captured.

I was very attentive when the elders were meeting, and it appeared that they were becoming more concerned about the safety of our village. Some wanted to just abandon it and set up another village further into the jungle, but the older ones had more power, and they had survived in the village for more than fifty years. They saw no reason for moving the village and having to learn a new area. I must admit that I thought it would be a great task to relocate the village, so I tended to agree with those elders. The village would also be more vulnerable as the people were moving to another location. As a junior warrior, I couldn't speak my thoughts, so I just listened. In the end, all the village members were content with staying where we were and simply adding more sentries to watch for intruders.

Then, one morning, as the sun was rising, the village was attacked. Our warriors held the intruders off until their second and third waves joined the fight. By the time the intruders were in control of the battle, we junior warriors had gotten the families of our village to the safe places, while hoping that we were indeed safe.

But that was a false hope. The intruders had apparently been planning to raid our village for years. They knew of many of the safe places, and they raided them, taking the women and children. It was then that we all realized that we, the people, were what the intruders wanted, not our weapons or belongings. Every person they caught was tied up as we tied up captured animals.

We had heard of tribes attacking smaller villages to imprison them to be sold as slaves, and it appeared that we were attacked for that reason. It was said that the captives were taken to a land far from our native land, so I knew I didn't want that to happen to my family. But as a sixteen-year-old boy, I knew that I was no match for the intruding warriors that had overpowered the greatest among us, the warriors who I still had so much to learn from.

I knew that I needed to protect my mother and my siblings, so I told Mother that I would lead the intruders away from them so that they could escape deeper into the jungle. She knew what that probably meant for me, so with tears in her eyes, she nodded, giving her approval.

I directed my younger brother to use all the skills he had been taught to take care of the family. I patted my heart to show him that I believed he could do it. Knowing that I might be killed or captured, I looked at my family one more time, knowing that it could be the last time that I would see them.

I left the safe place to lead the intruders away, knowing that I was taking a big chance. I was fearful that Father and my three older brothers had been captured or killed, so there were no other options for me. As I made myself an easy target for the intruders, I called on the Great Spirit Warrior to give me the strength and guidance to get the intruders to chase me and forget about my family.

I threw my spear, injured one of the intruders, and pulled my knife, taking the warrior attack position. As I watched the intruder fall with the spear in his heart, other intruders advanced. Knowing that I couldn't stop all of them, I only had one choice, one chance to get them away from my family.

Without thinking about it, I ran through the trees, leaping over anything that was in my way. I was a fast runner, so when I noticed they seemed to be falling further behind me, I taunted them, challenged them, and even injured one or two of them as I threw rocks at them. Nothing that I did seemed to change their plan to capture me. Then I ran into an open area, and it occurred to me that I had been herded into this opening just like we herded wild animals into our traps. They were all around me, careful not to injure me, which scared me even more somehow.

As I wondered why, I was running fast, intending to break through their circle to escape. Without warning, I was entangled and lifted off my feet in a trap. As the constraints got tighter and tighter, I could no longer move, and the weapons I had in my hands became useless.

I was screaming, cursing, and fussing, but mostly, I was realizing that I was now a captive. I was wishing for death, but I was in no danger of dying. I couldn't even do anything to bring death to myself; I was just at the mercy of the gods, and it appeared that the gods were not going to help me.

Suddenly I was just a boy again, the tears welling and overflowing, lip quivering until I broke into a full-blown wail. I was terrified. I was stuck and helpless and, worst of all, all alone. Never in my life had I been so isolated. I was used to being the rising star of junior warriors, to being surrounded by family and never further than a shout from someone who cared for me. The loss seemed to be tightening in my throat as the constraints tightened on my body. I was soon limp and gasping, the men around me talking and all but ignoring me while dismantling their trap to move me. I was invisible. Inhuman. No one was going to come to my rescue because everyone I knew needed to be rescued, too.

As I stared blankly at my captors, growing numb, a vision of the village elders came to me. They didn't say anything, just nodded, each holding the weapon they had taught me to use. My jaw set. I closed my eyes and called upon the Great Spirit Warrior to give me strength and guidance to survive. I knew that my childhood was behind me now, and I had to face life, embrace captivity, and survive. I was a warrior now, there were no other options for me anymore.

My captors were nearly finished dismantling the trap and pulling me out of it. It took six of them to restrain me and they were some strong warriors. I didn't recognize their tribal markings or attire, so they must have been from another area. As they stood me up to tie my hands, I tried running away. They were tired of my aggression, so they knocked me down, almost knocking me out. Then threaten to cut off my ears if I kept fighting, so I stopped cursing and let them tie my hands and my feet without contest. I could understand enough of their dialect to know that they wanted to punish me as they tied me to a long pole and handed it, and me, off to be carried between two men that appeared to be captives. Being carried like a dead pig destined to be spit-roasted, I could only hope that my family had escaped to safety. Any hopes of my own escape were gone for now.

I was taken with the rest of the captives of my village and many other villages. It took several days for us to reach the shore of the great body of water. I didn't know then that it was what the white men call the Atlantic Ocean. That was the last time that I saw my native land.

Since then, I had been on a journey that I didn't plan or want to take, much of which had unexpectedly enriched my life. Yet, occasionally I cried, for I still didn't know if my family had survived that attack on our village so many years ago.

A knock on the door brought me back to the here and now. *Who in the hell could be knocking on my door?*

"Who's there?" I bellowed, only to be greeted by the beautiful voice that I was so familiar with. I had been so deep in my past that I had lost track of time. I opened the door, and my lovely Sophie was smiling at me and reaching for the comfort of my arms, "I missed you so much."

I hugged her close and said, "I missed you too, beautiful."

She was a former slave who had been brought to the western frontier by a nice white family. She worked as a clerk in the dry goods store in town and managed to do well for herself. As usual, her trusted companion Juno, a mixed-breed dog, was wagging his tail as if greeting me too.

When we first met, I helped her a lot to make sure that she was safe and didn't end up at the whore house, servicing men or cleaning up after them. She had done too much of that when she was still a slave. My closest friends, the general and Jose, had told me I should marry her, and I just might do that once I was finished with scouting. I didn't want Sophie worrying herself silly every time me and Ole Lightning disappeared over the horizon.

Right now, she needed me for what she wanted, and I wanted what she loved to give me. Oh, how great it was to be the man of her dreams. There was nothing else to do, so I smiled as big as I could while my heart pounded in my chest as if it was trying to get out to show that it belonged to her. They told me that was love, and I thought it was the greatest thing that I had found in America or anywhere in my life.

Maybe I could have found it in my homeland. I just didn't know. Right now, even though the memory of my family still haunted me night after night, the thought of Sophie overshadowed those thoughts. My family probably thought I was with the Great Spirit Warrior in the sky, just as I thought that they were. Since I was alive, there was a chance that they were alive as well, but I didn't think I would ever know.

For now, Sophie was real and with me, comforting me, loving me, and inspiring me to come back to her. In a way, that was what drove me when I was on a mission for the army or just out on my own.

CHAPTER 3: COMING TO AMERICA

After drinking some whiskey, eating a great meal, and enjoying a night of intense lovemaking with Sophie, I woke up alone. Sophie always left me during the night so she could be in her home when the sun came up. With Juno by her side, I never worried about her safety because he was one hell of a protector. I was glad that he liked me because I had seen an ole boy that he didn't like. It took months for his leg and arm wounds to heal.

I touched my forehead and shook my head, placing my feet firmly on the floor. The world seemed to be spinning. I immediately knew that the last shot of whiskey last night was a mistake. I looked at the whiskey bottle, and it confirmed my suspicion. I couldn't believe that I drank that much.

The whiskey, my exhaustion from my trip and being with Sophie, were each enough to knock me out. But with all those things together, I had slept like a dead man.

After all the battles that I had survived, I often wished that my village elders and family could see what I had become. It had been almost twenty years since I last saw them, and those twenty years were full of trials. I was completely different now; I had become a man and a warrior.

Back in Africa, at age sixteen, I thought I was so close to being the warrior I had trained to be, until the intruders captured us and marched us up the gangplank and onto that ship. In some ways, I guess I was a warrior, because I stood tall, showed no fear, and walked as proudly as one could while wearing leg irons and shackles—both of which were cutting into my flesh.

That first step I took once aboard the ship changed how I thought of myself. I had been recognized for my abilities by the village elders, as well as by my family. Yet, the village warriors were not able to protect our village. The village elders had prepared me for being in such a predicament, so I knew the changes I needed to make. I could no longer think only like a warrior; I now needed to think first of survival. It was then that I resolved to become nameless. To keep my head held high, live my life on my own, and focus only on planning my escape from what I viewed as living hell.

As they pushed us down the ladders into the holding cell area of the ship, I could see that some of the younger elders from my village were chained up like me. As a warrior, I wanted to rush to their rescue, but I was helpless. That thought upset me, and a fierce rage started to build within me. Just then, I heard a scream and turned in time to see another captive get his head smashed to a pulp by one of the white men. The man had tried to attack the white man closest to him even though he was shackled, hands and feet. I guessed that, to him, death was better than being a captive. As I watched his body go limp, I became more determined to not let this situation be the last thing that I remembered in this lifetime. I would make it; I would survive this madness.

I kept telling myself that I was a nameless lone soul, over and over, until I started thinking that way. I knew that I was just a big boy, so I shouldn't have been so hard on myself. But I knew that a warrior should never feel sorry for himself, for doing so would blur his thinking and limit his chances to escape the difficult situation that he was in. No, warriors fight to the end. As a nameless lone soul, I knew I had to be the ultimate warrior and not a caring man.

As I turned from watching that head-smashing scene, I set to work accepting what had happened to me and figuring out how to live through it. Survival was all that mattered to me, for I was determined to live. I couldn't let the chains keep me from finding inner peace, that inner peace that would give me the strength to conquer my challenges.

The chains were heavy and tight, so they were cutting into my wrists and ankles. It hurt like hell, but I had to tell myself to get used to the discomfort. It took some time, but I did. I could see no way of getting out of this situation and based on the looks of defeat on the other captives' faces, they couldn't either.

The ship was larger than any boat I ever saw, but it wasn't too large to see throughout the hold. It had portholes with bars on them, so there was just enough light filtering in to see my surroundings. I concentrated on the situation and channeled all my energy into mentally cataloging what I could see. I noticed that the men were chained more tightly and with more restraints than the women. Women and children were in a separate compartment from the men. I noticed that there were no little children or babies. Younger men, like me, were separated from the older men. No men seemed to be older than about thirty-five or forty, and the women's ages ranged from early teens to mid-thirties. A closer evaluation of the captives revealed that all of us looked to be strong and in great health.

I didn't understand why at the time, but after arriving in America and being placed on the plantation, I understood the white man's plan. They wanted free labor to work their plantations, and they were stealing African people to do their work.

After assessing the situation, I knew there was nothing I could do except survive until I was at least on land. From the moment we left the shore, that ole ship rocked and creaked something awful. The white men were constantly yelling, what for, I didn't know, for at the time I didn't speak or understand their language. The captives constantly went from chanting in their native dialects to yelling and screaming in pain.

Minutes became hours, hours became days, and that ole ship kept rocking and creaking, our chains clanging with our every movement. Just when I felt comfortable with the rocking and creaking, something happened, and the ship rocked and creaked harder than before.

I was scared as hell, and as uncomfortable as the other captives, but I stayed calm and found a position that I could sit or lie in that brought me the least discomfort. I tried to maintain it as long as I felt was good for my body. I knew I needed to move as much as possible to keep my body conditioned for escape or a fight. In a way, lifting and resisting them ole chains gave the muscles a good workout.

The ship's hold was dark, damp, and I could tell that the air was extremely bad as soon as we were below the top deck. With all those unwashed bodies in captivity, the stench grew more and more unbearable. It was not something that I could get away from, so I forced myself to embrace it as a condition of this battle I was fighting.

I tried to make myself even like it, but that was going too far. I finally settled on seeing it as something to hate, something that I could use as a driving force when the time came for me to break away from this bondage. The only good thing about the situation was that I was so tired that I didn't have a hard time sleeping when it was quiet.

Just when I thought the voyage was as bad as it could get, it got worse. We were sick daily from the rocking motion of traveling on the sea. After a few days, some captives died, and I imagined that many of the captives who didn't die probably wished they had if they were as sick as I felt.

The constant rocking was so violent at times that it tossed us around like ragdolls. We were chained and had no way to brace ourselves from the motion of the ship, so we were banging into each other, slamming to the deck, and worst of all, the chains were cutting our ankles and wrists as our bodies moved more than the chains would allow.

We were a bloody mess by the time the violent rocking stopped. I surveyed my surroundings to see that the ship's hold deck was blood-soaked, and it was obvious that many of the captives had thrown up, pissed their pants, or crapped on themselves.

The scene and conditions made it very difficult to maintain the calmness that I kept willing myself to have. The violent rocking came in spells after that first time, never quite as bad or lasting quite as long, but we still got thrown around pretty bad. On each occasion, we could not do anything other than pray to our gods that it would stop as fast as it started.

The white men eventually changed the daily routine, and the captives were taken to the surface for some fresh air. The slave traders had everything planned, so we were chained in a way where about ten of us were taken up at a time. I guessed they didn't want us to have a chance to jump them. After being up on deck and seeing no land as I looked around, I knew that even if we were to overpower them, we could do nothing to save our lives.

If you couldn't see land, you couldn't swim to it. None of us had been on a ship, and we didn't know how to sail it, not to mention we didn't even know which way home was.

I asked myself, where was Africa? Where were we being taken? How long would it take to get there? And what would we be able to do if we could get to land? I had no answer to any of the questions. This wasn't comforting, but it at least confirmed that I had chosen the best way to deal with the situation.

That first day that I went up on deck, the ship captain arranged a little demonstration to help us understand that we had no way to escape this ship at sea. A couple of the dead captives were thrown overboard like trash. Standing near the rail, we watched as these massive fish tore into their bodies and ate them, bones and flesh. We learned a new word that day, and I thought of it every time that I was around water. The captain said "shark" while pointing to the sea creatures. That was the first English word that I remember understanding. I thought that if anyone had any idea of jumping overboard, that scene probably changed their mind.

After about a month, several of the captives in the section I was in died and became a meal for the sharks. It was hard to watch, and with each death, I had to wonder if I would meet the same fate. Just the thought of that made me more determined to survive, so I ate the bad food, exercised as much as I could, and stayed quiet and calm as captives were beaten, our women were raped, and anyone attempting to resist these white men was tortured.

There were captives from several villages on the ship. Even though the varying villages had their own dialects, there were enough commonalities that we were able to communicate. It wasn't long before we had a common chant that we used to pass the time. The elders would chant "keep the faith, my brother," and it gave us a certain amount of inspiration to develop other chants that were, in essence, our way of communicating what was happening to us, what we saw when we were taken up on deck, and most importantly, how our other village members were doing.

There were still many captives from my village, and we were able to get a general understanding of how many of us were there. Unfortunately, I learned that my brothers and father had died in the jungle, defending our village. It was tragic news, but at least now I knew of their fate and could pray that they were with the Great Spirit Warrior.

I also learned that my mother, brother, and sisters were not on this ship. Considering the sacrifice that I had made in that jungle, I so hoped that they had escaped a fate such as this and were grieving for the family members no longer with them. Hopefully, they knew that I was the only one taken captive. They could hope that I would survive and have a good life.

The food was terrible and in short supply, so I was always hungry, and I grew weaker by the day. About two months into the voyage, the ship's crew began to give us better food and improved the conditions of our living quarters, if you wanted to call them that. There were no comforts, no privacy, and, after a while, each of us knew all about the private parts of the captives around us.

We were not released to piss or take a dump. The piss would run into the cracks between the planks, and the ship's crew washed away the shit every morning. One thing was for sure—after what felt like forever on that ship, I would never complain about another person's body odor again. The funkiest person that I had ever smelled was a welcoming scent compared to the funk we smelled while in the hold of that ship.

About a week after they started feeding us better, there were a lot of sounds that we hadn't heard during the voyage. Apparently, something was happening because the ship's crew appeared to be happier and mistreated us less. For the first time, the ship captain came down below deck to look at us. He spoke to us through an African translator, a traitor. We were about to dock in America, and the voyage would be over. We would then be taken to the slave-trading exchange and sold to what they called "the highest bidder."

Of course, we had no idea what they were talking about, because no such things happened in Africa. If one village captured another, the captives would become the property of the captors. Later I would learn that we were the plantation owner's property. Only difference was, we were a very long way from our homeland, with no means of escaping or returning there. We had no idea where Africa was or where our villages were in Africa. I thought, *what is this place, America?*

I snapped back to the present as I heard the bugler playing first call In the fort next door, and I realized that I was shivering from the flashback. I got ahold of myself, wiped the tears from my eyes, and started my day as this new man had been doing for many years. I could not let my past dictate how I would face today and every day to come. I was alive, in great spirits, and I had a purpose that in some way ensured the safety of many people. It was exactly what I wanted to do for my village and family.

CHAPTER 4: WYOMING UPRISING

I had been in the fort for more than three months since my last mission to capture the gun runners. Not much was happening outside the walls of the fort, but within, the gun runners' trial had taken place. The general informed me that while questioning them, the army had gotten information about the people pulling the strings. Military and government men in other parts of the country had captured the other major players, and the gun running was slowed if not completely stopped.

I was surprised to receive a letter of recognition from the five-star general that the officers of this fort reported to. I was proud of that letter, even though the general was not publicizing the event at all. I knew that a black man who went on a manhunt, captured the white men that the army wanted, and brought them to justice was not a popular man in America as of yet, so I kept quiet about the letter as well.

I could see the hate in the eyes of the white settlers every time that I walked or rode down the streets of the little town. The hateful stares weren't much better inside the walls of the fort, but the soldiers knew the general would not tolerate any of them disrespecting me. This was the reason that I tried to avoid killing white men at all costs. Even though my success in capturing criminals benefitted all people out here in the West, I didn't think that the general and the few soldiers that were loyal to him could stop a mob wanting to hang a black man for killing a white man. That just was not an acceptable thing, even this far out in the western states.

The army wasted no time carrying out the sentences of the gun runners. The two deserters and the Indian scout were all hanged at the fort. The general allowed the youngest one to serve twenty years in prison, since he had joined the gang just before their last attempt to distribute guns to the Apaches. The deserters wouldn't tell who their boss was, but he had given the names of members higher up the pecking order, which led to the leaders being captured and hanged. His mother was happy that he was not hanged, but equally disappointed in him for getting mixed up in the gun-running scheme. I told the general how he helped me out on the trail, so he said he would try to get the sentence reduced. His mother thanked us, forced a smile and left for home.

I had been out on some routine patrol missions, but nothing of great importance, so I was getting bored, and Ole Lightning was getting too fat. I knew this quiet time would not last forever, so when I was called to the general's office, I was hopeful that he had another assignment for me that would be exciting and challenging.

I knew he didn't tolerate tardiness, so I was there early, waiting for him to arrive. There was some small talk going on between the officers, and I was surveying the room because I had not been there for a week or so. He walked in, looking like the best-dressed general in the army. Those medals of Honor pinned to his chest were polished and reflecting the sunlight that was coming through the window.

As the other officers came to attention, I stood to show the general that I respected him as well. He smiled at me as he usually did while saluting the officers. As the five officers stood silently, he inquired about my health and readiness to ride out again. I flashed that "I'm ready" smile as I rested my arms on the two pistols I carried. The officers chuckled to break the silence because the general was laughing at my little presentation of arms. I stood taller as I assured him that me and Ole Lightning were ready and willing to go wherever we were needed.

He dismissed most of the officers after giving them their orders for the day. The remaining officers were the two highest-ranking serving under him. Since I had seen him do this before, I knew my next assignment was a special one that required secrecy.

As the door closed behind the men leaving, the general stood up to give his assistant orders to not let anyone disturb us. When he returned to his desk, he didn't sit. This was unusual, so I became more attentive. Folding his arms behind his back, the general started the conversation by stating that what was about to be discussed must remain confidential between the persons in the room. He paused to look each of us in the eye, to see that we nodded to confirm we understood. I was the last one to get that stern look, and my head moved up and down. The general was a respectful person and never wanted to be looking down on his officers, me, or the soldiers, so he sat in his chair, leaned back and proceeded to tell us what had led up to this mission.

He said, "A small band of Sioux Indians jumped the reservation and have started raiding some of the small ranches and farms in western Wyoming. So far, several settlers are dead, a smaller town has been raided and more than twenty horses have been stolen. The Indians are small in number, but the army speculates that the renegades are actively recruiting to add to their band of braves. We all know that there are many Indians who do not live on reservations. Most live in the hills or mountains to avoid being seen by white men. But we've had growing numbers of Indians leaving reservations under leadership of rebellious superiors."

I knew that the general didn't like calling the Lakota Indians "Sioux" any more than I did, but that is how the army referred to them and he was a dedicated army officer. After calling them Sioux Indians once, he just referred to them as Indians during the rest of the meeting. As I sat listening to the general, I thought that Many Trails was the only Lakota

Indian that I knew that should be called a Sioux, which means snake in the Indian dialect.

I refocused as the general said, "The mission is to stop the renegades before their actions get popular enough with other Indians for them to join this band and eventually possibly cause a serious uprising."

There were Indian spies throughout the western states, so the army didn't want to utilize the soldiers from the closest fort. Since I had spent some time in Wyoming, the army and government had chosen me to lead the mission. The general said, "News of an Indian uprising travels fast and usually causes the settlers and local townsfolks to panic, so it is important to the army to keep this quiet and get the Indian raiders captured quickly."

The general ordered the two officers to tell anyone who asked that I was on special assignment at the request of the regional five-star general stationed in Colorado. They nodded to indicate that they understood the order.

I was to leave immediately, preferably today after sunset, to minimize the chance of being noticed by others. The general asked me what I would need for the mission. I took a few minutes to review the map that he had on his desk before I answered him. After about five minutes I told them what items I needed. One of the officers was writing it down as the general watched. I got that "what for" look from the other officer, but the general would not allow him to question my need for any of the items. The general informed me that the supplies and weapons that I requested would be crated and available before sunset. I requested that the supplies be in a locked box and given to Jose, to be left in Ole Lightning's barn. That questioning, new officer asked why. As the others laughed, I told him that there was no way that anyone except Jose and me would go into Ole Lightning's barn and come out alive.

Jose was used to the army leaving items for me, so he would know what he should do with the box. We were dismissed after discussing the mission more and agreeing on a plan of action and a contingency plan.

I left the general's office to start preparing to leave. I knew that getting me a dark colored packhorse that didn't wear the army brand would be the hardest thing for them to do so quickly. I couldn't travel that far with horses wearing the army brand without being questioned by someone. To keep the mission secret, I needed to be thought as a lone rider traveling. Hopefully there were some good packhorses in the adjacent town that could be bought and taking a horse from its owner would not be necessary.

I spent the rest of the day checking my weapons and making sure that I had everything that I should need. I had to study the available maps of the territory, known Indian reservations, towns, fort locations, and the best route for getting to western Wyoming. I spent some extra time doing this because I would be picking up five soldiers at a known army campsite near the Colorado/Wyoming border. I usually worked alone, so I needed to plan how to best use the soldiers.

From what I was told, they were a special group of buffalo soldiers, so I needed to make sure we would have what we needed and much more. I always wanted to have more than I needed because you could always bring what you didn't use back with you. On the other hand, if you didn't have what you needed, you might not be coming home again.

Sophie knew that when I came to the store where she worked during the day, she needed to get with me immediately once she got off work if she wanted to see me before I left. It was late-afternoon, the sun still visible in the west, when she showed up at my door. I could see that concerned look on her face.

I gave her a big hug and my best comforting smile as I said, "You are certainly looking as lovely as ever."

She replied, "You know that doesn't work with me. Tell me what's up."

"I am leaving just after dark for a mission in western Wyoming and I expect to be gone for as long as three months." I really expected to only be gone a month or a little more, but it was best to give someone that loved you the worst-case timeline.

She gave me that "it's okay" smile and started preparing the food that she brought for us to eat. I knew that meant that she wasn't as happy as she was trying to show, but there was little that I could do other than give her some space. As she prepared the food, I kept busy preparing for my mission as I briefed her on what was going on, leaving out any details that the general would consider to be confidential. We spent a couple of hours together, and as I prepared to leave, she just sat at the table pretending to be interested in the book she had in front of her. I wanted to hold her some more and I knew she wanted that as well, yet there was only silence. She had acted similarly the last few times that I was preparing to leave, so I hated to leave, hated that disappointed look on her face, hated knowing it would be months before I saw her again, but I was dedicated to my job and knew that the lives of many people were at stake. We both knew I had to go, so silence was our way of spending the last precious moments that we could together.

She didn't look worried, but I knew she always was concerned that I would not come back from a mission. She was a strong woman and knew that I didn't take chances when I left the fort. Yet, I was still wondering if I should go on this mission or stay with her. I was ready to leave so I went to her. She hugged me tightly and kissed me goodbye. As she stepped back, I could see her forced smile, and it made me question taking the chance that I knew this mission would pose. I knew that I was just a different, better man in her presence.

She whispered, "Be careful. I will be waiting for you to return."

I was feeling all good inside, so I nodded yes and left the house by the back door, as if going to check on Ole Lightning.

As I stepped out of the house, my heart was beating like a drum because so much of me wanted to stay with Sophie. I stopped in my tracks, took in a deep breath of fresh air as I looked around and listened for just a moment. I didn't hear or see anyone, so I took the few steps to

Ole Lightning's barn. It would have been difficult for anyone to see me in the dark, but taking chances was not something I practiced. I found Ole Lightning, my packhorse, and the other packhorse that I'd requested, eating and resting. I looked each of the horses over pretty good to make sure they were trail-ready, and then I got everything packed on the horses.

With the packhorses loaded, I saddled Ole Lightning, and we eased away from the fort and the adjacent settlement as quietly as possible. If anyone saw us, they probably were used to seeing me leave during the night, since we would leave in the night for training or real missions.

I didn't head north; I headed west instead. I would skirt around the settlement and head north on a back trail. A secret mission depended on some deception. I was sure that I would need to be somewhat deceptive several more times before I returned to the fort.

I rode at a good pace all night, and by sunrise I was out of the area and on my way to the Colorado/Wyoming border to meet the rest of the men. I could have stopped to sleep more, but lying down would lead to me thinking about Sophie, and I didn't need such thoughts on my mind while on a mission. I would take a longer noon stop and take a nap to make up for some of the time I missed sleeping the night before.

It would take about ten days of hard riding to reach the meeting place at the scheduled time. I didn't like long, boring rides, but at least I had time to evaluate the new packhorse and adjust how the packs were loaded. He had done well as I tested him with some long runs during the night. He didn't fight being led that fast nor did he appear to be tired after the runs. I felt that he could keep up under pressure, so I was able to travel a little faster.

I had figured in some extra traveling time, in case I experienced some trouble along the route. You could never tell when a river might be out of its banks, or a horse would come up lame, forcing you to slow your pace. This area was settled, for the most part, but many Indians and some outlaws were in the area.

A lone rider with packhorses would be seen as an easy target, but this time, lady luck was on my side, and all I saw were a few traveling farmers and a lot of farms, ranches, and small towns. I didn't need anything from those places, so I skirted around them, hoping that I was not noticed.

I arrived about half a day before the scheduled meeting time. The campsite was nothing special, but it was somewhat secluded and about a mile off the closest road in the area. There was a small stream and enough trees for shade and building a makeshift corral for the horses. I paused as I was about to enter the campsite because I smelled a campfire. Since I was expecting to meet men I didn't know, I proceeded fully alert and ready should I need to defend myself. Four of the soldiers I expected to meet were already there.

A tall, muscular man with big hands and a great smile approached me first as I dismounted. His voice boomed, "Hello! Welcome to our little camp. I'm the sergeant. Here are my credentials." He handed me his papers, "You can just call me Pewee or Sergeant."

The other soldiers laughed, so I knew that was his nickname.

"Afternoon, Sergeant. Pleasure to meet you and your men."

The second soldier outstretched his hand, introducing himself as Hammer. He was a short, skinny fellow, but I could tell that he was strong and a seasoned veteran. The third soldier was the quiet one. His eyes appeared to be searching one's soul. He carried a big hunting knife and a second pistol. He introduced himself as Skinner, so I immediately knew why he carried such a big knife. The fourth and final soldier was built like me and I could tell that he had survived many battles because of the scars on his neck and exposed forearms. Those forearms were like small tree trunks and he had legs to match them. He introduced himself as Tommy Fox and said that his friends called him Bigman. He told me that I could call him Bigman for he was honored to be on a mission with me.

I was not surprised to see that all of them were buffalo soldiers, because the general had told me that they would be. They were all grinning like kids that were about to get some candy. But since I didn't know any of them, I didn't ask why.

"It's a pleasure to meet you all," I said. "My name is—"

I was cut off as Peewee held up his hand gesturing for me to put my credentials away, "That isn't necessary. All of us volunteered for this mission to get the opportunity to work with and learn from the legendary living partnership of 'the Buffalo Scout' and 'Ole Lightning'."

My eyebrows were no doubt halfway up my forehead as Peewee continued with questions like he was meeting a celebrity.

"I know your Cherokee name is 'Running Dreamer'. How did you get that name?"

It had been a while since someone called me by my Cherokee Indian name, but I had to admit that it warmed my heart to hear it, because it reminded me of my special friend Sleeping Bird.

I responded, "I was running from slavery, hoping to find freedom in the West, so the Cherokee Indians named me that because of my journey. Then they took me into their camp and cared for me for several months."

I wasn't aware that my fame had spread this far away from my home fort, but judging from how these men were acting, it had. I didn't find much comfort in that knowledge, for being unknown was one of the edges I felt I needed to do the best job for the army. Such fame tended to make you seem larger than life and alerted bad guys of your abilities. Making a mental note of this, I would spend some time thinking about it.

For the next thirty minutes, they took turns telling me of the tales they had heard about me. Whoever was spreading the word was at least keeping most of the facts right. There appeared to be a little exaggeration thrown in to make the stories sound better, but I could live with that. I would have been very upset if the tales had become bigger-than-life, like those told about outlaws and gunmen.

I still considered myself to be a normal man, with exceptional survival skills and nothing more. I told the men that I appreciated them holding me in such high regard, but we needed to concentrate on making this current mission successful. We agreed to end the storytelling and make a new story that we all could be proud of.

After discussing our mission, making some basic plans, and eating supper, we went to sleep early. Ole Skinner was humming a sweet tune and it was making me sleepy. I wasn't upset because we had a long ride ahead of us and we were getting started a couple of hours before daybreak. We didn't know if others knew about us meeting here, and I didn't want to take the chance that someone was watching with the intent to follow us.

With this being an all-buffalo-soldiers mission, there was no way that I would allow us to take any chances that could cause us to fail. That Lakota raiding party was going to be found, caught, and returned to the reservation for punishment, or we were going to kill them.

We started for western Wyoming early the next morning and after a long and hard two days of riding, we could see that there was a big dust storm approaching us from the west. We knew we would need to shelter somewhere and let it pass. Judging from the building clouds, we had about an hour to find some shelter. Bigman knew the Lakota Indians in the area, so we made for their camp that was only a few miles away.

There were Indians racing into the camp from every direction, seeking shelter from the dust storm being driven by the thunderstorm. I had been caught out in one once, and I never wanted to go through that again.

We were racing the wind, and we could see that this dust storm was a big one. The western sky was almost black, the clouds building as far as we could see. The rain started as the Indian camp came into sight, so we felt that we could make it there before we got soaking wet.

Even with Indians rushing into the camp ahead of the storm, the camp looked somewhat deserted because everyone was in their teepees. There were no fires or other activities that you would normally see in an Indian camp. The sentries stopped us as we approached the camp. Once they saw Bigman they greeted him with smiles and let up proceed into the camp. By then, the wind was howling across the open plain, and the trees were bending in resistance against the force of the wind.

We had to talk with the chief and elders before we were accepted as guests. They were happy to see Bigman and they had heard of me. We talked until a squaw returned to let the chief know our teepees were ready. By the time we got in the teepees, it was raining like hell. After about an hour, it was not storming as much but it rained almost two days.

This gave us time to talk with the tribal leaders and get some information that we hoped would help us find our way around the territory and aid us in the capture of the Indian raiders we were chasing.

We didn't tell them about our mission, and hopefully they believed that we were scouting and making maps for the army and future settlers. I couldn't think of anything else to tell them, so that was the tale that came out of my lips. God knows we were carrying more than enough stuff on the packhorses to fool anyone who didn't understand what map makers needed to actually create a map. I was sure that we'd have a good laugh once we were on our way.

The two days of Indian hospitality and being stuck in that stuffy teepee had me feeling a bit guilty. I felt guilty for having to deceive the chief about our mission and I also felt guilty about accepting the kindness of the Indian squaw who kept me company while I was in the camp. I would talk to Sophie about us getting married when I returned to the fort. Then I would have a respectful excuse for refusing Indian squaws in the future.

When the storm passed, we said our goodbyes and got on the trail. Ole Lightning set a fast pace as if knowing that we had lost the two days. The men with me were swapping stories about what they had done in the Indian camp and making fun of each other. I glanced at Peewee and he got the message and quieted his men. I stopped to set us up in a tactical formation as we ventured into an area that neither of us were familiar with. Skinner was lagging a little behind the rest of us trying to make sure that we were not being followed. Bigman took off to scout out ahead of us and Hammer alternated riding about a quarter mile left or right of me and Peewee. I was at the mercy of the soldiers with me, and I didn't like that. Each had been attentive and seemed to be as excited about the mission as I was and at least one of them had lived in most of the areas we expected to be traveling through in search of the Indian raiders. With two more long days in the saddle behind us, we would meet up with the last soldier sometime today, but until we did, we would keep traveling in the tactical formation we were using.

I spotted a landmark shown on the maps that indicated that we were within five miles of the western most army fort. As expected, the last soldier joined us with the pack horse carrying the grain for our horses. There wasn't much grass in the area of the raids so having the good army oats was a must. Both horses were dark-colored geldings, as I had requested, so our team was complete. The soldier looked to be in his late thirties and his face showed signs of having been in the sun a lot. He was missing a tooth and that appeared to be his gateway to spit tobacco juice. His shirt was discolored except for the place where he once had a sergeant's bar. I remembered from the documents that the general gave me that he had gotten busted back for striking an officer. He introduced himself and said, "Just call me Bowlegs." He was sitting in the saddle so we couldn't tell just how bowlegged he was.

It was close enough to dinner hour and according to the map, there was a good watering hole just ahead of us, so we rode there to camp. Bowlegs rode with Pewee and me, so we got him caught up on the plan for the mission. Once we reached the waterhole, Bigman scouted the area and Skinner found the tallest rock in the area for a sentry position.

I was beginning to understand why they had been assigned to this mission. They were well trained, creative problem-solvers. They were good soldiers. Once Bigman returned, I signaled Skinner to come in as well. I knew that Ole Lightning would let me know if anything was approaching the waterhole.

It was best to not have a night fire so we would be eating a hot meal for dinner and our field rations for supper. As we ate at the waterhole, Bowlegs updated us on what had happened since we were assigned to the mission.

"A couple more homesteads have been attacked. One had been burned to the ground, everyone in it dead or gone, but the other homesteader managed to fight off the attack. He was injured and lucky to be alive."

Skinner replied, "That's good news, isn't it? That means that they aren't as good as they think, if a homesteader could fight them off."

Peewee responded before I could, "Maybe so, or maybe not. We can't be sure either way. Maybe the homesteader was ready for them or had training. We have to be prepared for the worst." I was impressed with how he handled the issue and my smile and slight nod indicated that I agreed with him.

We marked each place that the Indian raiders had attacked on our maps. Bowlegs was more familiar with this area, so he showed us the locations of waterholes, places to take a defensive position, the small towns, the fort and the remaining farms and ranches that had not been attacked yet. There appeared to be a pattern for the attacks, but we needed to do some scouting to be sure. We watered the horses one more time and spent the rest of the day and the following days at each of the sites searching for signs and clues that we could use in pursuing the raiders. As we rode, Skinner took to his normal trailing position and Bigman was out front scouting while Bowlegs continued to educate Peewee and me about the local area, what the army was doing about the raids and what the Indians on the reservations were saying.

As we scouted each of the homesteads that had been attacked weeks ago, most of the tracks had been aged by Father Time, but each of the soldiers was able to point out a disturbed area, a trail of broken grass stems, an overturned rock that was not bleached out by the sun like those around it, or brush marks in the dirt. I took note of their effort and told them that they did well. Since none of them pointed out all the things that I saw, I used each site as a training exercise, pointing out the things that looked normal until you studied them for a while. They didn't consider the lack of footprints in the areas they pointed out, so they didn't look any further for clues or tracks. I explained that those things didn't get disturbed all by themselves, so what happened to the footprints? It was like their eyes were opened for the first time and Bowlegs said, "That's what we need to figure out." They were all grinning, so I kept teaching.

Those broken grass stems and those overturned rocks were not natural occurrences. There were no animal tracks, so it was unlikely that an animal had disturbed them. I gave them a couple minutes to think on it. Then I showed them how to look beyond what they were seeing to find the clues we needed. As we went from site to site, each of the soldiers improved in seeing all the signs. Skinner did the best and Bigman had a renewed excitement about scouting. Peewee took lots of notes and told me how he would teach this new knowledge to his soldiers. Hammer and Bowlegs did better at each site, but my sixth sense told me that they were a little too proud to let their excitement show. These little exercises helped me decide how to split up the team if we needed to.

At the last site, I summed up what we had done the past days by telling them, "When men have something to hide, they will do their best to hide it. If they are successful, there will be no obvious clues for someone else to find and use to capture them."

I taught the soldiers to look for clues of the means and methods that men used in the cover-up process. I now felt that they could follow a trail better, because the winding-circle tactic will always lead to you finding the beginning of the deception and the other end of the deception.

I went on to say, "Once a person feels they have deceived a pursuer enough, they stop trying to deceive that pursuer. You just have to keep working at trying to find the trail until you find it."

The key to being a great tracker was being a patient and thorough reader of the trail. Indians were great trackers, which made them equally great at hiding their trails.

After we completed our investigation of the sixth homestead that had been attacked, we had a better understanding of the Indian raiders' tactics, and we had enough clues to make a good guess as to where the raiders would attack next. We had followed their exit trail from each of the sites, and we also had narrowed down the area we thought they might have their camp hidden to about five square miles.

The knowledge of the area that Bowlegs provided was instrumental in coming to those conclusions. We all thanked him and that grin on his face showed that he appreciated us doing that. I feared to think how far I would have gotten being all alone on this mission. I could read the signs, but not knowing the area would have prevented me from being able to anticipate the next attack. It would have prevented me from finding the Indians' hidden camp until I stumbled upon it. By then, I could have ended up dead and a meal for the buzzards.

Bowlegs knew of a good camping site close to where we were so we headed there to spend the night. There were enough rocks for a good defensive position and a small waterhole. Bigman did his usual scouting while Skinner took up a lookout position. Bigman returned so Skinner came into the camp as well. By then, Bowlegs and Peewee had gathered enough wood and buffalo chips to keep a small fire burning all night. Hammer was cooking. I didn't want to feel useless, so I watered and fed the horses. We ate and Bowlegs told us about finding this campsite while pursuing some hostile Indians.

Hammer asked, "Did you really find the hostiles buried in holes using a reed to breathe through?"

Bowlegs began the story, "The soldiers didn't know the Indians had buried themselves, but one of the mules side-stepped an area and pawed the ground while looking at the spot he stepped around. That exposed a corner of the blanket the Indian used to cover himself. Then all hell broke loose as the soldiers uncovered the four Indians. The one that had buried them left a false trail to follow, but he was captured as well." I committed that knowledge to memory because I had not seen that trick before.

After eating we compared notes, sharing what each had seen during the last few days, as well as reviewing where all the attacks had taken place. After an hour or so we had a plan for pursuing the raiders. We knew time was not on our side, so we decided to use a risky tactic to find the Indian camp.

Two of us would go to where we thought the raiders might attack next, in hopes of setting up an ambush. The other four would spread out across the area we felt the raiders would travel through to get back to their camp. If the plan worked, it would force the raiders to run, and the only safe place that they would have was their hideout camp. Bowlegs, Peewee, Skinner, and Bigman would be the intercepting group and Hammer would be with Ole Lightning and me.

Bowlegs knew of a small box canyon that was a great place to meet if our plan didn't work, so he marked it on our maps. We hid the pack animals there even though I hated to leave them there alone, but we couldn't execute the plan if we left a man with them. We needed to travel fast, and that was impossible while leading several pack horses. Hopefully, there were no big predators in the area and they would be okay.

We needed to stop the next raid before it got started because not another settler should have to suffer at the hands of these raiding assholes.

Hammer and I rode the rest of the day and just as the sun was setting, we arrived at the homestead that we felt would likely be the next to get attacked. We wanted to get there at night to ensure that we were not spotted if the raiders were watching. It was a small homestead with only a house, barn and some corrals with horses and a few cattle. We could see the light through the small windows in the house. They had their water well close to the back door and the yard was fenced to make it harder to attack the house. I was thinking that the homesteader was a smart man as Hammer commented on how well the homestead was set up. He was a quiet one in a group, but, as we rode together, he talked and asked questions. I nodded to show that I understood and answered his questions.

There were some sizable rocks within rifle range of the homestead on the west and east sides. Those on the west were a better defensive position, but we had taken up a position in those just east of the homestead to not be facing the morning sun. We were expecting the Indians to ride in from the south, so our position was ideal for the ambush we had planned. I hated to ambush anyone, but we expected to be outnumbered.

I could see that the rocks were not as good of a defensive position as I liked, but we didn't expect but six to eight raiders to show up. We dismounted, fed and watered the horses. We set up with Hammer being about six feet left of me. The horses were behind the larger rocks to protect them from stray bullets. We had extra guns and I had a couple sticks of dynamite in my back pocket just in case. I asked Hammer if he was ready.

Hammer whispered, "Them Indians are going to be really surprised when we spoil their fun." We continued with lots of small talk until it was time for us to take turns sleeping. I didn't expect the attack to happen before morning, so we loosened the cinches to allow the horses to be more comfortable. I told Ole Lightning, "Rest easy, partner. Tomorrow will be a busy day." As I waited to fall asleep, I thought that if we had guessed wrong, there were probably going to be more people murdered by the raiders. I guess I must have been dreaming about that when Hammer woke me up around midnight to take my turn watching, because it was still on my mind. I wanted the last shift so I could rethink our plan and care for my weapons. Around dusk, I eased over to the horses to tighten the saddle cinches. I gave them grain and water and spent some time searching the horizon for any signs of attackers. I saw nothing so I woke Hammer up so he could get ready for the battle we were hoping for. We had some cold field rations and water to wash it down. I wanted coffee, but we couldn't chance having a fire.

As the sun came up in the eastern sky, we didn't have to wait very long before we saw dust and then a little later, men on horses approaching over the southern horizon. Hammer and I exchanged grins over our small victory at guessing their next attack correctly. Not knowing if the homesteaders could provide any support for our attack, an ambush was our only asset to even the odds. The homesteaders didn't know we were there, and the raiders didn't either, judging from the way they were approaching.

They no doubt were not expecting much of a fight, knowing that they would have the homesteaders outnumbered and pinned down, so they were not overly cautious. They made the first tactical mistake by not proceeding with caution or scouting the area. In battle, if you made the first mistake, it was probably going to be your last one.

I had Ole Henry cocked and ready to fire at the first sign of a brewing conflict. My other rifle was close by and ready for firing. A quick glance assured me that Hammer had his rifle in a firing position, with a second one lying ready as well. He was awaiting my signal, and I was waiting for the raiders to come in close enough to make every shot count and be able to get off enough shots to ensure that no more than two of them rode away from the homestead.

We could tell that the homesteaders realized the raiders were approaching the house because they fired a warning shot. That was when the raiders started to attack. They never looked our way, positioned anyone to be a lookout, or attempted to flank the homesteader's house. It was a full-frontal attack by what they believed was a superior war party.

I had told Hammer that we would shoot the Indian that appeared to be the leader last because Indians tended to give up the attack when their leader was killed. He was to shoot those on the right and I would shoot the ones on the left. As expected, the Indian that appeared to be their leader was at the rear of the attackers. So, I sited in on the raider in the front of the attack. Once Ole Henry roared, the front raider was knocked backward off his horse.

The other raiders had not realized that the shot didn't come from the homestead, so they kept attacking. Ole Henry roared again, and another raider hit the dirt. Hammer was shooting as well, and I saw a third raider fall from his horse, get entangled, and spook the horse. That was one bad way to die, so I hoped that the shot had killed him.

One of the raiders pointed in our direction, so we were no longer a secret to them. His reward for pointing at me was a slug in the heart. I guessed the raiders figured that this was a bad fight because they took off in the direction they rode in from. I picked off the leader with the most feathers in his headband and a couple more before they were out of range.

I fired a couple more times to ensure that they would be riding fast. I didn't want to hit them, just have the bullets whistle by close enough for them to get an idea of my range. Ole Henry had them lying low on their horses' necks to be as small of a target as possible. Then, it got really quiet around the homestead.

I instructed Hammer to take off after them but not try to catch up to them since there were too many for him to hold off if they turned to engage in a fight. I told him to set a pace to allow him to throw a shot their way from time to time, to keep them moving. I reminded him of what to do when they got close to the trap we had planned.

The objective was to have the surviving raiders lead us to their hiding place. They would not do this if they thought we could follow them, so

Hammer was to fall back further and further as the fleeing raiders got away from the homestead. If they believed that they could lose the lone rider by covering their trail, they would go back to their hiding place, and since we knew their false trail tactics, we should still be able to follow their trail.

Once we knew the location of their hideout camp, we could scout it and plan our assault to capture them. Timing was the key to accomplishing this, so we had to move fast and not make any mistakes.

I rode down to the homestead and introduced myself. The homesteader's name was Amos Tucker and he said, "I'm grateful, but where in God's name did you come from?" I told him that I was sent by the army. After telling the homesteaders what had just happened, I suggested that they go to the nearest town or fort until all the raiders were captured. Judging from the look on the homesteader's face, the man was surprised that I was a black man and even disbelieving that we had saved his family and his life. He kept his gun pointed in my direction and kept asking how I happened to be on his land. I told him that I didn't have time to explain it all because I had to catch up with the other rider chasing after the raiders. He looked in that direction and cursed about there being black trespassers on his property. I had to take his insulting words because I represented the U.S. government, and in part because I was black. I would make sure that his rude behavior was recorded in my official army report.

I noticed that he had a wife and four children, two of which looked to be teenaged girls. They all appeared to be scared and appreciative. This helped me deal with his hateful words, but I was not happy. I guess his hatred for the black man was more important to him than being thankful that his family was still alive. I thought of something the general used to say, "Don't argue with a fool." I repeated my suggestion that he take his family to the fort or a town. Then, I mounted Ole Lightning and took off in pursuit of Hammer and the raiders he was trailing.

Ole Lightning was fresh after a good night's rest, so I pushed the pace and caught up with Hammer in about an hour. The terrain was very flat with scattered rocks and sandy soils. When we were within a few miles of where we expected the interceptor squad to be set up, we could tell by looking at the tacks that the raiders' horses were tiring something awful. Either their hiding place was very near, or they were so afraid of being captured that they were ignoring the fact that they were killing their horses.

I looked at Hammer's mount and noticed that he appeared to be okay. Ole Lightning was hot, but still ready to charge if it was necessary. Apparently, the raiders had ridden half of the night to get to the homestead, and their horses were not as fresh. I was holding Ole Lightning back, and he wasn't liking that because he was used to running down our enemies. I took a tighter grip on the reins to slow him a little more and told Hammer to do the same with his mount.

He gave me that "What the hell" look, so I reminded him that it was time to make the raiders think that our horses were done in, too. We needed them to think that they were getting away.

I said, "Remember, no Indian brave would lead the enemy back to the camp of his people, so we have to make them think they've lost us."

Hammer slapped his forehead and said, "Sometimes I just don't think," while showing me that big grin. He slowed to a pace to match Ole Lightning's and said, "Guess I wanted them too bad to think."

I said, "If we have this figured right, the Indians will do something to cover their tracks between here and where our interceptor soldiers are waiting. If not, finding their camp will be much harder."

I asked Hammer if he saw the wisdom in our plan now. He nodded in agreement, so we rode on in silence for a while.

I wanted to give him a chance to think about all that we had done tactically, and then I would discuss possible tactics we could employ moving forward. This was my way of training without insulting the other person.

After about three minutes of silence, Hammer said, "You are one slick-thinking rascal."

I just smiled and said, "I'm an experienced tracker and that makes me a good planner for tracking others."

"How do you come up with tactics and plans like we have been using since we met on the Colorado/Wyoming border?"

I had been saying to myself that I didn't think Hammer was paying enough attention to the when's and where's as we planned our every move. Boy, was I wrong. Hammer got it!

I told him more about my life journey and how so many events and folks had helped me learn to plan such tactics. I told him of the importance of not quitting when you faced uncertainty or a perceived superior foe. I ended by telling him that as long as you kept thinking and looking for the way to succeed, you had a chance.

Part of my answer was repeating what I had told them when we first me at the campsite, but with more details.

Afterward, I said, "When you have done what I just told you, you see everything a little differently. I use that experience and knowledge as my secret weapon in the battle to stay alive."

As we talked, I was watching the dust cloud created by the raiders' horses ahead of us. As expected, after about an hour, their dust cloud disappeared. We had traveled more than ten miles since leaving the homestead, so I figured that the raiders would be close to where our interceptors were waiting. I was feeling pretty smart and proud about thirty minutes later, when just as expected, the Indians' trail became increasingly harder to read, and then it just seemed to disappear like the morning dew on a sunny day.

Hammer started straining to see clues as to where the Indians had disappeared. I allowed him some time to work through the possibilities until he became outwardly irritated about the matter. I stopped Ole Lightning and gave him that look of "I got this."

"I've seen this trick played time and time again. Let's see what clues we can find." We had another training session, and within ten minutes, Hammer was able to decide our next move. I gave him the opportunity to be in charge for a while.

After traveling about ten minutes, we met up with the interceptor group. Just as planned, Peewee was stationed in the right place to see the trick the Indians pulled, and more importantly, see which way they went.

We found a shady spot, compared notes and shared details that we had learned while fighting and tracking the Indians. Then we finalized the plans for finding the hidden Indian camp and capturing the Indian raiders.

Knowing that the Indians would be expecting any pursuers to come from where we were, north of their hideout, we would split up again to approach the suspected area from three different directions. This would be a risky tactic, but we all agreed that this should be our plan of action.

Bowlegs set to work making maps to show key landmarks, water holes, and rock areas big enough to hide a camp in the nearby rocks. He and Skinner would continue following in the direction the Indians would expect a pursuit, and the rest of us would split up to approach the suspected hideout area from two other directions.

We still didn't know how many Indians were in the raiding party, and we didn't know how well armed they were. This was of little concern to me because I had a few surprises for them. Surprises that the soldiers with me didn't even know about yet. So, I sent Peewee and Bigman to go get our pack animals and meet the rest of us at a landmark that looked like twin towers in the middle of nowhere.

The Indians were probably feeling pretty good about laying that false trail and losing us. They didn't know about our interceptors, so they didn't know that we knew which way they really went. The interceptors had seen them dismount their horses, walk the rocks for about a quarter of a mile, and then sneak out across the prairie toward a big rocky area that was barely visible from our location. We felt their hiding place was located in those rocks. Then one brave lead the horses in a direction away from the trail they were taking on foot. This was their way of laying a false trail for us to follow. Those rascals had even tied rocks onto the horses to make it hard for a good tracker to know that there was no one riding the horses. A slick trick, but one that I had learned from the Cherokee Indians.

In fact, the braves that taught me how to do it also taught me how to tell if there were or were not riders on the horses. Since the soldiers weren't familiar with this tactic, they could not hide that they had no idea what I was talking about.

I told them "Indians are very smart, so they would have left rocks here that they could tie onto the horses as they dismounted on the rocks. One Indian would lead the string of horses away from the rocks, with the reins tied to the tail of the horse in front. Should anyone tracking them be good enough to follow them this far, they could easily be fooled by the trick and keep following a trail of empty horses right into an ambush." The soldiers now understood how the trick was planned and carried out, so they could use it and not be tricked by it in the future.

Once the whole team was back together, we ate, cared for the horses and talked about the big rocks that we thought the Indians' camp was located within.

Bowlegs had not scouted those rocks before, so he said, "I'm glad that you had me get the ropes. I believe our plan to climb the walls is tricky, but our best option." Skinner and Bigman volunteered to climb the walls using the ropes that we brought along just in case we needed them. "Hey Skinner, I bet you your lunch that I reach the top first."

"Now why would you make a pig-headed bet like that when you know I'm nimbler and a better climber, Bigman."

"Quit your joking, boys. Concentrate, or neither of you will make it to the top." Peewee was always good at getting them back on track.

Bowlegs and Peewee would circle wide of the rocks and approach them from the south. Hammer and I would follow a rock formation and approach from the northwest.

I said, "We will have to seal off the entrances once we locate them to trap the Indians in the canyon." We will seal it using dynamite."

Peewee and Bowlegs looked at each other anxiously. Before they could stammer out that they didn't bring any. I laughed out loud, got up and took the special canteen out of a sack, opened it and showed them the dynamite I brought with me. I told them, "I waited until now to reveal it, since some folks get very nervous to be around dynamite."

Skinner and Bigman had already taken a step backward, so Hammer was poking fun at them. I gave Peewee and Bowlegs three sticks tied together and three single sticks. The bundle was for dropping in the canyon entrance and the three single sticks were for emergency use if they were under attack. Bowlegs took the dynamite and put it in his saddle bags.

You won't be riding right next to me on the trail, Bowlegs," Peewee said. Everyone laughed at that.

"I have the skills to sneak around in the dark, so I will take out any sentries at the Indian camp." I was taking my boots off to slip into my moccasins to make that point stick. When I produced a miniature bow and arrow set, they were speechless. I set up a target at about thirty yards and hit it three out of three shots. "Woah, boss, where did you learn to do that?" Skinner's eyebrows were halfway up his face as he spoke.

I said, "My Cherokee friends taught me to use their weapons and it has benefitted me greatly through the years." After seeing that demonstration, everyone's spirits were high in anticipation of capturing the Indians.

We got some rest and waited for late afternoon to put our plan into action. Skinner wanted to be the lookout, so we let him do it while we rested.

***

At the appointed time, we split up as planned. Skinner and Bigman followed the false trail the Indians left for us to find. This was important since the Indians knew that two men had followed them from the homestead. The rest of us took the other two routes that would put us in position to approach the suspected location of the Indian raiders' camp just after dark.

We rode for most of the remaining daylight hours to reach the rocks that we felt they were camped and hiding in. This was some rough country, and if you didn't know it, you could get lost in a hurry and wander around until you died or were killed by someone or something. My head never stopped moving as I constantly scanned the rocks and horizon for any signs of danger. Hammer was doing the same thing since there was nothing more important for us to be doing. We lost sight of Peewee and Bowlegs after about fifteen minutes. They were on the longer route so they had to ride much faster than Hammer and me.

I had been studying the rocks for the past twenty minutes. Once we were only about a hundred yards from them, we stopped to study them more closely. Big rocky cliffs seemed to be shooting up out of the ground to form a canyon that looked more like a natural fortress. Very little vegetation was visible around the rocky area, and the soil was basically desert sand. It was so large that we had to study it for a while to determine how to get to the top of the rock walls. Hammer was stationed at a fort in northern Wyoming, so he knew more about finding a path up through the rocks than I did.

He spotted what he called a "goat trail" and said, "I think we can get almost to the top on that trail, but we will have to walk and climb the last section to reach the top." He pointed out an area up there where we could leave the horses so I knew he had been studying the rocks as we approached them. He continued, "I know rocks so that is why I wanted to be with you."

I smiled and said, "Thanks for doing a great job."

Hammer led the way up the trail and it didn't take long for us to get to the area where we had to leave the horses. I could tell that Ole Lightning wasn't liking being in a trailing position, because I had to pull his head back several times to keep him from biting the lead horse. Once we made it to where we would have to leave the horses, we had more time than we needed to find the best path for advancing on the Indians' camp. I knew that the Indians were probably watching the false trail that they left for us to find and we were on the opposite side of the rocks from where we expected their camp to be, yet we were as careful as we could be. We soon reached the top of the rocks, and were able to find an area with some big loose rocks where we could hole up and wait. We could also see the entrance into the canyon. It was too risky to try finding the camp before the sun went down, but Hammer and I had found what we were looking for. I had a big grin on my face as I now knew that a few sticks of dynamite would seal the entrance into the canyon.

As we looked at each other we were grinning from ear to ear, so I whispered, "Going to be some fireworks tonight."

Hammer laughed quietly and said, "I can't wait."

It was important that we didn't get surprised by any Indians that were out scouting for us or just hunting for game. I climbed to the highest rock that I could get to and was lying flat on it. I could see for miles, unobstructed. I could see what I believed to be the area within the rocks where the Indian camp had to be because it was the only open area within the rocks. I was surprised that I couldn't see any sentries, but I felt that the Indians probably didn't believe that the army or any whites knew of this hidden canyon.

As I surveyed this natural fortress, I thought of how the white man would continue moving west. Anything or anyone that tried to stop that progress would be the enemy of the white man and be killed or conquered. The Indians would be better off hiding from civilization and maintaining their lifestyle for as long as they possibly could. Fighting this losing battle was wiping them out.

Just before sundown, a lone Indian leading the horses of those that had dismounted in the rocks appeared on the horizon. Even though he was approaching from the west, he appeared to be skirting around the perimeter of the rocky area and not heading directly into the rocks. The only reason that I could think of for doing this was that there was no entrance to the Indians' camp from that direction. As he approached where he crossed our trail, I got a little tense, but the sun was setting and he was riding fast so he didn't see any prints that our shod horses may have made on the rocks.

In less than five minutes, I spotted two more Indian braves approaching the rocks from the east. They, too, appeared to be moving from the east in a northwestward direction, skirting the perimeter of the rocky area as well. That meant that there might only be one entrance into the area other than the one we had scouted.

Peewee and Bowlegs approached from the south side of this rocky area, so if they had done a good job of scouting, they should know if there is an entrance from that direction. They would know where it was and take action to seal it up when I gave the attack signal.

They had enough dynamite to seal up an entrance, which would stop, or at least slow, anyone attempting to exit the rocks in that direction.

The Indians would be easy pickings for the soldiers if they tried to run. Hopefully, they would know that trying to escape was a mistake and surrender rather than choose death. No more Indians approached before sundown, so it was time to put our plan in action.

Skinner and Bigman had been trailing the Indian leading the string of horses. They were to wait for the sun to set before they would approach the big rocky area from the southwest to take up their positions on that side. They didn't have dynamite, but they did have ropes that they would need to climb the rocks to reach the top. The knowledge that Bowlegs had of this area probably would be the reason we succeeded on this mission. He was spot on about this big rocky area and everything else that he told us.

We left our sentry position and took up a position just above the entrance to the canyon to wait for Skinner and Bigman to have the thirty minutes that they needed to climb to the top. My plan for silencing the Indian sentries that would be on night duty required me to sneak up on each of them to kill them and keep them from alerting the rest of the Indians.

I would shoot the sentries in the throat to make sure they couldn't cry out and alert the rest of the Indians. Doing so required great skill. I was pretty good with the bow, yet I knew I had to sneak up to within twenty yards of the targets to make the fatal shots. If I missed, it would most certainly be bad for our plan. Plan B: Hammer was ready to drop the dynamite in the entrance if he heard one of the sentries sound an alarm.

After spotting and taking out two sentries, I was just above their campsite. To my amazement, there was a perfect hiding place within the rocky area. There was a little water hole, with some native grass growing around it. It was about fifty yards wide and about a hundred yards long. The inside walls of the canyon were basically vertical, too, which was a welcome sight. The Indians could not climb their way out of the canyon, so that just left the narrow passage that we planned to close using the dynamite.

As I was surveying the canyon, I spotted the last sentry. He was on the rim just above the campsite. I could not take him out with the bow because he would fall into the camp area and alert the Indians that they were being attacked.

I was prepared for this quiet fighting, so I snuck up on the last sentry, slit his throat, and propped him up in a sitting position as he was when I killed him. I proceeded back to where Hammer was just above the canyon entrance.

In the dark, you cannot look for bodies as you can in the daylight, so I used a trick that I learned from the Cherokees. I found a lower position, which allowed me to scan the top of the canyon walls to see if the other soldiers had gotten into position for the attack.

Lying flat on the rocks, I looked at the stars in the directions that the soldiers should be stationed. If they did as instructed, they would be moving left to right in a crouching posture. Their movements would block the glow of the stars in the background, and I would see that and know that they were ready.

Once I spotted the other two groups of soldiers, I instructed Hammer to light the dynamite and drop it in the entrance to the canyon. The campsite was about thirty yards from the entrance and the path was a winding one, so I wasn't concerned about the blast injuring the Indians. Once Hammer dropped the dynamite, all hell broke loose. There was the noisy boom, followed by the horses trying to flee the noise. The Indians jumped to their feet, grabbed their weapons, and broke out in their native chatter, heads spinning in all directions searching for an enemy. Amidst the chaos, I put an arrow in the heart of the last Indian sentry that we had spotted on a ledge about ten feet above the canyon floor.

The dynamite blast was the best signal for a mission like this because the Indians would be confused and unprepared for the attack. While listening for a second blast that did not come, I noticed that the dynamite had done what we expected, and the entrance to the camp was sealed. The absence of another blast told me that there was not a second entrance to the camp below. The dynamite caused the loose rocks to fill the opening to stop any escape, so the Indians had no way to retreat. Hopefully, they would realize that they were sitting ducks and give up.

They made no effort to escape toward the south, so that confirmed our gamble. Instead, they crouched close to the ground, heads still spinning. We were lying flat on the rocks with our rifles ready to fire, but at this angle there wasn't enough moonlight to give our positions away.

The Indians had no way of knowing that I could understand them, so they made no attempt to communicate in another way. I was able to understand much of what they were saying. We needed to work fast because the shock of the attack would not last long, and the Indians were preparing to band together in defense of their camp.

I did my best to communicate with them, using as much of their native language as I knew. I told them that there was no way out because the dynamite had sealed up the entrance. They told me to die a terrible death and called my mother names that were hurtful. I called them murdering thieves and to insult them more, I called them slithering Sioux. Those with rifles fired toward my position, but I was far enough from the ledge that any bullets hit the rock face or went over my head.

I had each of the groups of soldiers light a match to let the Indians know that we had them surrounded. They could see that we had the superior position since we were up high, looking down on them. Most of the Indians had inferior weapons that were not accurate enough to be any threat to us, so they knew they were beat.

I yelled down, "Put down your weapons in a pile next to the fire and lay flat on the ground." I repeated that statement again and told them, "We have eyes on you from three different directions, so we will know if any weapons are not placed on the pile as instructed."

I saw one make a move to take a defensive position behind a rock, so I wounded his right shoulder as a warning to the rest. They were more than mad. We had humiliated them. They were cursing us, using every dirty word that I had ever heard come out of an Indian's mouth. In the glow caused by their large campfire, I knew that we could not just march down into the camp and tie their hands and feet, but I was worried that might be the only option. I needed to think.

Bowlegs recognized one of the Indians and shouted out his name. "Lone Cat, it's me, Bowlegs. Do as you were instructed."

Lone Cat turned toward where Bowlegs' voice came from and yelled, "Bowlegs is no longer my friend. I will kill you when I get the chance."

Bowlegs ignored him and yelled to me, "Lone Cat understands and speaks English well enough to communicate with us."

I said, "Lone Cat, this is the Buffalo Scout. We don't want to kill any of our Lakota brothers today. Make sure all of your braves give up their guns and start tying their hands and feet."

As we watched, Lone Cat said, "Buffalo Scout, we have heard of you. You have become our enemy."

I sent a Henry slug in the ground between his feet and said, "Do as you was instructed." He looked at one of the chiefs and the chief gave his nod to do as instructed.

There were more than twenty braves in the camp and a few squaws and children. All of the braves were wearing war paint, so we could not trust them to come along without trying to kill us. Only eight of the braves had blankets, shirts, pants, or knives that were government-issued to Indians on reservations, so it appeared that this group of Indians included plenty of braves who had never lived on a reservation. They never surrendered to the army and had continued to live hidden in the hills of their native land.

Bowlegs recognized a couple of Indians that had left the reservation to lead this band of renegades. Both were chiefs of their small tribes, but neither were great Lakota chiefs. I told Hammer that it looked like we got here just in time to prevent a serious outbreak of massacres. He nodded grimly.

With the guns in a pile next to the fire and the braves all tied up except for Lone Cat, I instructed Bigman to drop down into the canyon.

The Indians were surprised to see him rappelling down the face of the rocks on a rope. Skinner stayed up top to be our lookout. Bowlegs rappelled down on the south side of the canyon to give us two guns on the canyon floor. Pewee followed Bowlegs down the rope. He checked all the bound Indians to ensure that they were tied up good. Lone Cat had done a good job, and he was rewarded with a nice pair of handcuffs and some shiny leg irons. The same type that we put on the leaders of this band of raiders.

Once we had everything in the campsite under control, I told Hammer to go back down the way we came up to get his horse and take a sentry position at the entrance to the canyon. I wanted to tell him to take Ole Lightning with him, but Ole Lightning probably would have killed him. I lowered down the blasting powder and rappelled down to the canyon floor and greeted our prisoners. Only one of them was injured, so I had Bowlegs and Skinner use ropes to tie them all together in a big circle so they could watch the blasting show. Bowlegs tended to the wounded brave and advised that he was in no danger of dying.

Peewee gave me a puzzled look so I explained that I would use small amounts of black powder placed in the piles of rocks to make a lot of small rocks out of the big rocks that the dynamite had blasted into the entrance. They were relieved to hear that because there was no way to get out of the hidden canyon campsite with the entrance filled with big rocks.

We had to repeat the task several times to break up the larger rocks, but when we were done, most of the rocks were small enough for a man to lift and pull out of the way to make a passage. I had learned to use black powder for blasting on the plantation when removing tree stumps from the ground, and for the first time in a long time, that knowledge came in handy. The Indians and soldiers watched and said nothing. After the second blast, the soldiers had learned the importance of covering their ears and turning their faces away from the blast site. We had the Indians at the other end of the canyon and away from the blasting site to protect them from the blasting. The soldiers grinned as the entrance became more passable one blast at a time.

With the help of our newly captured Indian prisoners, the entrance was cleared of the rock debris just before daybreak.

We had the Indians tied off to each other like slaves were chained while in transit, so they were able to work and walk but not kick or run. I had Peewee and Bowlegs walk the Indians' horses around the canyon to calm them down before we mounted and tied each Indian to a horse. Some were cursing like hell because we didn't have them on their horse.

They were even more agitated when we made them allow the women and children to ride double with them, so we gagged them. With the Indians ready to travel, I rode double with Hammer to go get Ole Lightning. When we returned, Peewee showed his strength by going back up the rope to get his and Bowlegs' horses. Once we were ready to go, Skinner would bring their horses to the entrance. We brought one of the pack horses into the canyon to add any items that we could recover to the packs.

There were hairbrushes, jewelry, money, knives, silver pots, plates, and cutlery that the Indians had stolen. We hoped that they could be of use to some settlers. We took the firing pins out of all the guns that the Indians had, smashed the stocks on the rocks, and bent the barrels. After filling all the canteens, we salted the watering hole in the camp area. There was a steady flow of water entering it, so the water would only be undrinkable for a couple months but would then be back to normal.

Right now, we didn't need a new group of Indians using this campsite to build another band of renegades to start raiding again. At the very least, it would let any Indians that came to the camp know that the canyon was not a secret any longer.

The Indians had picked a great place to set up camp because the entrance was very hard to spot. Most riders would have passed it without even knowing that the entrance was behind a big ole rock. Chances were that a brave chasing game some time back had followed it into the entrance. One thing for sure, every Indian near this area probably knew of this hidden oasis because they shared such information. No army patrol looking at it would think that it was anything more than a bunch of big ole rocks.

Thanks to this mission, the U.S. government and the army knew about the site now and they would be able to check it for signs of occupancy as often as they felt was necessary. The soldiers made note of its location on their field maps, as I recorded it in my memory in case I was ever up this way again.

With the Indians securely tied onto their horses and all the horses tied together, our train left the campsite. Skinner left his post and joined us as we rode east to get back to the nearest army post. I led the group, with Peewee and Bowlegs as outriders, Hammer and Bigman took turns riding point, while Skinner was right where he wanted to be, riding drag. This was the best military formation we could use, with there being only six of us.

We had a long, hard three days of riding ahead of us that would be highlighted by sleepless nights before we reached the fort. We were crossing the open plains, so we couldn't take any chances. If we were discovered by other renegade Indians, things probably would not turn out in our favor.

The ride was tiresome, but uneventful apart from the soldiers' jokes and questions. We made it to the fort where Bowlegs was assigned in pretty good time and with all our limbs still attached. This was where we would leave the prisoners, no need to risk transporting them further.

Me and Bowlegs gave the details for the orderly to do the required reports. We left it up to the commanding officer to notify the higher-ranking officers about the particulars of the mission. Then we joined the others and had a good meal before going to bed to catch up on the sleep we missed during the mission. Even Ole Lightning welcomed the chance to rest and eat some good ole army oats.

The commanding officer in charge of the fort sent messages to the other forts where the rest of us were assigned. He would let them know that the mission was successful, that we were all okay, and that we were on our way back home. Bowlegs was home, so the next day, the rest of us said our goodbyes and headed east to return to our homes.

After the second day of riding, Bigman and Skinner headed northeast toward Laramie while the rest of us continued east. Once we got to the original place that we met up, Hammer and Peewee left in different directions to return to their home forts, and I turned south toward New

Mexico Territory. They were good soldiers, and good men, and I was proud to have worked with them, but I was ready to be home.

Using the eastern road made the trip longer, but there were mountains and a lot of untamed country in northwestern Colorado that a man would be foolish to attempt to cross. Renegade Indians and outlaws used the area as a hideout and didn't like army personnel or lawmen enough to ask their names before shooting them in an ambush.

With the packhorses carrying much less than they were on the trip up, we were able to make better time and travel longer, so I expected to get back two days faster than it took coming up. I loved traveling through this area because the views were breathtaking. The open plains were east of the road and the terrain went from rolling hills to the mountains west of the road. You could see for miles in any direction and the road was wide enough for wagons to pass each other. I had been gone for over a month and was looking forward to getting home.

I was met on the trail within ten miles of the fort by five soldiers I didn't know and Sergeant Williams. I greeted them and Sergeant Williams told me "We were sent out to escort you back to the fort." He got my best "Go to hell" stare as I asked, "Why?"

He said, "The Carson brothers that you helped capture a few years back escaped prison and have been seen in this area."

He relayed a few details of their crimes and I quickly remembered them and how all three of them promised to come kill me if they escaped. Until now, it didn't matter much to me, but right now I was wishing that I had killed them when I had the chance.

One gave me a very nasty knife scar on my left arm, and another kicked me in the nuts. I was lucky that I saw it coming and blocked most of the blow, while knocking the outlaw out with a hit to the side of his head from my rifle butt.

I said to myself, "Well, if they had come for me, they won't live very long. I just don't tolerate anyone threatening my life."

I knew that criminals like that bunch would kill the soldiers first, with the intent of making me suffer watching them die, all the while hoping that it would give them the edge they needed to kill me as well. I had outsmarted those outlaws the first time, and I planned to do the same this time.

I dismounted, as did the sergeant. He sent one soldier up the road about a hundred yards toward the fort and another out east of the road about fifty yards.

"How do you want to play this, Sergeant?" I asked. "I will ride by your side and we should have two soldiers out front, two behind and one east of us close to that ridge over there."

I nodded. He issued the orders to the soldiers and they took their positions as we got back on our horses and made our way back toward the fort with a renewed sense of caution.

In this formation, it would be hard for the outlaws to get to me without causing a ruckus. I had Ole Henry resting across my saddle horn, one pistol in the side holster, and one in the saddle holster. I felt a little naked since I wasn't armed with all my extra pistols and knives, but we were expecting only three outlaws. We were ready for them murdering bastards, and I had no reservations about sending them straight to hell a little sooner than they expected.

I wasn't as scared or concerned for myself as I was for the soldiers that appeared to be rather new recruits, led by an experienced Sergeant Williams.

We traveled about four miles, seeing nothing and no one. After another two or so miles, we saw what appeared to be a wagon loaded with supplies. That wasn't unusual while traveling this road. The driver had one of those big Mexican sombrero hats and was leaning forward as if falling asleep.

As the wagon passed me, I spoke, and he responded in broken English as most Mexicans did. We didn't expect any trouble from the wagon, so we paid very little attention to it, keeping our focus on the surrounding terrain.

As the wagon passed us, there was some movement that caught Ole Lightning's eye, so he shifted slightly, giving me a sign that something unusual had just happened.

As I turned in the saddle to see what could have spooked him, I saw movement in the wagon. I was surprised to see a rifle barrel and a face under the canvas cover. As I sounded an alarm for the soldiers, the two behind us were met with bullets from the man driving the wagon. The two soldiers behind me shot that asshole, knocking him off the wagon seat.

That spooked the mules pulling the wagon, and they started running. As the gunman, intent on killing me, attempted to get in position to get off a shot, the soldier riding flank put a bullet through the wagon sideboard, just inches from his head. As the outlaw attempted to take cover, I shot him, and the shock of being shot caused his torso to bend backward, so he almost looked like he was sitting up. That gave the flanking soldier a better target, so he drilled him good that time.

There was a second gunman in the wagon that was smarter, so he stayed low and got some shots off before I blew a bloody red spot in his chest, where his heart used to be. The two soldiers riding in front of us were back beside us and firing into the wagon just in case there were some more outlaws hiding under the canvas.

As I heard one of the soldiers tell the sergeant that I had been injured, I felt the pain for a split second, so I knew that I had been shot. The initial shock of it had blocked out the pain. I saw only darkness and felt only emptiness.

It was like I was back on the African shore, being forced to go somewhere that I knew nothing about, and I could do nothing. I could hear voices that seemed to be very concerned, and I could faintly tell that I was moving, yet I couldn't control my limbs; my eyes couldn't open; my chest hurt like hell; and my head, oh, how my head ached.

Then there was just darkness, and I could feel nothing. The Great Spirit Warrior was the only one who could help me now, so I tried to call on him.

CHAPTER 5: EXODUS FROM SLAVERY

In my not-fully-conscious state, I knew something wasn't right with me, yet I could not remember why or wake myself up. I was hurting something awful. I felt like I was being tormented by demons trying to keep me from meeting the Great Spirit Warrior. As I slipped back into an unconscious state, I was haunted by thoughts of the torments of slavery.

That era of my life was so tragic that I did everything in my power to forget it. But when I was in low places, those memories haunted me like a thief during the night, stealing my joy, dampening my spirits, and eating at the sanity that I tried so hard to maintain. I thought being captured and taken from my homeland was the worst I would endure, but once I was sold into slavery, I learned the true meaning of torture. The man who became our master was not a kind man in any sense of the word. He looked mean and unhappy all the time. He barked orders to his white employees and whipped us as soon as we were his property because he said he needed to get our attention. Lord, was that message loud and clear. That first introduction to the whip, the ole black snake, took a lot of hope from most of us captives, who had been thinking about overpowering the captors to escape.

Like the ship captain, the plantation owner had blacks that could speak our African language as well as his language. I would learn later that the language was English and that the master demanded that we learned it. He had his overseers use the whip to encourage us to learn.

They continued to use the whip to discourage us from trying to overpower the whites. That whip was one evil thing to use on humans. It would cut your flesh. It would strip your body of power, pride, and rebellion. Yet, you were still able to work, for that was your only value to the master.

After witnessing a runaway get whipped to death, I knew I was in one hell of a bad situation. We were chained but still watched so closely that escaping would be nearly impossible. Even if you escaped, you had to elude the slave hunters with their bloodhounds. You had to survive on what the land could provide because you couldn't get any supplies, and even if you could, you had to carry them while running, and that would slow you down and possibly cause you to be captured.

And if you ran, you would have to head up north or out west, hoping that you could get some help on the way. Knowing all the time that failing to elude the slave hunters would get you whipped to death or hanged.

It certainly made sense to stay in your place, be a good slave, and live out what you could of your life. I felt that was why so many slaves lost hope, lost their pride, and for some, lost their will to live.

We were treated like animals. The more attractive African women were used as house slaves and required to service the master and any other white man that desired to have sex with them. They couldn't fight or protest, or they would be beaten or killed. I knew of their pain, but none of the men were able to protect them as I had been taught to do as a warrior in Africa.

The mistress of the plantation didn't like it, but white women didn't seem to have much say about the matter. But they could take their hatred out on the black slave women as long as they didn't hurt them enough to compromise their value to the master.

I always wondered how those white women felt when they saw those slave women's half-white babies. Especially when the master seemed to be drawn to the slave women mothers. That was the only obvious show of humanity and caring that I ever saw in the master. I'm sure that the mistress could see it, too, so I guess that was why she was drunk so often.

The plantation owners would couple the black men and women based on a breeding program to produce the ultimate bucks and wenches. The slaves were not allowed to protest, and if the couples didn't produce babies year after year, they would be punished or sold.

The children would grow up and become a great source of income for the plantation owner, either working in the field or being sold. The biggest and strongest slave men were often forced to fight for the pleasure of the whites. They worked as other slaves did, but their job was to breed bigger and stronger slave children, so the best bucks would be mated to the stronger slave women. A male slave might never know how many children he fathered since some of the slave women were sold while with child.

There was no regard for family when it came to slaves. A slave was owned, and the master decided what would be done with each of them. If another plantation owner had a need for a slave, he picked the one he wanted out of those the master was willing to sell, paid the price, and that slave went with the other plantation owner. If it was a mother with children, the family was often separated, and another slave woman would be ordered to take care of the children left behind.

There were a lot of sad days, and there was a lot of crying on that plantation. How were we, as slaves, supposed to hold our heads up or be proud? I was determined to escape that life.

I learned a lot in those first years of being a slave, so I knew that slaves ran away often. Several escaped, but most were returned and treated even worse than they were before running away. I felt that I couldn't live that way for long. So, despite my fears and doubts, I knew that I had to plan my escape and get away with it the first time around because there wouldn't be a second chance.

It was late summer and hot as hell on the plantation. Crops were about ready to be harvested, so the overseers were pushing the slaves hard and allowing none of us any slack time. I was mad about the treatment and wanted to take off as soon as possible but picking the time to escape wasn't something to make a hasty decision about. Besides, I wasn't prepared to make a successful escape. For the next few weeks, I stayed busy with my chores, caring for the livestock and dogs, watching and learning everything that I could about the plantation and surrounding areas.

I knew that I needed to become a trusted slave because trusted slaves were not chained all the time and were allowed to leave the plantation with the overseers. It took all the willpower I had to take the punishments they continued to inflict on me to make sure that I was viewed as a good slave. This was difficult as I watched some of the other slaves being mutilated or killed for just trying to act like men. I watched it all, contained my rage and took my punishments because I needed to gain the trust of the overseers and the master.

After several month of being a good slave and caring for the animals, they had me training the dogs to track runaway slaves.

I was successful in becoming trusted because I trained the dogs well, helped track any runaway slaves, and never talked back or acted displeased about how I was treated. I was given more tasks that took me away from the plantation almost daily as I was loaned out to help on some of the neighboring plantations. I was with an overseer, but that didn't keep me from learning the area. I quickly became acquainted with nearby landmarks, plantations, farms, and towns. Since many runaway slaves were captured by neighboring plantation owners, I knew this information would help me to avoid them and have a better chance of escaping.

I knew that there were men that specialized in tracking runaway slaves, so that was who I was most desperate to spend time with. I needed to learn how they tracked. Doing this would not make me popular with the other slaves, but it would give me the opportunity to venture farther away from the plantation to learn about rivers, creeks, hills, and even swamplands. I would learn their tracking tactics and limitations. If I was to succeed in escaping, I needed to know the enemy and how he fought. I couldn't depend only on my warrior skills to get away.

After going on a couple of the runaway slave hunts, I could see how I could use the terrain, creeks, rivers, and trees to aid me in escaping because the dogs couldn't track a scent that they couldn't find. I learned more about the dogs and horses. I learned the weaknesses and strengths of the trackers. Yes, I could begin to see that I had a good chance to escape. I just needed the right opportunity to make my move.

I usually knew when slaves planned to escape since the woman, Betsy, they made me live with knew everything that went on in the slave quarters, and she liked to talk. On occasion, I even confused some of the trackers to give the slaves that I liked a better chance of escaping. Usually, it was all for nothing since few of the runaway slaves had any knowledge about the surrounding area, and those born into slavery didn't know how to survive on their own. Many would just run around in circles with no idea they were doing it. Fortunately, some slaves were assisted by the Underground Railroad, so they escaped up north to Canada.

I would also hear the white men talking about the West and all the adventures and opportunities out that way. I learned that slavery wasn't as popular out West and that Indians lived out there and had struggled to live with the white man. It didn't appear that the Indians would overpower the whites, but for now, they were more powerful than them in several unsettled areas. So, I decided I needed to go west as soon as I got a chance.

As the months passed, I became more trusted by the trackers and master, so I was not chained up anymore. I worked with the bloodhounds, so I had access to leather and steel. I had shoes since I had to travel with the trackers. I made some leather inner soles for them. I knew there were big rivers to cross, some large, mountain-like hills, and some dense forest with animals that could kill a man. I needed weapons, so I was able to hide small steel shanks in my shoes. I had the skills to make a knife or spear with them. I had been given a small knife and a honing stone to keep it sharp, so I could cut vines and small branches to use for making a spear.

I was a good listener, so I had learned about charting a path based on the stars as I was out with the trackers. That was probably the most important thing that I learned from them. Once I knew how to figure out where I was and where I was going without a map, I felt that I was ready to make my move.

As I was kneeling to drink water out of a creek, I was thinking about escaping. I thought about trying to get a gun, but they were very careful with those. I had learned how to load and shoot a gun by watching the overseers, but I had not actually fired one. If I was lucky enough to get one, I could figure out how to use it. The next best thing to do was to steal one once I got far enough away from this area.

I would probably have to take a life to get one, but I was prepared to do anything to escape slavery. Even though I hated that thought, the rage in me outweighed my pride. The life I knew back in Africa had been taken from me, and there was no way that I would get it back. I was walking and living in America. I had no joy without my freedom, my family, and my pride. Slavery had stolen all of that from me.

I was still thinking about escaping when we got back to the plantation. In fact, it was always on my mind, but I was careful to never tell anyone of my plan. Betsy didn't even know of my plan to leave. I didn't choose her, love her, or want to be the father of her children. I also knew she couldn't keep her mouth shut, and I couldn't take a chance that she would tell someone.

Because I helped track the runaways, all the slaves thought I was a traitor. That was exactly what I wanted them and the white men to think, for it was the one thing that would allow me to gain the opportunity to escape.

I was still on that plantation, waiting for my chance more than a year after I started planning my escape. One chilly late fall morning, several overseers were sick. There were tasks that had to be done to keep the plantation operating, so I was instructed to go get firewood for the main house and the cabins that the overseers lived in. I was being watched by a newly hired overseer that had not become as hateful as most of the other ones.

I had helped him when his ankle got caught in a trap, so he liked and trusted me. We were not far from the fields, so when the alarm sounded to alert the whole plantation that one of the slaves had run away, I became nervous. The overseer with me had to report to the master, so that left me alone, giving me the opportunity I needed to escape.

He threatened me as he rode off on his horse, promising to kill me if I tried to run while they were chasing the runaway. I promised him that I would do what I was out there to do. That reply was deceptive, but not entirely a lie. I was thankful that they had another slave to help with the tracking and didn't want me to go on the hunt because it would have cost me my chance. He left, looking back from time to time to check on me. Each glance was daring me to try something. I would smile and wave while loading wood on a wagon.

I knew that I would probably never get a better chance to run, but I hesitated, thinking of the danger I would be in. But I knew I could not continue to live like this.

I kept chopping and carrying the wood while listening to the hounds. They were tracking the slave that had run toward the north hoping to evade all white people until he got to Canada. I certainly hoped he was running straight north and not getting confused and just running around in circles. I hoped that he was a fast runner as well because the dogs and horses ran faster than a man could and I needed them to be busy hunting him while I headed west.

Once I could barely hear the hounds, I took a long look back toward the plantation house, hoping it would be the last time that I saw it, the fields, or the other slaves. No one was watch me, so I knew it was now or never. I pretended to be checking the harnesses on the horses, but I was actually cutting off the leather reins and any other leather or rope, because I knew I would need all that I could get to aid me in escaping.

The biggest threat to being caught was them damn bloodhounds. They could track a man no matter what he did to distract them. I had a trick or two planned, and if they worked, I would have a much better chance of escaping to the West.

I took the ax back into the woods as if to cut more wood. I chopped a dead tree trunk a few times, in case someone was close enough to hear or see me. Then I became the warrior that I was trained to be. A smart warrior knew when to move during a fierce battle, so I was moving from my last combat and racing toward the next one. More importantly, I was no slave for the first time in years and immediately, my pride was driving me, not that damn whip. I was not upset about leaving what had been home for the last several years. I was determined to right the wrong that caused me to be here in the first place.

The first day I just ran at a steady pace, taking short breaks to rest and listen for the sound of hounds. I could feel the morning sun on my back, so I knew I was heading west. The cold was welcomed as it helped me stay fresh. All the items that I was carrying were a little heavy, but I had carried such a load every day on that plantation or when tracking runaways. My body was very able to keep carrying it for several more hours, so I stayed focused on running.

As I ran, my thoughts returned to that plantation. To the white men, I looked like a good ole slave, and to the slaves, I looked like what they called an "Uncle Tom". I didn't really understand the term, but if it made me appear to be a trusted slave, I was all for it. That title let me get this far. I was being hunted, but I was free. I didn't know how far I would get, but I knew I was not a slave no more. I was a warrior again.

As I ran, I looked for trees that had grown big, with the limbs intertwining. My first trick to throw off the dogs was to climb a tree, use the limbs to transfer to another tree and use the rope to drag a piece of my clothing along the ground to give the dogs a false trail to follow. Once I had transferred from one tree to another and then maybe a several more, I would pull up that piece of clothing and that would be the end of my trail.

As I was performing the tactic, it occurred to me that I never thought that playtime in the trees in Africa would be helpful in escaping slavery in America.

The tactic would give the dogs fits. They would be confused, and the trackers would likely not know that I had gone up in a tree in the first place. I knew that they would figure it out after a while. But the time it took them to do that would allow me to get that much further ahead of them. Even if they did figure it out, they would have a much harder time determining which tree I climbed and which direction I took.

I knew I couldn't take any chances, so by using the rope tactic several times, I was able to make a false trail of several hundred yards in the trees before using the rope to lower myself down into a small creek where my scent would be masked by the water. I figured that I had traveled more than ten miles as the sun was setting. I used my warrior skills to make a spear and catch a few fish for supper. I had matches in a leather pouch tired around my waist so once I walked a little deeper into the forest I made a fire to cook and eat them.

Since I was at a small creek, I left another false trail heading north by leaving a few footprints along the eastern edge of the creek until I used my ropes to get up into the trees again. This time, I changed directions on the trackers while moving through the trees and headed directly west. They would be expecting me to head north, so if they lost my trail, they would look that way for a while before even considering that I might have gone in another direction.

When the dogs couldn't pick up my scent, they would have to figure out which direction I went, how and when I crossed the creek, and how to track what they were now probably thinking was a ghost.

Meanwhile, I was putting as much distance between them and me as I could. As I ran, I continued to listen for the dogs, but I never heard them. Even though I couldn't hear them, I knew that if a white man saw me, he would assume I was a runaway slave and attempt to capture me. I was in a battle with an unknown number of combatants and I would not be safe until I got to one of the western states I had heard about.

I remembered hearing the white men talking about the swamps to the west. They wanted to scare us with tales of poisonous snakes and alligators. I had heard stories about white men using small slave children as bait when hunting alligators. I so hoped that it was just a tale, but something within me believed it was true based on the cruelty that I had seen and experienced on that plantation.

I had met men that had seen the swamps and had even ventured out into them. Not one of them told of having an enjoyable experience. I wasn't sure of how I would handle that part of my travels west, but when I reached the swamps, I would find a way to get across them.

It took several days for me to get out of the area where the plantation was located. I figured that I had traveled about ten miles each day, so I should have been well west of the plantation, maybe in northwest Mississippi, near the Louisiana border.

It had taken me longer to get that far west than it should have, but I had to keep changing directions, just in case the dogs and trackers were still on my trail. I also knew that the trackers could contact trackers in other areas by telegram to alert them about a runaway slave. As I considered it more, I was making good time, but I also knew I could not outrun a message being sent that way, so deception was my best option, and I needed to be damn good at it.

What I needed was a new scent and some different clothing. I had been running in the forest for many days, so my clothes were basically rags, and they definitely identified me as a runaway slave. I couldn't roam around almost naked, so I needed to take the chance of finding some people in an isolated place and stealing some different clothes. I thought about using a skunk's musk to taint my scent, but I had no way of catching one without getting the smell all over me.

It was about dark, so I rested for a while. I was shivering from the cold and it woke me up early, so I started walking again. By late morning I smelled smoke, and then I spotted it just ahead and a little north of the direction I was traveling. It appeared to be somewhere close to the game trail I had been using to make my way through the thick forest I was in. The trees were so tall and thick that I could not see any structures, but I could tell that it was not a wildfire.

Using all the skills that I learned from the warriors of my village, I approached the area to scout it. I never heard any voices, and I didn't see or hear any dogs. My senses told me to stay still and wait. After about ten minutes, I saw movement.

It was a human, but what kind of human, I had no clue. I had never seen any people in America that looked like the person I was looking at.

I could tell that it was a man and that he was very old. He was about my size, so I felt that this was my opportunity to get those clothes and different shoes. My mind told me to rush him, but my instincts cautioned me to wait.

After about five minutes, he spoke in a language that I hadn't heard before, and a second person appeared. This was a woman, and she was dressed in the same type of clothing that I would later learn was buckskin. Hers was close to white and decorated with colored beads. She had what looked like feathers attached to her ears and a very colorful necklace of beads and colored stones. It was somewhat like clothing I had seen in Africa, so it was very appealing to me, and it certainly would give me a different appearance than the clothes I was wearing. They continued to talk, and she nodded right after she had turned a full circle, as if she was sensing something. She had long black hair that the slight breeze was blowing away from me. She looked strong and showed no signs of fear.

She placed the bowl she was holding on a little table next to her. As she turned my way, she spoke in English. "We know you are there," she said, "It would be best if you come out before we consider you a threat."

I was kneeling behind some thick underbrush, and I hadn't made any noise. I knew they could not see me, so I was wondering how they knew I was there.

I didn't know what weapons they had, so knowing that I had been discovered, I left my spear where I was kneeling so they would have no reason to think I was a threat. I stood up and walked out of the forest into the small open space that was just large enough for a house, a small shed, and a small garden. Apparently, this was their home because there was only one trail leading into the opening, and it was on the other side from where I entered.

I was not afraid of an old man and a woman. I was a warrior. I didn't feel threatened, but I proceeded slowly and carefully anyway. My eyes were darting left and right, looking for other people, but I didn't see any.

As I approached the woman, I could see that she wasn't as old as the man. He was giving me a good looking over, probably assessing if he could handle me in a fight. She had peaceful eyes and a slight smile that encouraged me to approach them.

As I got close, she continued in English, "Not many escaping slaves make it as far west as you have." She told me where I was which meant nothing to me and that we were more than thirty miles from the nearest whites or any towns.

I said, "I'm from a plantation near Hattiesburg and I'm heading west to live with the Indians."

"You're more than seventy miles west and slightly north of that city."

That was good news because it confirmed that I was heading in the right direction.

"What people are you?"

"We are Quapaw Indians. My name is Winter Wind. My father named me that because it was very windy the night I was born. This," she gestured to the older man, "is Fighting Bear. He was named that because his father was out hunting a Bear when he was born." She could see the questioning look in my eyes. "Most Indian names represent a key event that was happening when the child was born. We live isolated deep in the forest in hopes of not having to go to the reservation. As long as we don't cause any problems, the whites allow us to live in the forest."

I felt the woman's eyes looking me over again. This time she said, "Sit, rest." I was sure I looked awful tired, but I also was sure I was not comfortable with that. She could tell by my stiffness. "Don't worry, no whites ever venture this far into the forest. Sit. Eat." I eased up at the thought of a hot meal. They fed me and showed me nothing but kindness. I was surprised when Winter Wind started tending to my cuts and blistered feet. I had been running so long and been so focused on escaping that I hadn't noticed the cuts or paid any attention to the pain.

By mid-afternoon, Winter Wind had me feeling refreshed and ready to get back on the trail, but they convinced me to wait a few days to rest because the closest safe place was what the whites called "no man's land" in the Oklahoma Territory that was a far distance away, and it would take many days of walking to get there.

I told them I was bound for Texas and needed to cross the swamp. They told me that they knew the swamp and volunteered to help me get across it if I still wanted to go that way. They also told me that it was only one of several swamps that I would have to cross if I continued west. That was concerning to me because finding food and a safe place in the swamps to sleep would be very challenging. Winter Wind had food prepared by then, so we stopped talking about crossing the swamp.

While we ate supper, they explained Indian culture to me. I got a quick history lesson on the Native Americans that the whites called Indians. They told me that they knew I was near their camp because they could smell me. I knew that was possible, but since I expected the people to be whites, I didn't go downwind. Whites' noses were not as sensitive, and they tended to surround themselves with overpowering scents that kept them from smelling people. I made a mental note that I would need to be more careful as I traveled.

They gave me blankets and let me sleep on their porch. I hadn't slept much while running since the nights were chilly, and I didn't have anything to cover my body. Once I started feeling cold, I would walk to warm up. Thanks to my new friends, I got a decent night's sleep and was awake early the next morning.

The Indians were already up, with food cooked, and Fighting Bear was working on something that I was not familiar with. He was using animal skins and stitching them together. He was inserting some colored beads, feathers and what appeared to be hair in some of the stitches. He looked at me and smiled but never stopped working. I asked Winter Wind what he was making, and she smiled and said it was a surprise. She was weaving something that appeared to be a very colorful blanket. I watched for a while and then I got on my feet to walk some. I could feel their eyes watching me, but they said nothing. Later as we ate, they suggested that I utilize the Indian trails to go west and not go to Texas. They told me that the Indian trails would take me further north and would put me days ahead of where I would be if I went through the swamps.

They told me I would get to the big, wide Mississippi River before I got to the larger swamps. As she said, "It would be about impossible to cross the river this far south all by yourself," Fighting Bear nodded his head. Then she told me, "Even if you crossed the river, once you get to eastern Louisiana the swamps start, and they are much bigger as you go west toward Texas. The swamps are mainly in the southern half of Louisiana though, so taking the Indian trails avoids them altogether."

I didn't know one way or the other, but I needed to trust someone, and these people were helping me, feeding me, and caring for my aches and pains, so it was likely that they were giving me the best advice about traveling west. I made up my mind to trust them, so I no longer worried about them damn swamps.

As I refocused on what they were talking about, Fighting Bear said, "The other issue is that Texas is a slave state. There are many big open spaces that make it hard to hide if you don't want to be seen. I have heard that any black man with or without freedom papers could be, and often was, enslaved by the Texas whites." That was the last thing I expected to hear, but it certainly confirmed that I needed to trust these people.

During the next couple of days, they continued to work on the various animal skins that they were curing. I could tell that Fighting Bear was making clothing and stringing colorful beads onto thin strips of leather. Winter Wind appeared to be making something to go on the head because she kept putting it on Fighting Bear's head. They didn't talk much; they just worked steadily. Sometimes they would talk in their native language, and then she would ask or tell me something. I think it was their way of making me feel more comfortable. We had supper that evening, talked more, and decided that I should leave the next morning.

I woke up refreshed and ready to go north. I went to get my spear and when I returned, they surprised me with some of the buckskin clothes they wore and made me a headdress of feathers to cover my curly hair. It was then that I realized what they had been working on during the past two days. After putting on the clothing and headdress, I looked in the mirror and could tell that from a distance it would not be easy to tell that I was a black man and not an Indian. I felt that would be very helpful if I saw any whites. They also gave me some strings of beads and told me that the Indians along the trails would recognize them and in turn would allow me safe passage along the Indian trails.

I didn't know as much as they seemed to know about this area or the areas west and north of where we were, so I felt their suggestions would give me the best chance to get to the West. For now, my destination was eastern Oklahoma Territory, and thanks to my first Indian friends, I was well equipped to make the journey.

Winter Wind gave me the blanket that I had seen her weaving. It was colorful and heavy enough to keep me warm on the cold nights. I thanked them for their help and gifts. I had seen my village elders exchange gifts, so I felt bad because I didn't have anything of value to give them in return. They must have sensed that I felt like that, so they told me to remember their kindness and return it to someone else when I was given an opportunity to.

That reminded me of some of the wise things that the village elders used to tell us. I was a long way from Africa, yet the elders here demanded kindness of the young just like my village elders did. I swallowed my pride, thanked them again, and thanked the Great Spirit Warrior for guiding me to these good people. I looked down at the moccasins that were feeling so natural, smiled at my new friends and left the first place that I found joy since being in America.

For the first time, I felt that I had a good chance of making it to the West. I was in no hurry since I didn't think I was being pursued. Based on how far the Indians told me I had traveled from the plantation, it was unlikely that the trackers were still on my trail. I knew they were mad as hell, and I wondered what the people I was enslaved with back there on the plantation thought of this "Uncle Tom" now. Laughing to myself, I set a good pace and put some more miles between me and that plantation.

I traveled for days, using the landmarks that the Indians told me to follow. There were some tense moments when I was approached by other Indians along the trail, but once they saw the strings of beads that the Quapaw Indians gave me, they helped me find my way, took me down the trail, and provided me with food and shelter.

I knew I was taking a chance but dying out here at the hand of an Indian would allow me to die with honor. For now, I was feeling alive again for the first time since being captured in Africa and brought to

America. But the scars from the whippings and chains would always be a reminder of slavery and help me remember just how special freedom was.

***

The journey to western Mississippi took almost a month. Had it not been for the Indian trail and the Indians helping me to get through the forest, over the mountains, and avoid the farms and towns, the journey would have been nearly impossible.

Even with their guidance and help, I came close to being seen just outside of Natchez, Mississippi. It was the best place in this area to cross the Mississippi River, and there were people everywhere. The slave hunters were easy to spot because they were checking everything that came in and out of town. The river was close enough for me to see it. It was the widest river that I had seen in my life. If it was wider south of here, my Indians friends were right about not being able to cross it alone. The young Indian that was guiding me took me on a trail that only the Indians knew. The trail paralleled the main north-south road into Natchez but was a safe distance away and hidden by the thick forest. We still had to cross the east-west road, and that was where we were seen.

We could see some of the city as we waited for the chance to cross. I had never seen anything like that in my life. A white man on horseback came galloping around a building as we walked across the road. He saw us and took a shot at us while yelling out how he hated Indians. Luckily, he was too drunk to attempt chasing us into the forest. By myself and looking like a slave, I would probably have been caught.

But Natchez was behind me now, and I had traveled a few days, heading almost due north. I wasn't far from the Mississippi River, and at times I could see it from the top of one of the big hills. Those hills got bigger, and the terrain got a little more difficult to walk through as I got close to Arkansas. I had to go over or around the mountain ranges. I was thankful that they were not that tall, and even more thankful to have help from the Indians.

One Indian guided me along that part of the trail, and it was the first time that I had ridden a horse. Riding sure beat walking. Once we were out of the mountain ranges, I got good directions from the guide and followed the big Mississippi River as instructed.

Just as I was promised, an Indian spotted me and took me to their camp. They had special canoes that they used to get me across the Mississippi river during the night. I was met on the other side by other Indians that took me in for the next few days because it was storming. I learned that the Indians used smoke signals to communicate, and I was amazed to learn this existed.

I left that camp in eastern Arkansas and continued west. I was told that this was the last leg of the long journey from the Mississippi plantation to the Oklahoma Territory. I escaped in late fall, had survived some very cold nights, and it was early spring now. So, when the Indians told me that I should reach the Arkansas River in about fifteen days if I walked at a good pace from sunup to sundown, I knew my journey was about over. I did as instructed and met several Indians along the trail who helped me find my way to western Arkansas.

An Indian tribe camped near the Arkansas River took me in for the night. I ate with others for a change and was feeling rather blessed as I lay down to sleep in the teepee that they let me use. I knew I was so close to freedom, yet all of what had happened to me since leaving that plantation was weighing heavy on my heart.

I found myself thinking about home in Africa and that last vision of my mother with tears in her eyes. That was too much for me to handle in my state of mind, so I started crying. Someone must have heard me, so they sent someone to comfort me.

She was young and beautiful in the glow of the campfire. She didn't speak; she just came to me. I had been running for so long that I hadn't cared that I had not been with a woman since leaving the plantation.

Seeing her reminded me of how great I felt after pleasuring a woman. The tears dried up as I was with that beautiful Indian woman, yet I continued to think of all the good fortune that escaping slavery had brought my way.

The next morning some of the braves ferried me across the river in a canoe. As we were crossing the river, I thought to myself, if I would have had one of these canoes, maybe those swamps would have been easier to cross. It was just a thought occupying my mind as I could see the freedom land coming closer and closer. No, the trail that I had taken was the best route to freedom, because it was right in front of me. I learned of new people, saw some wonderful land, and if last night was any indication of how special life would be living with the Indians, I wanted it.

We said our goodbyes, and the Indians headed back across the Arkansas River, leaving me on what I believed to be freedom soil. Now that I was in eastern Oklahoma Territory, I felt much safer, but I was still a long way from the western states. I had learned some of the Quapaw, Choctaw, and Chickasaw dialects along the Indian trails, but communicating with the Indians was still difficult. I was concerned about being able to communicate with the Indians here in freedom land, but I was still so happy to be here. That was the moment when I declared that I was reborn, a full-grown man and a warrior, ready to fight to keep my freedom.

The Indians had told me about a large Indian camp that I should go to that was about ten miles from the river. So, I headed northwest as instructed, following a game trail. As night approached, I found a good spot near a sizable creek and I was too tired to explore the area, so I sat down.

CHAPTER 6: CHEROKEES, MY ADOPTED FAMILY

I thought I was still swimming through my memories when I started hearing voices. I didn't remember what had happened to me, but I had some serious pain in the rib area on the right side of my body, and my head ached as I began to blink back into consciousness.

I was hearing a woman speak to me. At first, I thought it was my mother's voice calling me home. Since I never expected to see her again, I feared that I was dying, so I started struggling to move, but something was restraining me.

That voice spoke to me again, and I finally woke up completely. I was relieved to see Sophie smiling at me because it meant that I was still alive and no longer reliving my fight for freedom so many years ago. I closed my eyes to say a short prayer before facing Sophie's smiling, loving face, and I started to get disoriented again. I was still so caught up in reliving my past.

Had I known how delirious I was, I probably would have kept my mouth shut. Ole proud me was trying to talk to the Great Spirit Warrior, who was telling me to get up and keep fighting. As I tried to get up, Sophie leaned in really close to me and yelled, "Stop it!"

She had never spoken to me like that before, so it brought me back to the present day fully. I stopped struggling to get up, and I shut my mouth.

Once I had shut up, she said, "I will do the talking, and you will listen."

That look in her eyes told me "That's the way it is going to be, mister," so I swallowed my pride and became as meek as a lamb. She always caused me to smile. How could such a beautiful, smiling face be so demanding and comforting at the same time?

She was smiling again and said, "You had us worried for a while there. We couldn't tell if you were fighting to live or not. Then something shifted and you were fighting again. I prayed a lot and I know that Jose did too. I tried to talk and she shook her head and said, "Jose is taking care of Lightning and the other livestock so you don't have to worry about that."

I looked around for him but did not see him. Sophie understood what I was doing. She said "Jose went to get the army doctor. You got shot in the ribs by one of those outlaws, so you have a small lung puncture that the doctor was very concerned about." She tried to hide her laugh as she said, "When you fell off Ole Lightning, you hit your head on the only rock within a twenty-yard radius, so you have a head injury too."

She tried but she couldn't hold it, she was laughing openly, so I wanted to laugh too, but it already hurt too much to just focus my eyes on her face. But inside, I was laughing and thinking how a rock is never around when you need one, but just fall and you'll hit it. Hearing all of that, I was thankful that I was feeling as good as I was.

I was still rather unstable and must have attempted to close my eyes because Sophie was shaking me and yelling at me to stay awake until the doctor got there. Sophie was so good to me that I would do anything that she wanted me to do, so I willed myself to stay awake even though I just wanted to close my eyes and sleep.

Had it not been for the joy I was feeling at seeing her smiling face, I know I would have drifted back into an unconscious state. The pain her shaking was causing in my hurt ribs was reminding me of that black snake whip back on that damn plantation, so I stayed alert to keep her from shaking me anymore. The good thing was, I now realized how much Sophie cared for me, so I thanked the Great Spirit Warrior and smiled at her.

There was a knock, and then the door opened and the doctor and Jose came in. I thought I instantly felt much better. Maybe I just wanted to look like I did. It didn't take long for me to realize that it was just in my head because when I moved my right arm, the pain in my side was worse than what I felt when I was shot with a flaming arrow by a renegade Apache three years ago.

The doctor looked me over, felt my forehead while checking my pulse and said, "You just need to lie still and rest." He looked over the top of his glasses, making eye contact as he reiterated, "No moving for several days, not even to sit up or roll over."

I didn't know how I could do that, and I guess he knew it as well but just had to say it to be professional. He had patched me up several times and knew how difficult it was to keep me in bed, so he was saying it more for Sophie than for me. I guess he felt that she could persuade me to follow his instructions. She gave me that "mother knows best" look, and I knew I wasn't going to get away with doing what I already had planned.

He went on to tell me that the head wound from hitting my head on that rock was more serious than the one to my ribs. I heard him say that I would be in and out of consciousness for a few days or longer. He was saying something else, but I could not tell what it was because I was out, gone from the present, falling deeper into another memory of another place at another time...

***

I had been on the trail as a runaway slave for almost four months, seeing few people along the way. I wasn't sure exactly where I was or if I was headed in the right direction. But I was sure that I was very tired, and the sun had gone down hours before. I ate the food I had and got ready to sleep.

I didn't think that I was close to any people, and I didn't hear anyone or smell any smoke. I was hot, so I put my blanket on the ground, got naked, and went to sleep.

I was hearing a woman's voice, and I thought I was dreaming of that Indian woman on the other side of that river who had comforted me. No, it was several women's voices I was hearing, so I suddenly became totally awake and alert.

I was looking up at several Indian women, and they were laughing and pointing at my privates since I had no blanket covering me.

They were smiling and laughing as I grabbed my clothes and put them on. Once I was dressed, they could see the items that Winter Wind and Fighting Bear had given me, so they quieted down and started chattering to each other. I took that opportunity to go pee.

I stepped back out of the trees, and one of the Indian women made the sign for me to follow them while another one took off. A couple of the women looked and acted differently. I would later learn that they were white women captives, and there were Indian women captives as well.

As we entered the camp, there was a lot of chatter. At first, I didn't understand why. Then I thought that maybe they hadn't seen a black man before. I was taken to the teepee of the chief, and things started to get as interesting as they were confusing.

After being on Indian trails for close to four months, I understood enough of their dialect to tell that they weren't talking about killing me, but I could also tell that the chief was not sure I was who and what I claimed to be.

I had heard about the clashes between Indians and white men being more common in this area, and I guessed that this made trusting anyone that wasn't a tribal member a seriously calculated game of chance. He was giving me a good looking over, and it was not a comfortable feeling. But I was still sure that anything was better than the life I left in Mississippi.

The chief spoke to me, but I didn't really understand much of what he said. I tried to respond, but their language was much different from that of the Indians that I had met on the trail and nothing like my native African dialect. Seeing the confusion on my face, he spoke, and one of the women left. She returned with one of the women captives that I had seen earlier. Once I realized that the woman was white, the hate I had for whites made me think, *serves her right to be on the opposite side of slavery*. That thought was forced out of my mind as my conscience reminded me that the village elders taught me to be more compassionate.

He spoke to her in their dialect, and she, speaking English, said, "The chief wants to know where you are from."

I responded, "I'm from Africa, but was a slave on a Mississippi plantation until I ran away about four months ago."

I saw her facial expression change when she heard that. As she told the chief what I said, his facial expressions changed as well. We talked for a while with her translating for us. Some of her first words confirmed that I was in the Cherokee Indian camp that the Indians in Arkansas had told me to come to. I had to smile at knowing that I had made it to an area of America that a black man had a chance to live free.

The conversation continued. As she communicated my story to the chief, he would smile, nod, or show facial expressions that let me know he was understanding. I would use similar expressions as she told me what he said or asked. Communicating like that was awkward and uncomfortable, but after a few minutes of conversing, the chief's facial expressions became friendlier. As she communicated the story about how I started on the Indian trail, they even laughed. It was refreshing to know that the Indians had a sense of humor. It was even better when I realized that they had some compassion for me.

I told him of my intent to go west. When she translated, he shook his head as if to say that was not a good idea. When the captive translated his words, I learned that the western Indians were in fierce wars with the white men, and the U.S. Army was out there to keep the peace. The chief told stories about battles with the army that ended very badly for the Indians. Even though he would not say it, I think he knew that the Indians were fighting a losing battle.

For a moment, I thought of us trying to defend our village in Africa. That didn't end well, and the survivors were taken by force here to America. That was bad enough, but I didn't want to think about dying right now after all I had done to stay alive and be free.

We spent the rest of the day talking, and by sundown, I had been accepted and adopted by the tribe. They asked me my name, and that was when I realized I didn't have an American name. On the plantation, the whites would just bark out "boy." I remembered my African name, so I told them that in my homeland, I was called Runihura, which means one that smashes to bits.

The chief pointed to his chest and said, "I am chief Buffalo Killer" in his dialect and the captive said, "He is Buffalo Killer and I am Sleeping Bird."

I nodded to indicate I liked their names.

Sleeping Bird said, "The chief liked your African name and told me that in this tribe you will be known as 'Running Dreamer' because you are running from the nightmares of yesterday to fulfill your dreams for tomorrow." I thought that was a fitting name, so from that moment I was proud when I was called Running Dreamer.

I was given a teepee, and as I was settling into it, I could hear some kind of dispute brewing. It was women's voices, so I just sat in my teepee, minding my own business. Then I heard the familiar voice of Buffalo Killer, and the noise stopped, leaving the camp in silence.

I felt that I was safe from being captured and enslaved again, but I was too excited to sleep, and to be honest, I was a little afraid as well. The Indians had treated me well so far, but if I was in their place, I would still have some reservations about a stranger.

I lay there, thinking and remembering how I had executed my plan to escape slavery and get here, and it occurred to me that I didn't know how to live as a free man here in America. I had been captured when I was about sixteen, so I had not experienced the responsibilities of providing for myself or a family. So much had happened to me since then, but none of it helped me understand love, marriage and living as a man.

I didn't understand relationships, other than those between family members. I knew that men and women became a family by being married, but I hadn't thought about that very much while I was a slave. I had heard about love, but I wasn't sure that I even understood what it was or how to accept it, enjoy it, and live with it. I had Betsy on the plantation, so I knew about being with a woman in the physical way. But how was I to get a woman to love and want me as a husband?

I thought, *a warrior is supposed to be strong, fierce, and never show compassion for the enemy. Then how is a warrior to love, marry, and live with a woman?* I knew my father did it, and I saw the slaves and white folks do it on the plantation. Well, I guessed when the time came, I would be able to do it as well.

That thought was comforting, but I had no idea of how to go about doing it. I wanted to marry someone I wanted to be with and not be forced to marry someone that others thought I should marry. I didn't have the answers now, but I knew I would when I got a little older and found a woman that I wanted.

I guess I must have drifted off to sleep because I didn't hear anyone come into the teepee. Then my keen senses alerted me that someone was next to me. I felt a warm body as a naked woman got into my sleeping blankets. She placed her hand over my mouth and gave me that universal "shush" to be silent.

She wasted no time doing what felt really great. I must have drifted off to sleep afterward because I didn't hear her leave. Smiling in the dark, I realized that it had been a great day, so I went back to sleep.

I thought I was dreaming about what had happened earlier when I felt a woman's hand cover my mouth. I felt that warmth engulf my manhood so I knew I was not dreaming.

When I reached out and touched the woman, I knew it was not the same one that I had pleasured earlier. She shushed me as well, so I let her have her way. As I drifted off to sleep, I thought, *I'm going to like living with the Indians.*

When I woke up the next morning, Sleeping Bird was in my teepee, preparing food she had brought with her. Hearing me moving around, she turned toward me and gave me a look. Then she smiled and broke out giggling, and I was not sure why.

I asked, "What's so funny?"

When she was finally able to stop herself from giggling, she said "There were Indian squaws fighting over which one would come into your teepee to pleasure you last night. I'm a light sleeper, so I heard the two different squaws sneak in to pleasure you." Grinning, she continued, "Both were making more noise than I had ever heard them make while pleasuring the braves."

I wanted to ask her how she knew that, but I didn't. There was nothing to do but start laughing too, so that's what we did while she prepared the food.

We talked while eating. I learned that her name was Anita Anderson, but she was called "Sleeping Bird" by the Indian tribe that had captured her about ten years earlier. She told the story of traveling west with her family on a wagon train. They were stopped in Kansas to rest the horses and have dinner. While squatting to pee, she was praying for her younger sister that was sick when the Indians took her captive. Since they didn't know about praying, they assumed she was sleeping, so they gave her that name.

She told me that she never saw her family again and often wondered if they had been attacked by the Indians because no one came looking for her. As she told the story, it sounded somewhat similar to what I had experienced, so I felt sorry for her. She told me that the Indians were moving their camp and passed by what appeared to be a wagon train that had been attacked and burned. She found some books and some pretty ribbons. She took them and had used them to remind her of life before captivity.

She talked about being born in a city called Boston. She said she was almost nineteen when she was captured and thought she was probably over thirty now but could not remember exactly how long she had been a captive. She told me of the great many hardships she had suffered at the hands of the Indians that captured her, but with this tribe, she was not treated as badly. With tears in her eyes, she told me of being taken by any brave that desired to have her and how she considered it to be a miracle that she didn't bear one of them a child. This was the same thing that happened to the slave women, so I understood her pain.

I could tell that she was a strong woman because the tears flowed, but her voice didn't change, and she didn't break down and cry like a baby.

I thought that her life was similar to mine, and if she felt anything like I did when I was a slave, she was one unhappy person inside.

As the weeks passed it was amazing how strong she always was around the Indians. The squaws would beat her often to make sure that she understood her place, but she would take it and not whine at all.

She told me that surviving was the important thing to her. She would smile while saying that "A little beating now and then didn't steal her joy but instead helped her realize that the squaws were in some ways jealous of her." I had to wonder if that was the case with white men on the plantations.

She was a pretty woman, even though she was dirty and in tattered clothing. She didn't have a brave to hunt for her, so she got new clothing when the chief instructed a brave to provide her with new skins. For her, it was a hard life, and I was hoping that I could help her as she was helping me. I hated white people, but I couldn't find any hate for this woman within me.

I asked Sleeping Bird about the constant late-night visits of the squaws since I just didn't understand it. She indicated that it was a traditional thing and as long as the squaws liked it, they would continue doing it until they were taken as wives. She told me that the chief only allowed it to happen with people that he liked. Hearing that made me feel a bit safer.

As the months passed, I became more accepted by the tribe and was allowed to go hunting with the young braves. The older braves were warriors, and they kept a curious eye on me until they felt that I wanted to be a part of their tribe. I was able to get skins for my clothing and for Sleeping Bird as well. We worked together to coexist with the Indians, making sure that we didn't do anything to make them think we would harm them. This was my temporary home, and I was liking it more and more as the days passed.

The Indians were constantly at war with the whites and other Indian tribes that tried to invade their territory or capture their women. I wasn't allowed to go on raids, but I was allowed to train with the braves and learn their tracking skills, their war tactics and the use of their weapons.

Sleeping Bird and I got really close as the weeks became months. She no longer came and went from my teepee; she lived in it with me. We would pass the time with her teaching me to read, write, and do numbers. Her favorite book was the Bible. Whites taught slaves religion using a Bible, but Sleeping Bird would read me stories that I had never heard while being a slave. She told me that it was common for slave owners to use the slave Bible and not the real Bible. Slave Bibles didn't include many of the books of the Old Testaments and omitted any chapters or verses that would allow a slave to believe that being a slave was not his or her sole purpose. This angered me greatly, but I did understand why they did it. I thought of all those blacks who didn't know what I had just learned.

I guessed that she didn't know that it was illegal to teach slaves to read and write, so I asked her about it. She said "Slavery was not well received where I'm from. In fact, Father was one of the northern leaders fighting to abolish slavery. I believe as my father did, and that is why I'm so diligent in teaching you. And plus, I found great favor with Chief Buffalo Killer when I started teaching English to the Indians in the tribe."

She flashed me a hopeful smile and indicated that slavery would be outlawed soon, and if I was to be successful in life, I needed to learn what she was teaching.

I just obeyed while thinking, *man, I am learning some interesting big words from her*. She was so patient with me and appeared to be more joyful than I was when I would get the number right or read from the books she had. I taught her African names for the basic things, animals and people so that we could communicate in secret if we needed to. It didn't equal what she was teaching me, but I felt a need to give her something.

Writing was more challenging, but she was strict in demanding that I get it right. We didn't have paper, so we used sticks to write in the sand of the teepee floor. I got better at writing as the months passed, but it was challenging!

That first winter was the coldest that I had ever known, and I was very happy as spring came. Sleeping Bird was too, because I could read, write, and do my numbers by then.

She knew of my plans to go west, so she told me that I must have an American name. Blacks without one were often taken back into slavery because it was obvious that they had run away. We settled on the name

"Raymond Dean Jackson." It took a while to get used to her calling me that, but it felt good to have a name that the American people would understand and hopefully respect.

One rainy day, we were in the teepee all day. We were restless because we didn't have anything to do. Without saying anything, she came to me, taking off her buckskin clothing. I was confused and scared at the same time because I knew slave bucks were killed for pleasuring a white woman.

She knew this as well, so as she knelt down next to me, she said, "The only sex that I have ever had was forced on me by the Indian braves. You are the only person I have truly cared for other than my family. I wish to pleasure you openly."

I knew I didn't have an argument that I thought would change her mind, and I had a desire to please this woman that had done so much for me. She was older and more experienced and pleasuring her was much more satisfying than pleasuring the sneaky squaws or slave women.

She introduced me to kissing and touching a woman in sensitive places and in sensitive ways that brought a woman pleasure. It was like performing the tribal dances back in Africa. Such joy, such pleasure, and all so prideful. I had no idea that pleasuring a woman could be so satisfying.

After we finished, she giggled and said, "I confess that I have been sneaking in some pleasuring for weeks by pretending to be one of the Indian squaws. I just couldn't resist after witnessing how happy the squaws seemed to be. I have waited a long time to feel happy about giving myself to a man I desired, so I wasn't passing up the chance to do it with you."

I didn't know what to say other than, "I'm honored and happy that you chose me."

***

By late fall, the conflicts between the Indians and whites had escalated, and the chief came to see me. As Sleeping Bird helped to translate the words he didn't know how to say in English, he said, "It was best that I be on my way west before the whites discovered the village in the hills that they had not explored yet."

He told me of the trails that the whites traveled by wagon train and suggested that I shadow their trails but not travel on them unless it was the only way to keep moving west. He thanked me for the warring tactics that I had taught his braves, and they showed their appreciation by giving me horses, clothing and other gifts that I would need to travel west.

I wanted Sleeping Bird to go with me, but I didn't have the nerve to ask. I had come to like her a lot, and I depended on her, so leaving her would be very hard for me. As the braves brought me the horses, there was another horse with Sleeping Bird sitting in the saddle.

Buffalo Killer looked at me with a big smile and said, "Sleeping Bird has taught my people to speak English, and some children have even learned to read, write, and do their numbers. She had convinced me that when the whites come, this knowledge could make the difference between us surviving or becoming one of the many Indian tribes that would be wiped out. Both of you have paid your way to be free." Chief "Buffalo Killer" was my American village elder, and I hoped he was as proud of me as I was of him and his people.

I said my goodbyes and mounted the fine horse that they had given me and headed out of the camp on the trail to the West. Me and Sleeping Bird looked like a couple of Indians, traveling along the same trails that whites used to go west. This was a troubling thought, but we were riding west anyway, determined to find our way together. After all, both of us were free again and willing to die to stay that way.

Knowing it would mean sudden death for us if our secret love affair was ever discovered by white men, Sleeping Bird kept her face dirty and continued to look like an Indian squaw, and I kept wearing buckskin and a specially designed headdress that concealed my African heritage. As long as we kept some distance between us and others, no one would know.

We both knew it probably wouldn't end well, but we were all that each other had.

***

I must have been smiling, as I was becoming more conscious, and as I became alert enough to smell, I could smell Sophie, so I was trying so hard to open my eyes. That was when I realized that my manhood was standing at attention, and Sophie knew it. She gave me that look of fury, and I knew she was working up one fierce case of scorn.

Her words were like daggers as she said, "Who is Sleeping Bird and did you enjoy pleasuring her?"

I knew the thing to do was to act like I didn't know what she was talking about, so I did, but it didn't work. She pressed me harder, and for once in my life I wanted to pass out, but just couldn't.

I was stronger now, so I did the manly thing and told her about Sleeping Bird since we were the only two in the room. I thought Sophie showed some compassion for how she thought I felt after losing someone who had done so much for me.

She smiled and went to get me some food. I thought to myself, *that was a close one!* So, as a big grin formed on my face, I said to myself, *I know my Sophie loves me now, because I'm still alive.*

She told me that I had been out for more than a day, so she was feeding me to keep me from starving. Good news was that I could move without feeling great pain in my side. I couldn't get up or do much, but I could sit up and move around a little without my head feeling like a hammer was beating my brains out.

Jose surprised me by bringing Ole Lightning to my window. He stuck his head through the open window and Sophie was nice enough to allow me to pet his nose a time or two before telling Jose and Lightning to get out and telling me "Lay back on your pillow, you need to rest."

I knew that Sophie was destined to claim me as the greatest prize of her lifetime. I hadn't told her yet, but I was planning the same thing for her. Dreaming about being with Sleeping Bird just reminded me of how great life could be when you got to share it with someone you loved.

For a fleeting moment, I had a vision of my father and mother and my happy family. I wanted to think of it some more, but after eating and being excited to see Ole Lightning and Jose, my head suddenly ached something fearful again. I was going back into my treasured memories of time and days gone by because my head didn't ache like hell when I was reliving yesterday.

CHAPTER 7: WINTER PASSAGE WEST

As I faded out of the here and now, I was listening to Sophie pleading with me to stay awake and talk with her. But I was on my way to that unconscious state of mind. As the pain faded away, I woke up in my unconscious state to the familiar sounds of Sleeping Bird doing what she always did to arouse me.

It was cold outside our makeshift shelter, but with a little fire burning inside and being under the blankets and furs, we were very comfortable. She seemed to be more excited this morning than on other mornings, for she kept wanting to do it over and over again. I thought I was going to go dry and never be able to pleasure her or any other woman again.

I kept wondering how far we had come and how long it would take to get to Wyoming. By my estimation of time and the miles we had traveled, I believed that we were still in western Kansas. That meant that we had a lot of miles to travel to get to Wyoming. I couldn't wait to see that big sky, the mountains, and all of that open and free land she always talked about.

As we rode west through the open plains, it seemed as if we would never get to the massive mountains that were barely visible on even the clearest day. We had faith in each other, and we were strong-willed, so we kept moving west, and those mountains appeared to be larger.

I had never seen real mountains before, so I was looking forward to getting closer to them. I had become more hopeful about getting to Wyoming and more confident that slavery was behind me. I was looking forward to a better future out here in the West.

I had taught Sleeping Bird how to hunt and fight. She had practiced each night, and I felt that she could defend herself as well as a young Indian brave could. I practiced as well to get better with the lance, bow and arrows and tomahawk.

We reached a beautiful flowing stream late one day and stopped to spend the night. Sleeping Bird was not feeling her best, so I was concerned for her and did all the work while she rested.

That was the day that I started learning to cook and care for myself and do the chores that women usually did. She insisted that I do that just in case something happened to her out here in the middle of nowhere, and I found myself all alone. She also showed me how to prepare the different medicines that the Cherokee medicine man had taught her.

We stayed there a few days until she was fit to travel, so, as Sleeping Bird slept, I would explore the area around the crystal-clear stream. The area was filled with game, and it was quiet. I thought to myself that if there were places in Wyoming as nice as this area, I was going to love it there.

With Sleeping Bird fit for traveling once more, we hit the trail. She kept practicing her fighting skills, and I kept practicing my cooking skills, so within a few days, I had a greater understanding of the medicines, and my cooking was much better.

Soon the mountains weren't so far off anymore. There was one thing I was certain of; they were massive and seemed to block the passage west. We knew Wyoming was on this side of the mountains, so I was sensing that our journey was almost over.

Winter was coming soon, and based on my experience in the Cherokee camp, I knew we had to find or build a good shelter to survive in through winter. The last travelers we met had indicated that we were only a day or so from the Wyoming border, and that was two days ago. We had made it to Wyoming, and we had done it in good time, but we had not found that special place we envisioned.

Once we spotted what appeared to be a well-traveled road going north and south, we decided to head southwest and find a good place to call home for the coming winter months. We had been traveling just south of the well-traveled road going east and west, so with Sleeping Bird's knowledge of how American towns and roads tied together, we were rather certain that we would be setting up camp less than twenty miles from a town.

We had traded some of the items that the Cherokee people gave us for money because Sleeping Bird knew we would need money to buy things. We had traded for some American clothes because it was not likely that Indians would be welcomed in towns, especially out here in the West where the army was still in fierce battles with the more hostile tribes.

We found a great location and worked together to build a suitable cabin to house us through the winter months. I would go out scouting in varying directions every day to locate towns and any farms or ranches in the area. After a couple weeks of doing this, I had discovered a town to the east, another to the northeast of us, and a third northwest of us. There were ranches scattered along the east/west road but very few farms.

I used a soft deerskin to make a map of the area, just in case something happened to me and Sleeping Bird had to go for help or needed to get to civilization again. We stored it in a hiding place after we had memorized it. The distances probably were not to scale, but the descriptions of landmarks would help anyone viewing it to find their way.

We built a lean-to shelter for the horses and a sizable holding pen so that they could get their exercise. The stallion that we stumbled upon just before finding this place was a spirited rascal. He was a big black thoroughbred about sixteen hands high, he was shod but not branded, and didn't have one blemish. He was just wandering around this area, so we felt he must have escaped from one of the wagon trains. He was so busy trying to get to our mare that was in heat that I was able to get a rope on him. Once I caught him, Sleeping Bird decided to name him Gvnige, meaning black. It had taken most of my spare time during the past weeks to gentle him and break him to the saddle.

We had been at our little home for about and month, not seeing anyone, then one morning, Gvnige sensed something and nickered. I didn't see anything that I considered to be danger, so I patted his shoulder and returned to the cabin. About two minutes later, I could hear several horses approaching the cabin, so we got prepared to defend our home.

It didn't appear that the riders were sneaking up to the house, and they were not charging like they expected a battle. To be safe, Sleeping Bird and I stayed in the cabin, peeking out through the slots in the shutters that we would use for firing rifles once we could buy some. Right now, all we had were bows and arrows and some well-made knives, tomahawks, and lances.

As the riders got closer, Sleeping Bird pointed out that they were wearing the uniforms of the U.S. Army. As they got closer, I noticed that they were black men. Neither of us had ever seen a black soldier before, so we didn't know what to make of what we were seeing. Sensing that we had less to be worried about than if the men were whites or Indians, we stepped out to greet them.

They gave us a very questioning look and asked who we were. Not yet trusting them, we used our Indian names. The one with stripes on his shirt sleeve asked, "Where are you from?" I answered, "A Cherokee camp in eastern Oklahoma. We came out here to get away from civilization." After hearing that we stole away from the Cherokees and headed west, they eased up with the questions.

I took this as my chance to ask them questions. They told us that they were an experimental group of soldiers that the Indians had given the name "buffalo soldiers." There were several groups of them scattered throughout the western states and territories since the army felt it was the best place to give the blacks an opportunity to be soldiers.

They told us that the southern states had seceded from the nation, causing a civil war. The war had been going on for a while, and it looked as if the South was losing. There was also talk of the president of the United States freeing all the slaves and making it illegal to own another human. That caused me to smile, and the leader of the group who they called "Sarge," which was short for Sergeant, gave me a quick, stern look.

He pulled his pistol and said, "I thought you were a little dark to be an Indian," and then directed me to take off my headdress. The cat was out of the bag for me, but they still believed that Sleeping Bird was an Indian squaw, so I was not alarmed about exposing my heritage. I would let them keep thinking that Sleeping Bird was an Indian squaw that had run away with me.

I had to do some explaining, so I told them my story. They were surprised to hear that I had escaped slavery and made my way this far west. During my explanation, I could see Sarge's facial expression changing. He even smiled as I told them about fooling the bloodhounds. His facial expressions were now hinting that he was proud of me. Most importantly, that pistol was now pointed toward the ground, and the other soldiers had followed his lead and held their guns in a nonthreatening position. Sarge formed a big grin on his face, put his pistol away, and things got much more comfortable as we talked about our lives.

Sleeping Bird was really smart, so she would always be looking down and she spoke with me in the Cherokee dialect. Once the soldiers knew that I could speak the Indian language, they got very interested in what I was planning to do. I had no plans, but I made up a tale about starting a horse ranch.

It was late afternoon by the time the tales were told, so they asked if they could camp near the house for the night. They told me that they had been trailing some renegade Indians that had been raiding some ranches west of our location and was heading back to the fort. I had a concerned look on my face. Sarge said, "You should be safe because they were in a hurry and heading southwest." I nodded to indicate my agreement. They were going to stay near us for a day or more, so they went off to set up their camp.

They knew we didn't have much, so they gave us some supplies as payment for Sleeping Bird serving them the first good hot meal they had eaten in more than a month. Sarge said, "Hey Shorty, this is real cooking. Maybe you should have her teach you a thing or two." Everyone laughed. They were so thankful that they chopping more wood than we could use in weeks and stacking it very close to the house.

They noticed Gvnige and commented on the fine colts he would make if he was bred to some good mares. I told them that was how we were planning to start the horse ranch. Sarge told us that the army would pay top dollar for good horses. Sarge said. "I will put in a good word for you with the commanding officer at the fort."

The next morning, they asked me if I had a gun. I told them that I didn't own one but that I was deadly with a lance and a bow and arrows. Sarge laughed at me and said, "Those weapons are useless here in Wyoming. They will not bring down an elk, and there are not many deer in this part of the country."

I didn't let on that I knew how to shoot, in hopes that they wouldn't see that as a threat. I told them we were prepared to eat smaller game until we could trade for a rifle. Sarge knew I would have a very hard time buying or trading for a rifle since I was a black man, and Sleeping Bird was an Indian. He also knew that I needed a rifle, and that caused him to do something that might not have been all right if their commanding officer was to find out about it.

Sarge said, "Look, we killed some of those renegade Indians and took their guns to keep other Indians from getting them. The guns are old, but in good working order, so we will leave them with you and spend a day teaching you to use and care for them before we return to the fort. And if there is trouble and you need help and can get to us, we are about five miles east of the main north-to-south road that you had to cross when you came out this way."

I told them that I knew of it from scouting the area when we settled here. Sarge also told me to go to the fort if we needed supplies or medical attention. He winked at me and advised that we should avoid all the towns. He pulled me to the side for some private words, so I went with him. He went on to say, "I'm a Negro, but I am smart enough to know that the woman with you is acting like an Indian squaw. When we were all laughing, I saw that her eyes are green; she be white, and you knows it." I couldn't deny it, so I told him the story about Sleeping Bird during the day as he taught Sleeping Bird and me to shoot.

He told me that he grew up in the northern states, where slavery was not as welcomed, but blacks were not treated very well there either. He came out west, somewhat indebted to a family on a wagon train of Northerners that had helped runaway slaves. He had worked for some of them, but he joined the army when there was no work for a black man to make a decent living.

The next day they rode out, promising to stop by from time to time to check on us. They confirmed that we had picked a great location because no one owned any of the land within thirty miles of us. That was good news to hear because our plans to be ranchers required a lot of grazing land.

We were alone again and had time to think about the past couple of days with the buffalo soldiers. If they knew what we thought was a secret, then we were not as deceptive as we had come to believe. We talked it over and knew that we would have to come up with a different story and arrangement, or we would have to split up in the near future.

We didn't like that idea, but what else could we do? Any white man probably would kill both of us if we were discovered. Afterward, we became much more aware of our surroundings. I would scout around our homestead daily in search of signs of other Indians or whites nearby.

The winter months brought much snow and bitter cold, so we spent a lot of time in the cabin, talking and educating ourselves. We practiced with our weapons but didn't practice too much with the guns because they made noise that could be heard from a distance.

We managed to stay warm and eat, and the livestock had enough shelter and hay to make it through. As the bitter days came farther and farther apart, we were really ready for spring with summer to follow.

I knew we needed more supplies and food, so I would have to go to the fort soon. I didn't like leaving Sleeping Bird there by herself, but she could shoot as well as I could, and as long as she stayed in the cabin, it would be very difficult for someone to break in. Those thick sod walls would stop any bullet fired at the house, and the door could be barred from the inside with the heavy timber logs that we cut for that sole purpose. The wood shutters were thick enough to protect the house during an attack. Since the cabin was covered with sod, it would be hard for someone to set it on fire from the outside. It even had an escape hole on the back side to allow us to get to the horses if there were too many attackers for us to hold off. Yes, I was uncomfortable, but out here in the West, you had to take chances, and leaving her by herself was the safest option.

I got up hours before daylight and left so I could make it back around sunset. It would be a hard ride, but it had to be done. I rode as fast as I felt the packhorse could be pushed as it trailed behind me on Gvnige, who I was not worried about because he was a magnificent horse. We could take it a little slower on the trip back to the cabin.

I reached the fort, found old Sarge, and he helped me get the supplies I needed. We talked a little while, so I was all caught up on the latest news. I mounted up and headed back to the cabin. The packhorse was carrying a load now, so we could not go as fast, but we still made good time. We were racing the sun, and it looked as if we had won the race. I knew I could make it to the cabin with some sunlight to spare.

As I approached the last ridge blocking my view to our little home, I could see what appeared to be chimney smoke. I had told Sleeping Bird to not light a fire while I was gone. I was saying to myself, *that woman has a mind of her own. She's going to do what she wants, and I guess there is nothing that I can do about it.*

As I topped the ridge, I knew I was wrong, and my heart seemed to be trying to jump out of my chest. Seeing that the cabin had been burned, my insides turned to mush; my heart was on fire. Smoke was coming out of the chimney and the door. The shutters were closed as I left them, but partially burned. The horses were gone and some of the furniture was scattered on the ground just outside the door. Then I saw Sleeping Bird's body lying lifeless next to the woodpile. My mind just didn't want to work. I couldn't comprehend what I was seeing. Sleeping Bird was dead. I just sat there in the saddle. I could feel the rage taking over my body and I didn't want to do anything to stop it.

I pulled my pistol, and I rode at a faster pace to cover the short distance to the cabin. I looked at Sleeping Bird lying by the woodpile with several arrows in her back. I was so sick and so mad that I just stared in disbelief as the rage within me grew out of control.

From a distance, the Indians would not have known that she was a woman. When we settled here, I insisted that she dress as much like a man as she could. I knew that if the attackers had known they were looking at a woman, her fate and last minutes of life would have been pure hell before the Indians allowed her to die. If she understood why I made the request, she never let on that she did, and she never complained. She even told me that she liked dressing that way.

Hopefully she understood why when that arrow pierced her heart, the heart that my heart had grown to love.

I buried her in an unmarked grave just a few yards from the cabin, in an area that she loved to spend time in. As I placed the dirt over her, my rage got worse with every shovel of dirt. I knew I had to get revenge on the murdering Indians. No one was going to treat me or anyone close to me like that and get away with it.

We kept the rifles hidden under a big log that doubled as a table, so the Indians didn't find them. That also told me that Sleeping Bird had no idea that she was walking into an ambush when she stepped out of the cabin.

I only allowed myself to ask one time...*why did I have to pick that day to leave her alone?* Then I replaced that with thinking I would need to track down the renegades that killed my Sleeping Bird.

For the first time since we started talking at the Cherokee camp, I spoke her American name. As I mounted Gvnige, my parting words were: "I will avenge you, Anita Anderson. They will die and die in an ugly way for their sins!" I was not able to do anything about the attack on our village in Africa, but I knew I had to do something about the attack on my first American home and the death of the only white person that had ever treated me like a man.

I collected the things of value to me that the packhorse and Gvnige could carry, and I rode away from my first American home in pursuit of the renegades who took it from me. I hoped that some other settlers would settle here as I did and live to see their dreams come true. Mine were shattered forevermore.

The tracks at the cabin were from three men on horses and my shod horses that they stole. They were riding south and made no attempt to cover their tracks, so I had no issue following them. Either they didn't expect to be followed or were too arrogant to cover their tracks. They were wrong, and it would be the last time they made such a mistake. I was sure I could handle three men on my own, so I wasn't overly cautious either.

I rode all night, all day and into the next night to catch up with those renegades. I spotted a campfire about the same time that I smelled the smoke, so I stopped and scouted the surrounding area. They had their camp surrounded by just enough trees to have a defensive stance if attacked. They were smart, but I was determined to avenge Sleeping Bird.

I tied Gvnige and the packhorse a far distance from their camp to keep them from giving us away. After determining the wind direction, I approached the camp from the downwind side, like those first Indians I met suggested. I started making my way to the camp with my bow and arrow ready to shoot. I had a rifle, but I wanted them to die by the same type of weapon that they used to kill Sleeping Bird.

I spotted all three of them and catalogued their appearances so I would never forget them. One was skinny and wearing Sleeping Bird's necklace. Another one was short and fat. My Cherokee lance was resting in his lap. The third one was about my size and he was sitting on my blanket and smoking my pipe. I didn't even smoke my pipe! I knew I had the right men. I chose the order of my targets and got in position to shoot quickly and accurately. I didn't want the first arrow to kill them because I had something special in mind for them. I sighted in on the skinny one and shot him, placing the arrow left of his heart. As expected, the other two were startled by the sight, and as the one sitting on my blanket stood up, I shot him in the chest as well, narrowly missing his heart. The fat one had been sitting on the ground, so I saved him for last. I shot him in the lower back as he attempted to run away, carrying my lance. The arrow entered his spine, and he fell screaming in pain.

I came into the camp and saw all three of them writhing in pain in the dirt. The Cherokees had told me that most plains Indians shared a dialect, so I should be able to communicate with the Indians in Wyoming. I spoke to them in that Indian dialect and told them how much I cared for Sleeping Bird and how nice she was. I poked at their wounds with the tip of an arrow as I told them how she had enriched my life.

As I tied their hands and feet, I was certain that they understood my pain, for I tied them so tight that the leather straps would cut off the circulation within their limbs. It was cruel, but I would get crueler. As I told them what was coming next, I could see the fear in their eyes even as they tried to show that they were brave. For the next few minutes, I became the savage they wished they had never met.

When I was finished avenging Sleeping Bird, I looked to the sky and thanked the Great Spirit Warrior for protecting me. I asked him for forgiveness, and as I fell to my knees, I cried in hopes of releasing the grief I felt. I gathered up all my things that they had stolen and retrieved my horses. I took their horses too. Those horses weren't payment for what I had lost, but I could sell them to make the money I would need to move on. I had made up my mind that this part of Wyoming could no longer be home.

***

Sophie's yelling was what brought me back that time, "Hold onto life because I need you!" I opened my eyes. My fists were clinched so tight that I had to wiggle my fingers to get the blood circulating again. Sophie wiped the sweat from my forehead and said, "It's okay baby, I'm here."

There was a look of relief on her face when I sat up and smiled. "I'm sorry for putting you through all of this. I will stay alive and stay in the here and now with you."

She smiled and said, "As long as you keep waking up, there is nothing I'm not willing to do to help you recover."

I reached for her hand, realizing that never again would I be able to reach out to Sleeping Bird. I would never forget her, for there were too many great memories to relive. Looking into Sophie's eyes, I swore to myself to inflict an even worse death upon anyone that did anything to my Sophie.

CHAPTER 8: CIVIL WAR IN NEW MEXICO

Sophie left to get me some food since I had been out for most of the day. As I thought about what I was dreaming, this time, I tried to think of a reason why I had dreamt it.

Sophie came back after a while and fed me like I was a baby. She talked to me as well, but my thoughts were about what that last dream meant. Was avenging Sleeping Bird's death the beginning of the rage that had been driving me all those years, or was it just magnifying the rage that started when I was captured in Africa?

I didn't know for certain, but if it was, it had kept me alive in times when most men would have been killed. I hoped it would continue to drive me, because I needed to live not just for me but for Sophie as well. She deserved a better life than she had been living, and I planned to give it to her. I knew of her being a slave and having to do what most slave women were forced to do. Some nights when we were together, she would cry. I knew why, knew I couldn't make those memories go away, so I would lay there feeling useless.

She was talking to me, "Your high fever broke while you were out. The doctor thinks you should be getting better now."

The doctor had told her what to watch for, and I could tell that she was living with a renewed hope since her smile had more joy in it; that sparkle was back. That smile! I knew I couldn't let that hope slip away again because she was one beautiful sight when she was smiling at me. That made me even more determined to live and make life much better for her.

In the following days I stayed in the here and now for most of the day but continued to have dreams about events of years gone by as I slept.

With me being better, Sophie was able to return to her normal life, leaving me to heal and get back on my feet. I spent a lot of time by myself, thinking, as I was building up my strength. I could tell that I was mending because each day I was able to do more of my normal activities, and each day I felt better. My head was better, so my vision was much clearer. My ribs didn't even hurt when I got up and moved around. I was tempted to take Ole Lightning out for a ride, but Sophie's words of warning kept ringing in my ears, "Do NOT get on no horse."

I did go out and brush him daily because that was exercise that I needed. I took every opportunity to slowly work my body back into the condition it needed to be in to continue doing my job. Scouting and capturing criminals were the only things that satisfied my warrior drive.

I always used past experiences to strengthen me, so as I slept at night, for some reason, I continued my journey through my past. At this point in time, I was very aware that I was reliving my life, but I still had no idea why. I felt that the only way to find the answer was to continue dreaming until the reason was revealed to me by the Great Spirit Warrior or God. I was beginning to hope that they were the same because the Bible taught that you could only serve one master.

As I drifted off to my yesteryears once more, I found myself back in Wyoming. After avenging Sleeping Bird's murder, I needed to change everything that was a constant reminder of her. I took a trip to the fort to report the incident to Sarge just in case they were out where the cabin was and expected to stop in on us. He and the other buffalo soldiers that had visited with us were really sorry about what happened to Sleeping Bird.

They wanted to go looking for the Indians, but I assured them that they didn't need to do that. Either the way I said it or something that they saw in my eyes caused them to give me a look of surprise and admiration at the same time. I could tell that they knew I had dealt with the situation. They didn't ask any questions, and I didn't offer any details. We just went and had a drink in their barracks and told some old tales about our past.

"Sarge, I have to get out of Wyoming. I'm going to leave tomorrow or as soon as possible." He shook his head in disbelief. "You are one brave man. Tell me. Have you ever considered a career in the U.S. Army?"

Truthfully, I had never thought of doing it, all I had ever thought about was getting far enough west, keeping my head down, and staying out of slavery. I never thought working a job like that was in the cards for me. But if the army was wiping out hostile Indians like the ones I killed, it just might be the place for me.

I asked him some questions, and his answers made me feel that army life could be a good option. We discussed the difficulties that blacks had as they served for the Union Army back east. I could understand how difficult the situation would be if they faced the Southern soldiers that still saw blacks as property and not U.S. citizens. The sight of a black soldier killing a white man would make the Southerners mad as hell. That was why being in the army out west was a better situation for a black man.

Sarge said, "The commanding officer is out on a patrol and will be back in a couple days. I will talk to him then to find out if the U.S. Army is still recruiting buffalo soldiers in northern New Mexico Territory." I stayed in the barracks to wait until the commanding officer returned. Two days later, he returned and Sarge went to talk with him about me. Within the hour he sent for me to come to the commanding officer's quarters. When I entered the room, Sarge was smiling. Once I sat down as instructed, the commanding officer began, "It is good to meet you, Sarge has told me of your troubles and desire to leave Wyoming. You should be able to enlist in New Mexico Territory." I beamed. This was the perfect fresh start. He held up his hand at my excitement, "But! There's a chance that the army might stop recruiting blacks for a while, so don't get your hopes up."

"Yes, sir I understand. I'll go down to New Mexico Territory as quickly as I can to see if I can enlist."

"Good, I will send them a message via dispatch, and I'll write you a letter you can show to any military or other person that may stop you along the way to question you. You'll also get enough provisions to get you there and a map of the territory between here and there. You will be on official army business so no funny business, we're trusting you to make it there and do as you say you will.

"Yes, sir. Thank you for your help. I will go straight there. No funny business." I went to find Sarge and tell him the good news. He was happy for me and we had a drink after he was off duty. I picked up the letter the next morning, said my goodbyes, and started my journey to New Mexico Territory.

I had sold the other horses and the Indian ponies so I had some money should I need it. Gvnige was very spirited, and we set a good pace that the packhorse could endure as we headed south. I rode just east of the main road to minimize encounters with travelers. White men still did not like to see a black man with anything that was better than they had. I didn't have a bill of sale for Gvnige and figured I would be hanged as a horse thief if I was spotted by white men that wanted him.

The terrain was rather flat, with just enough trees to make it harder for someone to spot a lone rider. I stayed about four hundred yards away from that main road and spent a lot of hours in the saddle to shorten the number of days I had to spend on the trail.

The trip took days, so I had lots of time to think. My thoughts returned to the conversation that I had with Sarge and the commanding officer back at the fort about the current status of the Civil War. The war had extended out west and was a growing issue for the settlers out here. I just didn't understand people hating each other just because they were different. Neighbors fighting neighbors who they had been friends with for years. I tried, but I just didn't understand all that mess. Hopefully the war would be over soon, and America would be a united country once more.

After several days of traveling, I was in southern Colorado, and, based off what I could tell from my map and the landmarks, I should be at my destination in a few days. I continued to skirt around towns. I didn't have any freedom papers, so I didn't want to run into any unwanted trouble, especially when I was so close to my destination. I was never going back to being a slave, and after killing in rage to avenge someone I loved, I knew I could do it again, especially for my freedom.

Just before crossing the Colorado/New Mexico border, the land was pretty flat, so I could see a lot of the landscape from my elevated position sitting on Gvnige. Sarge had given me a pair of old field glasses, and they enabled me to see even further. I would use them when I wanted to get a closer look at a landmark or something of interest along the trail.

I was looking at a deer, hoping I could get close enough to him to take a shot, when something spooked him. Then I spotted several Indians traveling in a parallel path to the one I was on. I scanned the area behind them and then that in front of them to determine if they were alone or scouting for a larger war party.

I didn't see anything behind them, but if they continued their current course, they were headed for an isolated homestead. After watching them for a couple of minutes, I was sure they were headed for the homestead.

I could see that it consisted of a small house, a barn, and pens with horses and cattle. I didn't see any people, but there had to be some around to keep the homestead looking well-kept.

I picked up my pace and dropped down in a gully that would take me closer. I wanted to watch the Indians. If it looked like they were going to attack the settlers, I would help the settlers. With the death of Sleeping Bird fresh on my mind, I wanted to kill any bad Indians that I encountered.

There was high grass all around and a little hill to block the Indians' view of me. I didn't expect them to have field glasses as I did, but in case they did, I didn't want to be discovered before seeing what they were up to. When I got closer, I could see that there were eight of them.

I looked through the field glasses again to see what weapons they had. They had no guns, but they were wearing war paint, and I knew that was not good for the settlers.

Their focus was on the house and livestock, so they had no idea that I was near. That would be the edge I needed to help the settlers. I dismounted about a hundred yards from the house and got in a good position to shoot the Indians if they started anything. About then I heard the first war cry, and they started the attack.

I aimed and fired at the last Indian in the group. He was knocked off his horse, so I aimed at the one just ahead of him, and he fell as well. I wanted to kill the ones in the back first because the leaders would be focused on the homestead ahead of them. I fired again, and another one fell, leaving five. That was when they realized that someone else had joined the fight in support of the homesteaders.

As they turned their attention to me, I dropped another one, and then I heard rifle fire from the house, another Indian dropped, going screaming to his spirit in the sky.

I started firing again and dropped two more while the shooter in the house dropped the last Indian. Suddenly, it was very quiet again, as if nothing had happened. Once my rage was back under control, I surveyed the battlefield.

With the Indians all lying dead in the field, I mounted Gvnige and walked him up to the settlers' yard. Even though I knew that those eight

Indians would not see their families again, I had no pity for them since they were trying to kill without being provoked by the settlers.

Warriors should only attack warriors, not families. Yet I still hoped that their families would mourn for them to help their souls find the way to the spirit in the sky that they worshiped.

As I approached the house, to my surprise, a woman stepped out to greet me. She was lean, wearing a worn dress and carrying a rifle. Her face was well-tanned, so I knew she was used to working outside. I waited, but no man came out of the house. I had noted how someone in the house had shot some of the Indians, so I didn't take any chances. I had already put my weapons away before approaching the house, because I didn't want to appear to be a threat.

She had a surprised look on her face, and I didn't know if it was because of the Indian attack or seeing me, a black man. Even though I had helped save her and her family, she still held the rifle, and I could see that she could point and shoot with little effort. I cautiously took a few steps closer and said, "Woah! Don't shoot! My name is Raymond Jackson. I was just passing by on my way to the U.S. Army fort in New Mexico and saw those Indians coming for your homestead. I can show you my papers if you like."

She said, "I'm Susan Moore and I am glad you happened to be around. I've heard of the buffalo soldiers and I am thankful that you was able to help my family." She lowered her weapon. "Is everyone all right?" "The children are scared but not hurt." "Good. I will bury the Indians and then continue on my way. She was thankful for that because it was not something a woman and kids should have to do.

"If you don't mind me asking, ma'am, where are your men?" She started crying so I continued, "Oh I'm sorry ma'am, I shouldn't have pried." A couple teenage kids came out to comfort her. The boy said, "Father was killed a week ago when another group of Indians raided the homestead." "I am so sorry." "We were preparing to move closer to a town for safety, and that's why we were all in the house and not watching out for more Indians." He held out his arm toward the dead

Indians and said, "I have learned a very valuable lesson and will never let my guard down again." I smiled to show him that I liked that thinking.

The boy couldn't be older than about fifteen but was large despite his baby face. He was strong and tanned from the hard work it took to care of a homestead, so I said, "I can see that your family has worked hard to make your homestead a good home." The boy thanked me sheepishly as did his mother. "Here, let me help you bury them." The boy offered.

With his help, it didn't take too long to finish that undesirable task. By then the mother had food prepared, and she invited me to eat with them. Being that they were white and I was black, I expected to eat outside by myself. She surprised me by demanding that I eat with them in the house. The kids didn't seem to mind having me eat with them, so I was on my best behavior, the way Sleeping Bird had taught me, as I ate that good meal.

The hate that some people have is so intense that they would never allow a black person to eat with them, but this family was different. As we ate, I learned that they were from the northeast, in eastern Ohio. They were against slavery and had moved out to Colorado to get away from the fighting between the northern and southern states.

Her husband had helped many of the slaves traveling on the Underground Railroad, and that was one of the reasons that they had to get out of Ohio before the Civil War started. They had been out here several years and really loved living in Colorado.

While I was washing up before we ate, I noticed that they had some mighty fine horses. Several of them were mares, and I thought about what Sarge had said about how my stallion would produce some fine foals.

After the meal, I said, "Susan, I noticed those fine mares you have in the corral. Would you be interested in selling me one of them?" Susan said, "Just take the one you want. Had it not been for what you did, all of us would be dead, and the Indians would have taken the horses. I figure that having the life of all my children puts me miles ahead of where I would be had you not come along."

This was an unexpected gesture, and it was the best thing that any whites had done for me or for any black person that I knew. For some reason, I just didn't consider Sleeping Bird to be white. To me, she was a Cherokee Indian. I thanked her and went outside with the boy to help with the chores. After finishing up, I asked the mother to write me a bill of sale for the mare. She said she would. I told her, "I found that stallion near the house I had in Wyoming. I would appreciate it if you would write me a bill of sale for him as well." She smiled and got her paper and pen to write the bill of sale for both horses. My grin showed my appreciation for that, but I still said thank you.

I stood watch that night, in case some Indians came looking for their missing braves. I didn't see or hear anything, so I took a little nap in that nice rocking chair on her porch once I noticed that the family was moving around in the house. I didn't think that there would be any other Indians in the area, but I waited for them to finish packing. I told the mother that I would help her son drive the livestock to the town that was only about ten miles away.

That town wasn't exactly on the trail I had been traveling, but it didn't take me too far out of my way. I would not have been able to sleep or live with myself if I didn't make sure that nice family was in a safer place. To me, those values that I learned in Africa should apply to everyone, everywhere.

We left late that day, spent the night on the trail and reached the town the next day. The mother reported the incident to the town lawman. That old fart didn't look capable to do anything but eat and sleep, but he gave me the typical hateful look that I expected. He appeared to be getting ready to question me, and she cut him off, knowing his intentions. Her son and me said our goodbyes and he told me that he would never forget what I did for his family. His mother nodded to indicate she felt the same. I said my goodbye to her and rode out of town to camp along the trail to New Mexico Territory. I hoped that none of the townsfolk would trail me and try to return me to slavery because I wasn't going to let that happen.

Before sunrise the next morning, I was on my way, and judging from Gvnige's reactions, he was satisfied with his new lady friend. She was a fine thoroughbred with a coal black shiny coat. She had long strong legs and if she had a blemish, I couldn't see it. I decided to call her Lady.

I picked up the pace to get a better idea of what kind of horse Lady was. After the incident with the town lawman, I was glad that the mother had volunteered to give me a bill of sale for Lady and Gvnige. Both were fine specimen of horseflesh.

I knew if I ran into some evil white men, the bill of sale might not be worth the paper it was written on, but it was better than nothing. Right now, that didn't matter because there were none of them in sight.

As I admired the gait of Lady, I thought to myself that I should get a mighty fine colt out of my two fine horses. Life wasn't always good, so I was enjoying it being good to me right now.

I didn't know when I crossed into New Mexico Territory, but if the map was right and I was reading the landmarks correctly, I would arrive at the fort sometime the next day. That thought excited me, and once again, I picked up the pace. I wanted to give the horses a little extra exercise before camping for the night.

About noon the next day, the fort was just ahead of me, and from my position, it didn't look like much of a fort. I had heard that most of the Indians in this part of New Mexico Territory had settled into reservation life and no longer raided and killed in rage.

Either way, I didn't plan to be a peacekeeping soldier. I was going to do what it took to get to where the army was fighting Indians. I knew that inside, I was a warrior, and I wanted to protect and defend, not just live out my days. I knew I had to make a life for myself out here in the West. Even if it meant protecting the very people that stole me from my homeland.

As I entered the fort, I noticed that most of the soldiers were buffalo soldiers and man, did they look elegant in their army uniforms. This stirred up excitement in me that I had not felt since being a boy in Africa. It was a feeling that I loved, so I looked up the commanding officer. His office was small and very neat. I was escorted to his office and I smiled and said, "Excuse me, sir? I'm Raymond Jackson." He returned my smile and said, "General John Miller. What can I do for you?" I gave him the letter written by the commanding officer at the Wyoming fort and waited while he read it.

The letter was in a sealed envelope, and the other commanding officer in Wyoming didn't tell me what he wrote. As I waited, I watched his facial expressions, hoping to read his thoughts as he read the letter.

I took note of the varying facial expressions and I didn't like what I was seeing. I was reading his body language as well, and what I read was not encouraging, yet it was not negative.

When he finished reading the letter, he looked up at me and sat there in his chair, saying nothing. I could tell that he was studying me. I wasn't expecting that, so I wasn't sure what I should do, so I did nothing but wait. He broke the silence at last and asked, "Are you comfortable with killing another person?"

I calculated my response carefully. "I don't like killing, but I would do it if it was necessary to protect others or myself."

He asked about my family, and I told him that I didn't have any here in America. He frowned and stayed silent. I said, "I was stolen from Africa as a boy, brought to America and enslaved. I escaped, came out west and settled in Wyoming. My woman was killed by renegade Indians, so I left there to start a new life."

It was encouraging to see his nods of agreement or appreciation of my story, so I was feeling better. He said, "The army could use a good man like you." I showed a big ole grin and said, "I want to be a soldier."

He called another officer into the office and ordered him to swear me in to make me a member of the U.S. Army. The other officer gave him some papers that had just arrived by military dispatch, so he opened them while I was being sworn in.

Just minutes later, I was a member of the U.S. Army and excited as hell. I turned to look at the commanding officer, and he now had a grim look on his face. He indicated that one of the dispatches was from the commanding officer at the Wyoming fort, and then he told me that I must have impressed that commanding officer a lot.

He told me that they seldom received such a recommendation for blacks looking to enlist in the army. I could even see the beginnings of a smile as he said that, and I thanked him.

He also told me "One of the other dispatches came from the War Department in Washington, DC, and it advised that Washington had put a freeze on enlisting Negros due to the ongoing Civil War that had spread west, including New Mexico Territory."

I was stuck on hearing him refer to me as a Negro because most whites referred to us as boys or less kind terms. So, I had to refocus on what he was saying. He said, "I wish I had read that before swearing you in because I now have a serious problem that I have to resolve."

He asked me to leave to give him time to work out the issue because the army needed men like me out here in the West, and he didn't want to let me get caught up in the normal disappointing opportunities that the local whites would give a Negro.

He instructed the other officer to have someone take me to the Negro barracks, where I was to wait until he sent for me. I was a bit confused, but I was in no position to argue, so I did as instructed.

As I walked, I started to get angry. I was so close to being a buffalo soldier, and yet, it appeared that I might not get to be one. I knew that nothing that was worth having come to you easily, so waiting was not a big issue as long as I eventually ended up fighting Indians and injustice. I was walking with contempt in my stride as I reached the Negro barracks. I entered and was greeted by an aging buffalo soldier.

He gave me a good looking over and said, "Hey, my handle is Flat Foot Johnny, but you can just call me Flats." Of course, I had to look at his feet. He noticed me doing that and started laughing. He said, "My feet are fine; it was a nickname given to me as a child because I was a fast runner." I smiled and had to laugh with him about it.

The white soldier left, so once I was alone with Flats, he got brave and started to talk and ask me questions about myself. He was making cornbread batter, and I could smell beans cooking. He was a little chubby, and there was a lot of gray in his hair and beard. As I answered the questions that I wanted to, I watched his facial expressions. He was never rude, but I didn't like talking too much because people had the tendency to run their mouths. There were things in my past that needed to be my business only.

He was one talkative rascal, and I was stuck with him until the general sent for me. I was tired of his mouth running, so I was hoping that it would not be too long before I heard from the commanding officer. But the more Flats talked about his military experience, the more I started thinking of him as a warrior. He had been a soldier for several years and had been out here in New Mexico Territory as one of the original buffalo soldiers. He told some fascinating stories about those early years. The story about surviving an Apache attack in western New Mexico Territory was a great one. I could see myself in that fierce battle fighting to survive. I was hoping that I would get the chance to live such adventures.

Then he started talking about the more recent years, and several times he mentioned a scout. I stopped him and asked "Flats, what does a scout do and how do you get to be one?" He explained, "You needed to know the landscape of the area you are assigned to scout, and you had to be able to read signs, especially Indian signs."

As he explained a scout's duties, I was thinking about how I could read signs and had been reading them since I was about fourteen years old. After escaping slavery, I had learned about Indian signs and to track while living with the Cherokees. The buffalo soldiers in Wyoming were experts at tracking the Lakota Indians, and I learned from them, then used all the knowledge I had to track those renegade Indians that killed Sleeping Bird. I felt that I knew most of what it took to be an army scout. As I was still listening to Flats, in my mind, I felt that the only thing I would have to do was learn the area, and then I would be the man to take an army scout position. I would think more about this when I was alone and able to concentrate.

Another soldier came in, and I recognized that the stripes on his uniform were the same as Sarge had on his uniform. Flats greeted him as Sergeant Thompson as they started talking about what was cooking for dinner. Sergeant Thompson was talking to Flats as he looked me up and down and then asked Flats, "Who is this fellow and why is he here?" Flats looked a little confused, so I said, "Sergeant Thompson, my name is Raymond Jackson. I'm here waiting for General Miller to send for me. I want to enlist."

He had been told that the army was not enlisting any new Negro recruits, so he said, "You are wasting your time." "I know that I cannot enlist right now, but I'm waiting here until General Miller sends for me." He nodded, and the three of us continued to talk about not much of anything as I waited to hear from the general.

It was easy to read in the sergeant's body language that he didn't like me. I wasn't too concerned about his feelings since I knew I could not become a soldier and wouldn't have to serve under him. So, I matched his hateful looks and threatening body language. It had been a while since I had fought anyone close range, so I was hoping for a battle.

A few minutes later another soldier came into the barracks. He was one of the buffalo soldiers that had visited the cabin when I lived in Wyoming. He greeted me with a big smile, and we had a laugh or two about old times. The sergeant stopped the happy time and demanded that the soldier tell him what he knew about me. So the soldier did, leaving out the part about me living with a white woman passing for an Indian.

I was still in the barracks at supper time, talking to the soldiers and resting. By then, the barracks were almost full of soldiers, and they were laughing and singing songs that were so sweet and sad. I had heard most of the songs on the plantation, so I was familiar with them. The slaves used the songs as a means of making their captivity seem more manageable and felt that they helped them pass the time day after day. They sounded so much more spiritual hearing them as a free man. I felt sadness for those still enslaved and hoped that the president would free them all soon.

Sergeant Thompson had left about an hour earlier, and I had not seen that Wyoming soldier in a while either. A sentry came into the barracks, and everyone got quiet. He told me to report to General Miller at once, so I made tracks in a hurry.

I arrived at General Miller's quarters, and to my surprise, there were several officers in his office with him. Sergeant Thompson and the Wyoming buffalo soldier were there as well. They all looked me over as if trying to find answers to a question written in my body language. My excitement became concern, and I had the feeling that this was not going to go as I had hoped.

Even though all the officers and soldiers were standing, General Miller asked me to be seated as he started the conversation. His body language and tone were much different from earlier, so I knew this was going to be a serious conversation.

His first question was, "Who are you, and why are you here?" I knew this was no time to play games, so I told them my story, leaving out some names and events to protect the innocent, namely me. I didn't know how these white men would feel about Sleeping Bird being white, so I was taking no chances.

I summarized it all by saying that I came to New Mexico Territory to become a buffalo soldier or become the best scout that the army had ever had. He nodded and said, "What makes you think you can do that?"

I told them about my time with the Cherokees and my training in Africa. They seemed to get real interested during my story about escaping slavery and making my way westward all the way to Oklahoma Territory without ever seeing a tracker or hearing their hound dogs.

One of the officers wanted more details about how I did that, but General Miller denied his request. I was relieved because I didn't want to reveal my tactics just yet. Slavery was still very real in the southern states, and if such information was to be communicated to the plantation owners and their trackers, it could compromise a slave's attempt to escape.

After telling me that the story of my escape and making it to Wyoming seemed too good to be true, General Miller said, "The buffalo soldier from Wyoming told us about the woman that was with you and that you always spoke to each other using your Indian names." I was hoping that he didn't ask any questions about Sleeping Bird since I wasn't prepared to discuss her.

He said, "I believe you because your story matches that of the soldier from Wyoming. There was another letter from Wyoming about some renegade Indians being killed." He paused, gauging my response. "Tell us how you killed those three renegade Indians and why you treated them as you did."

I was thinking, "Apparently Sarge had sent some soldiers to find the renegades that I killed and reported it to his commanding officer. That Wyoming buffalo soldier must have ridden fast and long to get here so fast with that dispatch." Then I remembered that I spent three days at that Wyoming fort and I lost another two days helping the settler.

I knew the cat was out of the bag for certain, so I looked at the buffalo soldier from Wyoming and Sergeant Thompson. Neither made eye contact with me, so I answered General Miller and I didn't hide the rage I still had as I told them the facts.

After I finished, he said "No ordinary man would have done what you did." "I don't consider myself to be ordinary in any way. I was raised to be an African warrior, and I am determined to protect others here in America as I would have in Africa. They killed someone that had done nothing to them and didn't threaten them in any way. She didn't even know she was in danger. They shot her in the back like cowards."

General Miller stood up and dismissed the officers, Sergeant Thompson, and the buffalo soldier. Once they left, he said, "You appear to be very confident in yourself." I could only smile and say, "I train daily to be a protector of people, and that is all that I want to do."

He said, "Well, there's a possible opportunity in western New Mexico Territory for a man with skills like yours. They need another scout that can track and who doesn't mind fighting or bringing criminals to justice. I cannot send a military dispatch to the fort in western New Mexico territory, but I will send a personal letter with you, asking the commanding officer, General Tommy Foster, to give you an opportunity to be a scout."

I'm sure that the grin on my face told him everything he needed to know, but I still said, "This is exactly what I've been hoping for, thank you."

He continued, "Scouts can be government employees or soldiers, so there should be no problem for you to get hired with my recommendation. The letter will explain that the only option the army had to get you on our side was for you to become a scout. The catch to all of this is that you have to return to this fort after the Civil War is over. Then you will enlist in the buffalo soldier regiment."

This was exactly what I wanted, to prove my fighting skills. The western New Mexico Territory tour of duty as a scout would allow me to do it, so I was hoping that the Civil War lasted a long time. I managed an even bigger smile and asked,

"When do I leave?" "The letter will be waiting for you tomorrow morning, and you can leave afterward." I was dismissed, so I left and headed back to the Negro barracks, where I was to spend the night.

I was so overjoyed that I had to find a quiet place to thank the Great Spirit Warrior for my good fortunes. I was almost a scout, a protector of the people. They were not my people, but they were the only people around, and they needed all the protection they could get.

I took my time making that walk. I wanted to keep the smile on my face for as long as I could. I felt somewhat betrayed, so a part of me was upset with Sergeant Thompson and the Wyoming buffalo soldier for telling the commanding officer about my Wyoming troubles, but had they not done what they did, I might not have gotten this opportunity.

Seeing them would be awkward, but I would be the bigger man and thank them for their help. I was one step closer to being the warrior that my father wanted me to be. Father died in battle, and if I were to die, I knew there was no greater honor than dying protecting the people that depend on you.

I ate and spent some quality time with some of the soldiers. Sergeant Thompson even seemed to be nicer to me. That Wyoming buffalo soldier made eye contact with me, and we had a silent exchange. He was proud and supportive of me, and I was thankful to him for not revealing the big secret of Sleeping Bird's heritage.

Then, for some reason, I remembered her last words to me. I had been in such a state of rage that, until now, I hadn't remembered her telling me that she would have a surprise for me when I returned. Now I would never know what that surprise was...

***

The sun was up, and I felt better after some restful sleep for the first time since being shot. I was refreshed and more determined after reliving the events that brought me here. Thanks to the army doctor and Sophie, I was getting back on my feet. At this rate, I would be up and about, doing my daily routines in no time.

There was a knock on the door, and Jose came in, smiling as usual. He gave me an update on my livestock and asked if I needed anything.

Between his wife and Sophie, I had all the food I could eat and some food that I didn't want to eat but knew better than to turn down.

We talked for a while and he left to go tend to his daily tasks. About an hour later, the general came by to see me. He never came to my house, so I knew he must have some real important reason for showing up. He told me that one of the killers was not with the group that attacked me and was still running loose.

He had a soldier on duty outside my house because they didn't want to take any chances. I knew from Jose that they had posted soldiers close to my house since I was shot but kept them out of my sight. I thanked him and asked him to make sure that Sophie was protected as well, but without her knowing. He winked and told me that it was already done, and then he left.

I didn't want to think about it right then, so I started reading some of the books I had collected over the years. Reading was something that I enjoyed a lot because, as Sleeping Bird told me, reading leads to a better you. One could continue to learn if he continued to read, so I often wondered what Mother would think of me if she could see me now.

CHAPTER 9: U.S. CAVALRY, SPECIAL ASSIGNMENT

About three weeks later, after a long day of working myself back into warrior shape, I retired to my house early, with a lot on my mind. My life was still being threatened by someone. The soldier stationed outside my house was a brave man, but I was still a little uneasy. I trusted the army, but when an outlaw was determined to do something, he usually kept trying until it was done.

I checked my weapons before getting ready for bed. I always slept with a pistol under my pillow and one in the holster hanging from the post of my headboard for anyone to see. I was a light sleeper, so the faintest noise would wake me, alerting me of any potential danger. If the outlaw got past the sentry, I would send him to reunite with his friends in hell.

As I waited to fall asleep, I was thinking that history might not tell my story, but I would always remember my homeland, family, and the journey I had been on since coming to America. As I drifted off to sleep, I was thinking about getting back on my feet and resuming my duties, then, I was continuing to dream about the past years of my life leading up to me being where I was today. After making a similar journey several times before, I embraced it, allowing it to consume my every thought and allowing myself to dream about some of the best years of my life.

***

I was back on my journey to the fort in western New Mexico Territory. I had enjoyed my stay at the eastern fort, but I didn't care much for Sergeant Thompson. He reminded me of the slaves that were called "Uncle Tom" on the plantation. I think he meant well, but he wasn't missing an opportunity to advance his rank at the fort. I hoped that he would become as successful as he desired.

That morning as I left, Gvnige was very spirited after resting for a few days. Lady was somewhat spirited as well and didn't seem to like the pack she was carrying. Maybe if she knew it had the grain that she would eat each evening, she wouldn't have put up as much of a fight.

My other packhorse was carrying more of a load, including our water, but he didn't show any indication that he was not happy about it. We had a two-week ride ahead of us, and with the maps General Miller had given me, I should be able to get across the mountains to the west and find the fort in Apache territory.

On the second day on the trail, Lady started coming into heat, and Gvnige could smell that she was, so he was getting harder to control as we rode west. I learned a lot about breeding horses while I was a slave, so I knew it wasn't time for breeding today. Tomorrow or the next day would be the best days. Gvnige didn't know it, but I was saving him some pain by not letting him at the mare.

After getting very little sleep during the night with Gvnige fussing up a storm, we were traveling again. About mid-afternoon I found a stream at the foot of the mountain range that had a cluster of trees that would allow me to make a small corral to let the horses mate. I camped there for the rest of the day even though there were hours of daylight left.

I woke up early the next morning and hit the trail. We made better time now that Gvnige had his mind on traveling. I pushed him a little harder than usual to make up the time we had lost by stopping early the day before. All three horses were well-rested, and Lady seemed to be more satisfied than on previous days, so we made very good time for a couple days.

We reached a little town that was marked on the map, and I spent just enough time there to water the horses and verify where I was. The folks appeared to be friendly, and many of them appeared to be Indians or Mexican. I felt a little safer but remained cautious.

As I walked from the general store, I saw a document that interested me. I was pretending to just lean on the post across from the document as I read it. I wasn't ready for any other people to know that I could read. As I read the article, I had to repeat what I read to myself, "The president freed the slaves."

I smiled, as that was the first time that I thought of America as being a place where I belonged. As I read other information in the document, outlaws were stealing and killing all over this territory, so I became more dedicated to being a protector of the people in this land that was now home. I looked to the sky and silently asked the Great Spirit Warrior to strengthen and protect me. I was not living a bad life; in fact, it was the best life I had lived so far.

With slavery being a thing of the past, it was much more comforting to be a black man in America. But, as I thought about it some more, I knew it would take a lot of years for the black man to rise above slavery. We were free, but most blacks had nothing and would have to settle for living almost as enslaved as before. America was not going to send the blacks back to Africa. America was not going to make up for all the black lives that it had destroyed. I questioned if anything would be done to help the newly freed people. Yes, we were free to just lie down and die or accept a different form of enslavement just to survive. Coming out west was an option for free blacks, so I now had more of a reason to fight to make this land safe for the settlers that would come. I took a deep breath, refocused on my mission to get to the fort, and headed for my horses.

I was a new me, a prouder me, and I was liking myself much better now. I knew this would be the edge I needed to become a great army scout, and I only needed to get to the fort and start working at it. I mounted up and headed out of the town, intending to make it to a friendly Indian village that was only supposed to be about ten miles west.

When you are riding alone, you have lots of time to think, so I recalled how so many of the slaves talked of their ancestors being born here in America for as long as they could remember. I was one of a few blacks who had actually been born in Africa, so I was blessed to know of the homeland. I told many of the slaves about life there. I would never forget the pride that they showed when I told of the great battles our village warriors had with other tribes.

So many of the slaves were enslaved internally, with shackles and chains that no one could see. The shackles of ignorance and fear were as strong, if not stronger, than any chains that the white man had placed on their legs and arms. The saddest thing was that they didn't even know it!

The white man was responsible, and he would do all he could to keep blacks enslaved. Sadly, most of the blacks would stay enslaved, having no choice except to accept the treatment of the whites. It was sad, but mostly this was how I felt life in America would be for blacks for many years to come.

Those thoughts troubled me, so I rode in silence. About an hour later the weather started getting bad, so I had to slow our pace, which caused us to get to the Indian camp just after dark. As I approached the camp, I slowed our pace to almost a crawl because it was not too smart to come rushing into any place out west after dark. There were sentries at the edge of the camp, so I stopped to greet them. Using the Indian dialect that I knew, I spoke to them, and they allowed me to enter the camp.

These Indians looked much different from most Indians that I had seen so far. They tended to be shorter and thicker than others. I stopped at the first structure and studied it for a while since it was the first one of that type that I had seen. It appeared to be made of wood or straw mixed with sod. It was round, but it had a domed top that looked nothing like the teepees I had seen. The man that emerged through the doorway spoke broken English, but we were able to communicate.

I told him where I was coming from and where I was going. He confirmed that I was on the right trail and told me that it would take another week or more to get there. He said that the village would welcome me for the night and that I could camp at the western edge of the village.

He issued commands in their dialect as I rode toward the west end of the camp. He had confirmed that I was making good time, and I was glad because my butt needed a softer surface. One more week wasn't that long to wait, so I focused on getting settled for the night.

I was thankful that the rain had stopped just as I entered the village. I got the horses unsaddled, fed, and tied up good. I even hobbled them, just in case one of the Indians was more taken with them than they should be. You could never be too careful with fine horses.

I started a fire on the village side of where the horses were bedded down. If one of them rascals wanted to attempt to steal my horses, they would have to come by me. I knew that Gvnige would give a warning if someone was approaching and that would wake me. The horses were my partners, and we had to protect each other.

Just as I was about to start cooking, two Indian squaws came walking into the camp with food for me. I thanked them for their generosity but was pretty sure they couldn't understand me. They left soon after and I spread out my bedroll and went to check on the horses before turning in for the night.

I woke up alert and feeling more rested than I had since my journey started. As I prepared to break camp, the same two squaws came back carrying food, and both were all smiles. I thanked them and expected to hear nothing in return, so I just smiled and said my goodbyes.

The rest of the trip was rather uneventful, and I arrived at the fort and adjacent town just about the time that I had expected to. I saw some troubling stares as I rode through the town, so I was glad that it wasn't much of a town. I was stopped by the sentries at the gate of the fort and after stating my business, I was directed to the commanding officer's, General Tommy Foster, office. I presented him with the letter, and after reading it, he looked up and asked if his friend John Miller, was doing well.

I said he was in good health and seemed to be well respected by his troops. After some more small talk to get to know each other better, we discussed the responsibilities of a scout. Afterward, he called in a junior officer and had him start the process of hiring me as a scout.

I thanked him, and he laughed as he told me, "I hope that you will be as happy in the coming months and possibly years as the smile on your face shows now." I assured him that it would be an improvement from my life thus far and that I looked forward to any challenges that the position would bring my way.

I started talking about how happy I was to be in Apache territory, so he told me some stories about hundreds of soldiers being killed and gave me some advice about not becoming overconfident.

He had been out here in New Mexico Territory for more than ten years. He told me to always refer to him just as "General" because out in this territory it isn't good for the Apaches to know the commanding officers' names. I thought about it for a split second and tended to agree with the rule. I said, "Yes, sir, General." Afterward, I realized that was the first time that I had said "Yes, sir" out of respect for a white man and not just out of obligation or fear.

Someone was waiting to see him, so he dismissed me and told me to camp just outside the fort for the night, and he would see to me having more suitable housing the next day. He ordered a couple of soldiers to camp near me to ensure that I wasn't troubled by any of the settlers of the nearby town. We bonded in those few minutes, and I left his office with a new sense of pride. I knew that we would become good friends and prove to be great allies on the battlefield.

As I left his office, I thought about him, and I had a warm feeling. It was easy to see that he was different from the whites I knew back in Mississippi. This man was more like the elders of my village back in Africa. Yes, I could and would respect this man and protect him with my life. That night, I asked the Great Spirit Warrior for the strength and guidance that I would need to protect the people in this land.

In the following weeks, I met the soldiers and the other scouts. Most of the soldiers were white, but sometimes, there were a few visiting buffalo soldiers as well. Man, did they look magnificent in them uniforms. I wanted one but knew that I was not allowed to have one until Washington allowed the enlisting of more blacks. For now, I would settle for buckskin clothing up top, with American pants and the fine black boots that came almost up to my knees. They were made of very smooth leather that shone enough for you to see your reflection if the sun was in the right position. The army wanted its riders to be comfortable on a horse and able to walk or run if on foot, so they had flat heels. Those boots were the best thing I had felt on my feet in my life.

One of the scouts was a Lakota Indian named Many Trails because he was more knowledgeable about the western Lakota country than anyone that the army knew about. He had come here with Major Roberts from up north.

I was told that Major Roberts held him in high regard and protected him as if he was related to him. They had been at this fort for a couple of years and had proven to be of great benefit in training recruits, experienced soldiers, and scouts. I made a mental note of this pair since I wanted to learn from them as quickly and often as I could.

For the next three years, we went on many missions and fought many battles with the Apaches. The Apaches were brave warriors and reminded me of my African village warriors in many ways. They were fighting to hold their land, continue their way of life and drive away the white man. They didn't hate the buffalo soldiers as much as the whites, but they knew that all soldiers were a threat to their way of life. I was getting to protect others as I always wanted to, so maybe being here was what the Great Spirit Warrior wanted for me.

As the Apache tribes became smaller, many of the missions were training missions, and others were to scout and make maps of unexplored areas. We even had to end a few Apache uprisings and those were the times when I felt that I was doing what the Great Spirit Warrior wanted me to do.

There was one thing I knew for sure; those Apaches were mean and determined to hold their land and never go to reservations. I could understand that, but I hoped that they would have realized that they were fighting a losing battle. The white man was determined to settle the West, and he was not going to allow the Apaches or anything else to stop him.

In a way, I was now one of the white man's weapons, so I was just as guilty. Deep within my heart, I felt sorry for the Apaches. Yet, when I thought about how Indians had killed my Sleeping Bird, there was still enough rage within my soul to kill the bad Indians and end the battles that had claimed so many lives.

On one particular mission, I was riding with Many Trails and a couple of other scouts. We were scouting for a large campaign to make sure that we knew the whereabouts of all the major Apache camps. The Apaches didn't like this, and many of the tribes came together to attack us.

As we were riding at the foot of a mountain range, I noticed that no birds were flying anywhere near us, and no desert critters were around either. Quickly, I realized we had ridden right into an ambush. I alerted the commanding officer, and he told me that he sensed danger as well. He issued orders to deploy the appropriate army tactics to defend our position, and the soldiers responded accordingly. I didn't have time to fret over it then since the Apaches had started attacking; I would do that later.

The commanding officer was wounded during the initial attack and couldn't do much except try to keep breathing. The next officer in command rallied the troops, and we managed to dig in to make a stand against the Apaches. As their numbers dwindled, we were able to get the wounded patched up and ready to head back to the fort. A lot of the soldiers and Apaches were killed in that bloody battle, so I was mad as hell.

Many Trails was the lead scout that day, and he was nowhere to be found until the battle was over. My early warning saved many lives in that battle, including the commanding officer's, so as we waited for darkness to make our return to the fort, I revisited what had happened. I needed to commit it to memory to ensure that it didn't happen again. The Apaches came at us from three directions. Some had apparently been lying flat on the desert floor or under the scrub brush since they were no more than a hundred yards from us, and we didn't see them. We had superior weapons and worked as a single unit, so the Apaches were either killed or pushed back by our rifles and pistols.

After the battle was over, I advised the commanding officer of my suspicion related to Many Trails, and he indicated that he would look into it once we were back at the fort. I never trusted Many Trails again. I made a mental note to always make a scouting plan of my own to compare to what Many Trails came up with.

After narrowly escaping death that time, on occasion, I had to point out flaws in Many Trails' scouting plans. The general took note of this, and after a while, the general made me the lead scout for all of his missions. I could tell that didn't please Many Trails or Major Roberts, but my life was more important to me than their pride.

Many Trails and I were scouting on another mission, and we were jumped by a band of about twenty renegade Apaches, so they outnumbered us, and pinned us down in a bad place. Many of the soldiers were killed or injured. After tending to the wounded, we knew that we couldn't stay where we were, so we made a break for it just after dark.

The only way that we could sneak away was in the opposite direction from the fort. Six of us took off from that place, and only two of us made it back to the fort. Many Trails took an arrow high in the right shoulder, so I had to ride beside him to keep him in the saddle as we rode to stay ahead of the Apaches.

As we rode into unfamiliar areas, I was concerned for our safety but knew that we had to get away from the Apaches. They were not going to let us head back to the fort, so we kept riding and taking every opportunity to pick one of them off when they tried to come take our scalps. There were less than ten of them left, so they had become much less aggressive. However, they were still mad and out for revenge.

We found a secluded area that had water and good protection for us if we had to fight, so we settled in, hoping the Apaches didn't know about the place and were not able to trail us to it in the dark. We had good cover behind some rocks, a stand of trees to hide the horses, and most of all, shade.

Even at night, the desert heat could kill you in a more painful way than the Apaches, so finding the shade gave us an advantage. If they found us, they would have to fight in the heat. That desert sand was too hot for them to lie in, so they would stay on their horses or walk. Hopefully that heat would sour their desire to kill two enemies.

I used what Sleeping Bird taught me to save Many Trails' life and patch him up. He was out of danger of dying, but still not able to help with the fighting. I felt I needed to get him back to the fort soon, or his chances of surviving would be slim. He was in and out of consciousness, babbling and chanting in his Lakota dialect, so I knew he was in a bad way. He finally quieted down and slept, so I ate and got a little rest as well. I knew the horses would alert us if another horse or person came anywhere near us, but I stayed awake anyway.

Around midnight, I heard approaching horses just as Gvnige nickered. The moon was bright and high in the sky, so as the riders approached, I could see that the man was not an Apache. I let him come into the camp and got the drop on him as he was studying Many Trails, lying in agony.

He was dressed in buckskin, but he was a white man. An Indian squaw was riding the other horse. I spoke to him from cover saying, "Hey mister, I have you covered, so don't try anything." He slowly turned to face me and said, "I am not with the Apaches, and in fact we were running from some that had jumped us."

Just then we could hear horses approaching, and it was the Apaches that he spoke of. There were six of them, and they appeared to be those remaining in the group that had attacked me and Many Trails a few hours earlier.

They were approaching fast, as if not expecting to find anyone anytime soon. We started shooting, and the Apaches were knocked off their horses, falling dead on the desert floor. We felt that we had gotten all of them in that hail of bullets, but Apaches were known for faking death.

They would allow the enemy to come within killing range of their weapons and spring a surprise attack. So, after waiting longer than we expected any human to be able to lie out in the hot desert sand, the stranger went out to make sure that they were all dead.

After about ten minutes, he returned to the camp carrying the guns that the Apaches had. He had blood splatters on his lower pant legs and immediately proceeded to clean his big Bowie knife. I didn't say anything, but that was a sign that he had made sure all the Apaches were dead. I just nodded, and as he sat down, we were finally able to introduce ourselves.

He was one of the tallest men that I had ever seen. There was gray hair in his beard, and several of his dirty teeth were missing. He had battle scars on his face, neck, hands, and the parts of his arms that I could see. But those sky-blue eyes were like the entry into his soul. He said, "I'm called Tall Knives."

It was then that I noticed that he had several knives. One was about a foot long and appeared to be the butt end of a cavalry saber. He had hunting knives strapped to the outside of each leg. He smelled bad, but I could tell that he had a warrior's heart.

I told him that the scout was the Lakota called Many Trails. He spat on the ground right next to Many Trails and said, "I have heard of him and don't like what I have heard." I wanted to ask him questions, but I would wait until we were alone. I wasn't certain that Many Trails was completely unconscious.

I introduced myself as the Buffalo Scout, and Tall Knives showed all his rotten teeth as he smiled. He said he had heard of me as well and said he felt honored to be in battle with me. We continued with some small talk and told a couple of tales.

Although he didn't like Many Trails, he looked at his wounds and declared him to be fit to ride.

He said "It's best that we don't stay where we are. I know of a secret place that I am certain that the Apaches don't know of. We could go there and hole up until Many Trails could travel to the fort."

He indicated that there was a shortcut from the secret place to the fort, but we couldn't go back right away.

Then he went on to say, "The Apaches would be on the warpath because of the death of their brothers and would be even angrier when they found the six that were lying on the desert floor around our camp. They probably wouldn't settle down for a few days."

I had been scouting the area for years and felt that I knew about every canyon, rock pile, and watering hole in it. His talk about a secret place was a surprise and one that I was looking forward to seeing. Many Trails was barely conscious, so we tied him in the saddle and blindfolded him at the demand of Tall Knives. This was a further indication that Tall Knives didn't trust Many Trails. I would have to ask him why when the time was right.

We headed to the "secret canyon," as he called it. The moon had gone down, and it was dark, so I could not chart landmarks to find my way to or from the hidden place. We were riding fast, so keeping Many Trails in the saddle took a lot of effort. Once he was totally passed out, we just tied him across the saddle.

Tall Knives indicated that we were not too far from the secret canyon, so Many Trails should survive the ride. After riding for another half hour, we arrived at the entrance to the secret canyon that had to be a blind canyon based on the big ole rock blocking our path. It was not quite day yet, but I could see that the walls were at least two hundred feet tall and almost vertical. No person or animal could climb the walls I was looking at.

There were other big rock formations at the base of the walls too, and many of them were twenty to thirty feet tall. If there was an entrance into that place, I could not see it. Tall Knives must have sensed my thoughts because he told me that I would not see the entrance until we were in it. He said, "The entrance isn't very wide, and you certainly cannot see it from a distance because of the rock formations at the base of the canyon." He told the squaw to fall back behind me and Many Trails, and he proceeded into the canyon, through the entrance that appeared after we maneuvered around three of the rock formations.

Once we were inside the entrance, he stopped to make sure that Many Trail's blindfold was still in place. As he did this, I noticed that there were multiple trails just ahead of us. As we rode, I noticed that some of them were dead ends or too narrow for a horse to pass through. I was still storing the path we were on in my memory when we went around that last curve and entered the secret canyon.

Even in poor light, I stopped, sucked in some air, and blinked my eyes several times to make sure I wasn't dreaming. The view was amazing. I understood why Tall Knives thought so much of the place. It was beautiful in the early dawn light, but once the sun was up, I could see just how functional it really was. He told me that he'd stumbled upon this canyon while traveling at night on foot after some Apaches had shot his horse out from under him.

Wearing his dark buckskin clothing, the Apaches couldn't see Tall Knives. He was lying behind some big rocks to keep the moon glow from glistening off the beads on his buckskin shirt, and they passed right by him.

He showed me his rifle and told me of the coating he used to cover the shiny parts to keep them from reflecting light. I thought, *this fellow is a survivor*. I needed to learn from him and use the knowledge to stay alive, so I did exactly that for the few days that I spent with him in the secret canyon.

I learned some more Indian secrets about medicine from the squaw, and I got Tall Knives caught up on the latest happenings in the country. He was not happy to hear about how rapidly the West was being settled, but he was happy to be in the loop.

We became friends during those few days. He was as happy as anyone that I had ever met in my life. He had no need for money, for he lived off the land and desired nothing but his freedom to hunt and live out under the big western sky.

We exchanged some tales, and he told me some of the things he had heard about me. Some came from whites, but most came from the Indians, including the Apaches. They hated me as much as they hated the whites but had the ultimate respect for me as a warrior.

His words made me feel rather good about myself and confirmed that I was doing what I wanted to do. I was protecting those that couldn't protect themselves. I was indeed a warrior.

We waited for Many Trails to wake, but he was so feverish that it didn't happen. We decided that if we didn't get him to the fort soon, he would die. That thought didn't upset Tall Knives, so I knew that his hate for Many Trails went mighty deep.

We left the canyon the next morning, using a trail that was not on the army maps, and to my amazement, we could see the fort in about half the time that I had expected it to take. Tall Knives didn't want to get too close to civilization, so he said goodbye and told me that the two of us were the only ones that knew of the secret canyon. He also said something that I didn't understand, but since I didn't know if I would ever get back to that secret canyon, I didn't really think too much on it.

But I did hear him say it twice, "One day, you will discover the secret of this canyon, and it will change your life forever." I wanted to think about it, but I was more interested in storing the details and landmarks of this trail in my memory. Knowing this route could be most helpful in the future, I decided to keep it a secret for now, since I still had that uneasy feeling about Many Trails.

I got Many Trails back to the fort, and the doctor was able to save his life. The general was happy to see me, as were the soldiers. With Many Trails injured and recovering, I became the lead scout for the army in Apache territory. This made me the happiest black man in this part of the country.

The Apaches had settled down some, and there was even talk of a peace treaty with them. I certainly hoped the day would come soon, because those Apaches were some mean and savage killers when they were mad.

As soon as I was dismissed by the general, I headed over to the stables to see how Ole Lightning was doing. He had been born about three years earlier, and I was counting the days until I could retire Gvnige and start riding Lightning. Gvnige was a great horse, but Ole Lightning was something special.

I thought Gvnige and Lady were fine horses until she dropped Ole Lightning. He was beautiful when he was born and seemed to get more beautiful every day. His coat was always as shiny as any that I had seen. He was spirited, tall, strong, and faster than any horse that anyone at this fort had ever seen. He was a jewel, and he was mine.

I had often been asked to prove that I owned Gvnige, Lady, and Ole Lightning. Each time I was asked, I was thankful that Susan had given me the bills of sale for Gvnige and Lady. I didn't need one for Lightning since he was their offspring. Some of the white settlers tried to give me a lot of trouble about owning such fine horses, but the general put an end to their tactics, and I was never challenged again.

My friend Jose was in charge of the stables, so he cared for my animals when I was away. Jose was the only person who could get close to Ole Lightning besides me. I didn't know why he liked Jose and nobody else, but if he stayed that way, he would be hard to steal.

Jose met me with a smile and gave me an update on the progress Ole Lightning was making in his training. The two of us had put our heads together and came up with a plan to train Ole Lightning based on army and other special requirements that the two of us kept secret from everybody else. He had to stand tall to be mounted, stay calm in battle, charge when urged, be sure-footed in close-contact fighting for the army, lie down when signaled by tapping his front leg, kneel to allow me to mount him if I was injured, come to me when I whistled, and not let anyone else ride him. The last one was the hardest to train.

Jose had Ole Lightning demonstrate the tricks and I was thrilled when he did them all perfectly. I thought to myself, *if I were to become the greatest scout ever, I would need the greatest horse in the West to accomplish that honor. And Ole Lightning is that horse.*

The Civil War was over and the general finally received that dispatch from Washington, allowing the army to once again enlist black soldiers. He had a very hard decision to make because he had promised his friend that he would send me back to the fort in eastern New Mexico to join the buffalo soldiers there.

He waited to hear from General Miller, and when he did not, he contacted him. As it turned out, his friend got transferred to Washington to take a position in the main War Department office. In his haste to leave, he had overlooked notifying the general.

The general came to see me, all smiles, and gave me the news, and it made me feel special to know that he wanted me here. The general had tried to use his friendship and distinguished record to get permission to have a buffalo soldier regiment here, but it was denied. We did host some of the buffalo soldiers occasionally for training as they escorted wagon trains to the western states or territories.

He told me that until the War Department had experimented and found the best solutions in the northern and eastern states; the existing buffalo soldier regiments would remain as they were and where they were.

He smiled and said, "The good news was that you get to remain here as a U.S. government employee assigned as lead scout for this fort." Those words, oh, how they would echo in my mind from time to time, bringing me joy even years later.

***

The sunlight coming through the window caused me to wake from the dream. I got up, and it didn't really hurt to walk around. It occurred to me that Sophie wasn't here, so I could do what I wanted to do, and I did just what the mischievous little boy inside of me wanted to do…I had whiskey with breakfast.

CHAPTER 10: BUFFALO SOLDIER, TOUR OF DUTY

I went out to spend a little time with Ole Lightning. Damn, that sun was bright and hot this morning. It's amazing how quickly your eyes can get sensitive to bright light when you are not out in the sun. I was glad that my other senses seemed to be working just fine, and my body felt strong and ready for battle.

Ole Lightning was happy to see me, so he was prancing and snorting as he ran around the corral. He was thinking we were going for a ride, and I certainly wished that we could go out. Sophie had promised to finish killing me if I got on a horse, so I gave him some treats, brushed his coat, and fed him. I looked him over good, and although he wasn't old, he also wasn't a colt anymore. Even at his age, he was more horse than any I had ever seen. I checked on Lady as well since she was expecting another foal.

I didn't expect another like Ole Lightning, but I knew it would be a fine horse. Gvnige was older now and probably didn't have too many years left. Jose had been exercising him and teaching him new tricks to keep him battle-ready, but I truly hoped he would not need to do anything except service the mares, eat, and keep growing old.

I had made a lot of money breeding him and Ole Lightning with the mares of the local folks. They had produced some really nice foals, improving the quality of horses in this area. It would be a sad day for me when he died, but I knew that day would come. I was thankful for Ole Lightning and hoped he would live a lot longer than Gvnige.

I made a mental note to go to Nebraska to buy some mares to breed with Ole Lightning when I was back on my feet. The owner of the mares had them picked out for me, and he was just waiting for them to get old enough for breeding.

He had offered to ship them by rail since the railroad had expanded to within a few miles of the fort. Considering how long of a ride it would be and the possibility of encountering outlaws, I would be smart to take him up on that offer. After all, I wasn't getting any younger.

I headed back inside because my eyes were having a hard time focusing in the bright sunlight. I knew I had to keep following the doctor's orders as well, and I could tell that my body was not ready to deal with the heat. Besides, Sophie was coming by later today, and if I looked tired or uncomfortable, she was going to give me hell.

I was bored, so I got my books out and read some more and spent some time thinking about what it would take to get a horse ranch started out here. I had saved some money, thanks to the reward money that I collected for bringing in criminals and felt that I had enough to start the ranch. There was lots of open range that I could homestead. I had enough mares to start the ranch, and if I could get Jose to throw in with me, there would be nothing to keep us from being successful. With all the scouting I had done, I had spotted several great sites for such a ranch, and I knew I needed to get it started before Ole Lightning got too old to produce fine colts. Hopefully, the foal that the mare birthed would be a fine stallion, just like Ole Lightning, and I would have two great stallions on the ranch. I knew I would have to buy some new stallions as the herd grew, to minimize inbreeding, but I would deal with that when the time came.

The Apaches were about done fighting, so it was much safer to live in an isolated area now. Plus, the general was talking about retiring, and I wasn't looking forward to breaking in another commanding officer.

Sophie came by when she'd finished work, and she looked as lovely as ever. Her smile told me that she was pleased to see me resting. She hugged me and said, "What have you been up to all day, mister?" I told her, "I went out to care for Ole Lightning and I have been in the house reading and making plans for a ranch." The books were still on the table along with the paper and pencil that I had been making plans with, so she believed me.

She asked what I was planning, so I told her, leaving out the part about the role I wanted her to play. She told me that she thought it was a good plan as long as I was not too far from the settlement. I knew what she meant, so I smiled and kissed her.

After having a fine meal that she cooked, she let me pleasure her just like I had hoped. I was thinking that if I pleasured her real good, she might not be so strict on me. I was tired of this damn house, and I needed her to agree that I could spend some quality time outside.

I must have done a good job because she left happy, smiling, and without telling me to stay in the house. That wasn't exactly approval to venture out, but it appeared that she left the door open. I would make my own decisions and figure out how to calm her down if she got mad at me. I was feeling a little tired, so I got into bed and tried to hold onto the latest memory of Sophie making sweet love to me...

***

This time when I started dreaming, Sophie was still in my life. It was about three years earlier and she had just arrived out here with the nice family from the East. Once I got to know her, she told me that they found her on the road as she was leaving the South for what she believed would be a better life in the North. They were on their way out west and offered her employment. They had just arrived in New Mexico Territory and were busy getting their general store business set up.

I was returning from a scouting mission for the army, living my dream. Blacks were still not the most popular soldiers when in the settlement, so I tended to just ride through, keeping my eyes on the road ahead, so I paid little attention to the new store with a sign in the window saying that it was opening soon.

A couple of weeks later we were heading out on a routine patrol, and as we went through town, the general paused to greet the new family opening the store. It was then that I saw her for the first time. She was the first fine black woman that I had seen in these parts, and I was so happy to be able to see her. She was lean and looked strong. She was focused on doing her job, so I wasn't sure if she had even seen me. My heart skipped a beat as I focused my attention on her. The general was talking, I could hear him, but I couldn't have repeated a word he said.

I was glad that I was sitting on Ole Lightning, the finest horse around, because I knew if she looked our way, Ole Lightning would attract her attention even if I didn't.

She did look our way, and I was grinning from ear to ear, knowing that I was not to speak unless the general asked me to. She smiled back at me, and I was like that Arabian genie, floating on a cloud. I was hoping that our patrol was not out too long because I needed to get back here to see this fine woman again.

The mission was a short one, and we returned to the fort after being out only one night. As we rode through the settlement, I was glancing toward that store in hopes of seeing that woman again, but I didn't. So, I was not a happy man as we rode on to the fort. I spent the rest of the day thinking of how I could get to meet that woman and how I could get her to want me. As I was falling asleep, I still didn't have my answers, so I prayed to the Great Spirit Warrior for guidance and settled for dreaming of her.

A week later, I was still working up the nerves to go talk to her. I had even tried once, but as I walked around the store getting the things that I needed she was busy, so I missed out. A few days later I was still on a mission to meet her. By then, I knew her name was Sophie and I felt that I had made some progress. Jose came by and told me that he was having a supper party for his wife, Maria the next day and I must be there. I agreed and went to the party in my finest clothing because Jose and Maria were my good friends. Jose greeted me at the door and had the biggest grin on his face. I said, "Why you grinning like that?" He said, "Oh no reason, I'm just glad that you could make this special occasion."

I walked through the door and Jose led me to the back porch as he usually did. I was surprised that Maria was not in the kitchen but thought little of it since Jose had said the party was for her birthday. I could smell the food and I had been starving myself all day to be able to eat a lot. I saw Maria and she had a similar grin on her face. I was thinking to myself "Something is up." I walked up to her and gave her a big bear hug and she kissed me on the cheek. Stepping back, she said, "I think you are going to be as happy as I am about this birthday supper." I said, "Oh yeah, why?"

I was looking at the table and noticed that it was set for four people. Jose called my name and as I turned to look at him, there she was. Sophie was smiling and there was nothing for me to do but smile and introduce myself properly. I said, "I'm Raymond Jackson, known as the Buffalo Scout by the local folks and Indians." She said, "I know, and I am happy to finally meet you."

Maria interrupted the moment to tell us to set down and eat. I gave Jose that "I appreciate you, but I'm going to get even" look so he just laughed. After we were seated at the table, Maria told me how this dinner came to be. I had told Jose about Sophie and Maria had met her, found out that she was available and interested and planned this surprise. Then she confessed, "It's not my birthday, it's Sophie's birthday." I looked at Sophie and said, "Happy birthday. I am so happy to share it with you and my best friends."

She smiled and that is when I saw the sparkle in her eyes and knew that we would become friends and hopefully a lot more.

I was right, and I would see Sophie often. I usually walked her home after work because she was a fine lady and I would notice the men looking at her. Being the protector that I was, I had to do all that I could to protect her because she was my lady now. Most men didn't want to tangle with me, because they knew that would include tangling with the general and army as well. When I was out on missions Jose and Maria would watch out for her.

I found an injured dog one day when I was on my way back to the fort. I thought of how he could be a good companion and maybe a good protector for Sophie, so I patched him up and presented him to her as a gift. It was love at first sight and she pushed me out of the door saying, "I have to take care of my Juno, so I will see you later." I left feeling like I had just shot myself in the foot. But it was still best that she had someone to protect her when I wasn't around.

***

The territory was relatively safe now, but the army was still keeping the peace and escorting wagon trains. The buffalo soldiers continued to escort some wagon trains and they would drill and trains with the soldiers at the fort. The white soldiers didn't want any blacks to bunk, eat, or drink with them, but they were mighty happy to have me, a black scout, riding out in front of them to read signs and keep them from getting killed.

On occasion, one of the buffalo soldier units came over to drill with the white soldiers. It took me a while to figure that one out. But then one day it occurred to me that when there was word of the meanest Apaches being on the loose, the buffalo soldiers would go on patrol with the white soldiers. After a day or two, the white soldiers would return to the fort, and I would remain with the buffalo soldiers until we located and captured the renegade Apaches. Truth be told, the buffalo soldiers didn't mind, and I didn't either. We would not be recognized as such, but we were the best soldiers for those types of missions.

On one such mission, we were in hot pursuit of some Apaches that had raided a remote homestead. My ability to read Apache smoke signals alerted us that some captives were being tortured. It didn't take long to find the place that they were doing the torturing. We snuck up on the four Apaches we were trailing, torturing a couple hiders that they had caught killing buffalos for their hides. To Apaches, this was the ultimate crime because the buffalos were their main source of meat.

The Apaches were so focused on their task that they had no lookout posted. Lying flat on the rocks, we could see them no more than forty yards away. They were basically skinning the men alive to make the last minutes of their lives living hell.

One of the hiders appeared to have passed out, so all the Apaches were concentrating their torture skills on the one lively hider. One Apache was peeling the skin off the top of his left foot; one was peeling the skin off his right cheek; and one was peeling the skin off his chest. The last Apache was using hot coals from a fire to cook his privates.

They must have been enjoying it because they were whooping and hollering, yet we could hear the screams of the hider, pleading for mercy. Mercy that we knew he would never get.

There were three buffalo soldiers with me, so I had each of them choose their target, site in, and fire on my signal. I had instructed the soldiers to shoot to disable each of the Apaches so that they would be alive but not able to do anything to harm us when we got to them. They were all good marksmen, so each of the Apaches stopped what they were doing and hit the dirt, now moaning in pain and probably wishing for death.

I had one of the soldiers remain up on the rocks as a lookout while the rest of us went down to see if there was any chance for the two hiders.

Neither of the hiders was dead, but neither one of them would live to see the sunset. The one that the Apaches were working on when we arrived had spilled all his innards where he was sitting, since the hot coals had burned away his skin and muscles down there. He was minutes away from death.

The Apaches were shocked to see us and even more shocked to be shot and bleeding. I had no intention of allowing them to bleed to death because they were going to experience the same torture that they were performing on the hiders.

While I was checking on the hiders, I told the buffalo soldiers to bind the four Apaches in the same spread-eagled position the hiders were in. I patched their wounds as if we were going to take them back with us. Then I sent the buffalo soldiers to get our horses and dig graves for the hiders.

By then, one of the hiders had died, so I went to check on the second hider who had passed out. That hider had died a terrible death too.

The army had warned hiders on more than one occasion to not practice their trade in Apache territory. I'm sure that they were wishing that they had listened as the torturing stole their last breaths.

With each of the Apaches staked upright on a flat rock as they had done to the hiders, I was ready to do what not many men were capable of doing. They had a good fire burning, so I already had hot coals.

Since I didn't want the soldiers to get in trouble or see what I was going to do, I sent them to bury the two hiders under some trees and out of sight of what I was doing.

With the soldiers out of view of the torture site, the torturing began again; the only difference was that the Apaches were the ones getting their privates and innards burned out.

I let them smoke the wrong end of some burning sticks to keep them from screaming to their gods. I even used their clothing to stuff their mouths to make sure that the burning sticks didn't fall out.

I did most of what I did because I wanted the Apaches to know that someone with more hate than they possessed was in this part of New Mexico Territory. As I walked away from them, I couldn't help asking myself, *are you any better than they are?*

As I was about to leave the camp, I remembered that the men were hiders. I knew I needed to find their weapons to ensure that the Apaches didn't get them. They had left the everyday rifles and pistols visible but had done a great job of hiding the finest weapons. I knew they had them, yet I could not find them.

The hiders' mule team was still hitched up to the wagon, so I tied Ole Lightning to the tailgate and drove the wagon away from a site that most men would gag at seeing. Not me. I was a warrior, and it was okay for the enemy to die by the weapons that they would have used to kill us.

I drove the wagon around the rocks to meet up with the buffalo soldiers. They were finishing the graves, so they looked up at me, sitting in the wagon seat, but said nothing. I told them that I left the Apaches tied up and alive with gags in their mouths.

I was thinking, "If the sun didn't kill them, either their wounds or the desert animals would." I didn't tell the whole story, but sometimes that was the best thing to do. I just hoped that the Apaches' horses would eventually find their way back to the Apache camp and not just roam the desert until they died.

I told the buffalo soldiers that we needed to make tracks for the fort in case there were Apaches close enough to have heard the shots and came to investigate. Besides, we had to get back to the fort and do something with the fine-grade buffalo hides. I knew that the fine rifles were hidden in the wagon, so I would get Jose to help me dismantle the wagon to get to them once we got back.

The fort was probably a day's ride if we went back the way that the map showed. I knew the shortcut that I had learned from Tall Knives, so I headed in a direction to save us a half day in the saddle or on that bouncy wagon seat. The buffalo soldiers were stationed close to the Texas border so they didn't know the route was a secret and I didn't expect them to remember it or be around to tell anyone about it.

One soldier asked what we would do with the hides. I told him that we were buffalo soldiers, so it was only fitting that we have heavy buffalo robes for when it got really cold. They all smiled, and we headed back to the fort.

As we approached the fort, it was about dark, so I had one of the soldiers take the wagon to my house, and I went in to do my report and see the general. It was a routine check-in, so I was out of there in thirty minutes. The general didn't like long reports any more than I liked writing them, so mine was brief yet detailed.

I mounted Ole Lightning and headed home to see what I could find hidden in that wagon. The buffalo hides would make great winter robes for those cold winter days that this ole boy hated, but the real treasure I was sure we were yet to find.

Once I got back to my house, I dismissed the soldiers, and they went to the tent area where visiting black soldiers were required to stay, each with a nice buffalo hide. I took my time looking at that wagon because something didn't look right to me. Jose was walking by, so I called him over to get his opinion because he knew a lot more about wagons than I ever wanted to know.

He took a quick look at the wagon and snapped his fingers. He said, "I know what it is. This wagon has a false bottom." I asked, "What does that mean?" He said, "It's easier to show you than explain."

There were about fifteen prime buffalo hides in the wagon, so we unloaded them, and since they appeared to be cured out, we stacked them in the hayloft of the barn.

Then Jose pointed to the bottom of the wagon and said, "This looks like the bottom, but it isn't." He got some tools and started disassembling the false wagon floor to expose a secret compartment. As he found the bolts that were holding the second floor in place, he pointed them out to me. I had seen them earlier but had no idea what I was looking at.

When he removed the bolts, we were able to lift the false bottom. Once it was out of the way, we both sucked in air and our hearts skipped a few beats. Lying in the secret compartment were the finest two Henry repeating rifles that were ever made. We had heard of them, but we hadn't seen one with our own eyes.

They were in separate well-crafted wooden cases with glass covers, and there were four cases of ammunition, each containing one hundred shells. This was a great find, so great that I was unsure of what to do next.

We took the rifles and shells into the house and stored them in the place where I hid things of value. Jose and I were partners, and I trusted him with my life, so I knew he would keep quiet about the rifles until I had told the general about our find.

The next day I reported finding the guns to the general. He asked if there were any identification papers on anything in the wagon. I told him that I could not find anything in the wagon or the gun cases that would identify the men. He thought for a minute and then said there was no way to find out who the men were or where they came from.

He said if no one reported them missing within the next six months, all that I had found would become my property. I liked that decision and promised to keep quiet about it until he got back to me at the end of six months. I rushed out to tell Jose the good news, and we had a great laugh and a drink of some fine whiskey.

***

I was dreaming of that treasure when I became aware of unusual sounds outside my window. I reached for the pistol under my pillow, while moving around as if I hadn't heard a sound. Then there it was again: that faint sound of leather on sand. It was the only warning that I had, so it was important that the person making it thought that I hadn't heard it.

Someone was attempting to sneak up on me, and I was not going to be as surprised as they wanted me to be. I moaned and started making snoring sounds to make it hard for the person to hear the hammer of my pistol lock in the cocked position or me easing out of the bed. I was ready for the intruder, so I concentrated more to see if I could hear if there was more than one.

The snoring sound must have been what the person was waiting to hear because the window next to the bed started sliding up slowly, making almost no sound at all. In fact, if I hadn't been looking at it, I would not have known it was moving.

I had gotten out of bed and used the pillows to make a form similar to a sleeping person where I usually slept. In the dark, the intruder would not be able to tell that it wasn't a person. It was an old trick, but it still worked more often than not. If the intruder peeked in the window, he would see a pistol in the gun holster hanging on the post of the bed headboard. That would add to the deception and help keep him focused on the form in the bed.

From my position along the wall and next to the window, I could see a gun barrel being poked through the window that had been opened about six inches. The gun barrel was inched in further and further until I could see the hand on the butt of the gun. I could tell from the fingers that it was a right-handed person, so that meant I needed to aim to the left of the gun to shoot the person holding it in the chest.

Once I saw a good portion of the arm extend into the house, I hesitated to pull the trigger. If this sucker tried to come in, I would capture him in the act and work him over with my gun butt. I already had too many dead men on my list of bad doings for my liking, so if I could avoid adding this one, I would feel better.

The arm stopped moving once the elbow was inside the house far enough to aim at the form in the bed, so I shot that elbow instead of killing the man. The gun dropped, and the person cried out in pain. By then I was out the door and on him in time to trip the criminal as he tried running away. The soldier that was supposed to be on duty came running from behind the barn, carrying a lantern. Had he been any faster or not been carrying that lantern, I probably would have shot him as well.

I told him, "Call out before approaching such a scene in the future if you want to live to be an old man." He nodded in agreement and helped me get the criminal to the army fort for medical attention. He was the last of the murdering brothers that had tried to kill me. Had I known this when that arm was sticking through my window, I would have ended his life and saved the general the trouble of hanging him.

It was about daybreak by the time we got the mess cleaned up, and the army had the last of the renegade killers securely locked up in the fort stockade. It was too late to try going back to sleep, too early to be up and about, so I just lay back down because my head was starting to ache from all the excitement.

It was moments like this when I truly missed my mother and Sleeping Bird since they both would know exactly what to do to comfort me.

CHAPTER 11: THE LAKOTA WINTER CAMP

With the murder attempt behind me, I had my little house and barn to myself, and that was just the way I liked it. I grew up with too many people in my village, crowding all around me, and too many family members in a small hut. Then I had been forced to live with people I didn't know or like on that damn plantation until I ran away to come out west.

Those times when I was alone on the trail from Mississippi to the Oklahoma Territory were some special times for me. Warriors liked it when they knew who the enemy was, and when you are all alone, everybody and everything is an enemy until they prove not to be. Besides, I could think when I wanted to without being interrupted or tempted to do anything else.

I suspected that was why people say I'm hard to deal with or get close to. They were right, and I planned to keep it that way until I knew I could trust them like I trusted the general, Sophie and Jose. I didn't have to worry about either of them doing anything that was not good for me.

Sophie and I were getting closer and spending more time together, and I really liked being around her. She was a welcome addition to my American family, and I knew that I would die trying to protect her and would do everything that I could to make her happy.

Jose was like a brother or warrior companion to me. I considered them to be all the family that I had in America. Not knowing if I had any family left alive in Africa, I accepted the fact that without them, I was all alone in this world.

Jose was born in the New Mexico Territory and had lived out here all his life. He had suffered some of the same hatred from whites that I had, so I guessed that was why we got along so well.

Jose and I had been keeping a keen eye on Lady because she was about to drop that foal. She had already dropped Ole Lightning and two of which were now young mares so this was her fourth. We were excited and worried at the same time because she seemed to be having problems with this one. As the sun was setting, I went out to check on her and found that she was down.

I knew that meant that it was about time for the foal to be born, so I went to get Jose. She was in pain, but we knew we couldn't do much to help her. Together we watched and waited as she tried to bring that foal into the world.

I guess Jose needed to get his mind off her pain, so he asked me to tell him a story about one of my many missions. Normally I would have tried to get out of it, but I needed to get my mind off Lady's pain as well because I was getting a little misty-eyed. I smiled, and we both took a good long drink of whiskey to get in the right frame of mind for one of my tales of my life of yesterday.

I decided to tell him about being in northwest Wyoming and southern Montana Territory about seven years earlier, helping the army find a Lakota winter camp. I had not spent much time in that area, but between the tall tales Tall Knives had told me and the help of a local scout and a buffalo soldier that the Lakota trusted, we were confident that we would find the camp.

The Lakota were small in numbers in those days and were not at war anymore. They had their way with Custer and his troops, but the U.S. Army sent more troops and basically wiped them out.

We needed to find one of the oldest and most respected chiefs so he could attend a meeting with the War Department representative. The meeting was to verify that the Indians were being treated right and given everything that the peace treaty stated.

After leaving the fort, I was able to catch a train and get up there in less than four days. I was thankful that I didn't have to sit in the saddle the three weeks that it would have taken to ride by horseback from New Mexico Territory up there. They had cars that hauled livestock as well, but I didn't want to put Ole Lightning through such an adventure at such a young age.

Once we got off the train, we did some hard riding for days. The snow got deeper, and it got colder as we climbed to higher altitudes. Some of the snowdrifts were up to the horses' bellies, causing them to get tired quickly. And plus, none of these horses were Ole Lightning.

I was concerned because we couldn't see the trail under all the snow. I certainly hoped that the scout knew the landmarks well enough to get us to the camp. He did, and we reached it on the fifth day. We probably would have ridden right by it if one of the Lakota braves that knew the buffalo soldier hadn't called out to him.

After exchanging greetings and stating our business, we were led to the camp by the brave. They had picked a great location for their winter camp. It was amazing how there were fires everywhere, and we were only a quarter mile from it and had not seen or smelled the smoke.

I guessed that the trees were so close to each other that we couldn't see through them, and the wind was at our backs, so it was carrying the smoke scent in the opposite direction. There wasn't much of a chance that I would be coming back up this way, but it was possible, so I made a mental note to pay closer attention to the landmarks as we made our way back to the fort.

The chief greeted us with a big smile after he hugged the buffalo soldier, so I knew they had great respect for each other. He inquired about me, and the soldier told him of my adventures and why the army had sent me.

The chief turned to me and said, "I have heard of a brave buffalo warrior such as you that had tracked renegade Indians in eastern Wyoming. They had been killed in a bad way."

Most of the eyes in the camp were on me, so I was careful to not smile while recalling the experience, but the chief was able to see enough of the personal aspiration on my face to point at me and ask, "Was it you that did those things?"

I wasn't sure of how I should answer him, but I knew that lying would not have been the right thing to do. I just stood tall and emotionless and told him why it happened. He was not happy that I had killed some Lakota, but he respected me for telling the truth and referring to them as Lakota and not Sioux.

After that conversation, I wanted to find somewhere to hide. I could see that not all the braves were happy with the whys of my account of killing those Lakota Indians.

The chief sensed what some of his tribal members were thinking, so he raised his arms and, in their dialect, declared that from that day forward, the Lakota would know that the unknown warrior would be called "the Buffalo Scout" and that he was not the enemy of the Lakota Indians.

The local scout translated his words for us and showed a slight smile to let me know that I had nothing to worry about. I scanned the braves and tried to meet their stares with the best warrior stare that I could make.

I didn't know if I should be thankful or concerned for my life, but I knew that I couldn't show any fear or one of the braves might take that as an invitation to lift my hair during the night.

The chief then told all in the camp that we were his guests, and no harm was to come to us. Some of the braves showed their disapproval, but none of them would dishonor the tribe by harming people that were not their enemies.

Since it didn't appear that any brave would try anything, I took a moment to think about the name the chief tagged me with, "the Buffalo Scout." I liked it. In fact, I loved it and would choose to use it forever.

I left out a lot of the details that I remembered and ended the story by telling Jose that the trip back down the mountain was uneventful, and the chief met with the War Department fellow. Both returned to their homes, and there was still peace between the Lakota and whites.

Jose seemed to enjoy the story, and by then, Lady was doing much better. The foal was about halfway out, and Jose felt it was safe for us to help her finish the job. Jose was really good with horses, so he did the delicate work while I stood ready to assist at his request. It was a healthy yet wobbly, long-legged newborn colt. I certainly hoped he would turn out to be a fine stallion or even a great stallion like Ole Lightning.

Lady seemed to be doing okay, so we got her back on her feet so the colt could get some milk. That was when Jose declared that it was the perfect time for another drink, and I had no reason to argue with him. We seldom stopped at one, and with that being a special occasion, we had all that we wanted as we watched the colt stumble around on those long legs.

As we walked to the house, I told him about my first train ride to get under his skin a little. As I did, I couldn't help but wonder if the people in my homeland of Africa were progressing as the people here in America were.

CHAPTER 12: THE APACHE CHIEFS

It had been more than seven months since I was shot and laid up. The dreams became less frequent, and then stopped about five months ago. I saw this as a good sign that I was back to normal. My senses were sharp, my vision was good, and my mind had me focused on my warrior skills.

Many of the soldiers would watch as I did my warrior training drills, but not being as committed as I was, they never did anything more than watch. I certainly hoped that their lives would not be threatened due to their lack of training for battle.

Several of the younger soldiers took an interest in my training and joined me in my daily routines. Each of them would comment on the benefits they were getting from them and felt that they could protect themselves better during a hand-to-hand combat situation. It wasn't a surprise to me to see them excel ahead of the other soldiers that only did what the army required of them and nothing more.

My body felt as strong as ever, and as I rode my horses and trained with my weapons, I felt I had made a full recovery. I no longer felt any pain in my body where I had been injured. But mostly, I was bored and ready for some action.

I was going to do something, even if I had to make my own mission. I had leave time, so if I didn't get an assignment soon, I would go out to the secret canyon and work on the plans for the cabin and corrals.

I had been trying to talk the general into letting me go out with the patrols for about a month, but he wasn't buying it. He always had a tactical reason for not letting me go, but I knew he just wanted to give me some extra time to heal and get back my strength.

He did let me go on some training missions that were not going to require an overnight stay away from the fort. I was to observe the troops and intervene to test and help the scouts that were in training and nothing more.

It wasn't as exciting as tracking the enemy and ending any threats that they were attempting to carry out, but it was much better than hanging around the fort, watching other people do what I loved to do.

I had to admit that I had more opportunities to see and be with Sophie, and that made me happy. Thinking of Sophie made me realize that it was getting late on Sunday and I hadn't seen or heard from her all day.

That was not like her, so I decided to check on her. Jose knocked on my door and asked me to come back to his house and help him with one of his horses that had been a little lame. I knew that I could find Sophie later, so I got in stride with Jose as we headed to his house. We treated his horse even though the horse didn't appear to be lame. Jose knew more about horses than I did so I just held the horse's head as he was doing something to one of its back legs. We finished that chore, had some cold lemonade that Maria had left for us as we rested in the rocking chairs on the porch. I told him I was going to see Sophie so he said, "Hey, I want to look at the buffalo robe that you have hanging in your barn before you go." I said, "What for?" "I want to check the inner side to compare it with one that I bought the other day." He went to get the buffalo robe and we headed to my house.

We headed directly for the barn, and as we entered the barn, my closest friends were standing there, wishing me a happy birthday. I had attended other birthday parties but had never celebrated my own birthday. My emotions were high and my mind took me on a short journey of my past. I didn't know the date of my birth; in fact, I wasn't exactly sure of how old I was.

When I arrived at the fort, I had to give the U.S. government a birth date and age to become a government employee, so I had given them October 22 as my birthday. To the best of my knowledge, that was the day that I crossed the Arkansas River to enter the Oklahoma Territory. To me, that was the day I was born here in America. All my previous days in America, I was a captive. To me, those were days I didn't count as living. I wasn't sure of my age either, so we agreed on the theory that I was probably older than sixteen when I arrived in America, so my age was recorded accordingly. It meant so little to me that I didn't even remember that it was my birthday.

I had been in America longer than I lived in Africa, and I had done much to protect the people of this land. The time had passed quickly for me, except for those years when I was a slave. Lately, it seemed to be flying by so fast that I couldn't remember a lot of what happened, even just a few years back.

Looking at Sophie and seeing how happy she looked, I knew it was time for us to plan to live the rest of our lives together. They tell me that when you are in love, It is like that. After all these people left, I was going to spend some quality time with her.

In fact, I just might take her on a little trip with me if I didn't get an assignment soon. It was time to put my sorrows of yesterday behind me and have a family of my own, just like my folks had back in Africa.

I knew I couldn't keep fighting an unknown enemy, but that enemy still stalked me, denying Sophie and me the chance to be a family. Lately, going on missions was not as exciting as it once was. The West was about settled, so it was time for me to settle down to normal life as well. I needed to live as an American. This was home now, and it was hard for me to imagine that the people in Africa were doing as well as the other black people I knew were doing here in the west. I knew that most blacks suffered great hardships and even died unjustly here in America, but I had seen the same thing happen in Africa, and there were very few white men there.

For years I thought and prayed that the African people would come take us slaves from the whites to return us to the homeland of our ancestors. I wondered why they didn't do anything after the Civil War. There had to be recently freed blacks that would have gone to Africa if they had any way of doing so.

The blacks were an abandoned people, stuck in a country that no longer appreciated them simply because it was now illegal to enslave them. How sad it must have been for all those freed slaves. I got off easy because I escaped, and now I had a job, a place to live, and food to eat.

I owed my good fortunes to my survival skills, to Sleeping Bird, and to the general. Yes, two whites had helped me become the great man that I am today. Hopefully they represented the true Americans. Sure, I had worked hard and had taken lots of chances through the years, and I was so thankful that the Great Spirit Warrior protected me.

Sophie's kiss on my cheek brought me out of my head and back to now. I joined the guests in the celebration and had a grand time. I would get Jose for tricking me as soon as I got the chance. For now, I had a more important thing to do. It was my birthday, and I knew that Sophie would give me some special loving tonight.

***

A few days later, I did what I had told myself to do. Sophie was at my house, so I sat her down at my table, looked in her eyes and said, "We love each other, and I want you to be my wife."

She was immediately out of her chair, jumping up and down saying, "Yes I will marry you!" After I kissed her over and over, she said, "I'm a little surprised, but so happy."

I saw the tears in her eyes and knew they were tears of joy so I told her, "I promise to only cause you to cry tears of joy for the rest of our lives." I couldn't hold back my tears. She wiped them off my check and said, "I promise to only cause you to cry tears of joy for the rest of our lives." My heart was beating fast, and I could feel hers beating to match mine. That was all I needed to confirm that I was doing the right thing.

She wanted some time to plan for the wedding, so I told her to take all the time she wanted. I went to tell Jose and Maria and then I was bragging with pride to anyone and everyone I could get to listen about her agreeing to be my wife. I was so excited that she said yes that I forgot all about going out on a mission.

I went to give the general the good news, and he jumped up out of his chair, came around the desk and hugged me, saying, "It's about time for you to marry that wonderful woman." I could see the excitement in his eyes and hoped that I wouldn't cry. I knew I had done the right thing, and he, the man I admired and trusted the most, had just confirmed it for me.

I could tell that my emotions were running very high, so I needed a distraction. I guess he needed one, too, because the general told me he was about to send for me anyway. He needed me to go on a short mission. He had received a report that several of the Apache chiefs had been meeting secretly, and the army didn't want an uprising after having several years of peace.

He wanted me and a couple of his senior officers to go visit each of the chiefs to get an understanding of their state of comfort with the peace treaty and the Indian Agency representatives.

I didn't want to disagree with him, but the senior officers that he wanted to send were new to the West, and the Apache chiefs didn't like strangers. I pointed this out to the general, and with a smile, he told me that he was hoping I would say that.

He knew that his original request was flawed, so he was testing my sharpness after being off duty as long as I had been. We both had a laugh about it and continued discussing the mission.

We agreed that I should go alone or take someone to keep me company. As he continued talking, I thought about all the years of service that Jose had put in, stuck here in the fort, caring for the livestock. We were best friends, and I wanted him to have an adventure that he could tell tales about in his latter days. So, when the general paused, I told him that I would like him to find someone to do Jose's chores so that he could go with me.

The general smiled and agreed as if he had been thinking the same thing. He reminded me that Jose had been training several soldiers to do his job, and there was no better time than now to see if they could handle it.

He went on to say that the timing was perfect for Jose to go on the mission. He admitted that he had wanted to give Jose a chance to get out on the open range but just hadn't seen the opportunity before now.

I left the general's office and went to give Jose the good news. Both of us were very surprised that Maria was all for him going on the mission with me. He was excited, so I told him what time we were leaving in the morning and headed to see Sophie to give her the news.

The next morning, the general had the maps showing the locations of each of the Apache chiefs, based on the latest sightings. I purposely charted a route to start in the desert areas first and end up in the hills after going through the mountains.

I had a little surprise in mind for Jose that I thought he would like as much as I did when I discovered it. He was going to be the next man to know of the secret canyon and the first to know of my plans to build us a ranch around it.

We swapped some big tales as we rode, because it helped to pass the time and certainly kept our minds off the heat. As we rode into each tribal camp, we were met by peaceful and prideful Apaches of all ages.

We would assess their appearances, clothing, and lodging to get a feel for how life was for them.

I knew that reservation life was not as bad for them as slavery had been for me, but their pride had been stripped away from them. I doubted that it would ever be restored in the adults. The children would hopefully grow up knowing the strength of their ancestors and live proudly.

It was important that we verified that the Apaches were in good health and had all they needed to survive in this country. Most were healthy, and some had taken to being educated. A few were even Christians, because of white and Mexican missionaries in the area.

They were growing crops and raising mainly sheep. They had the right tools, and it appeared that they knew how to take care of all that they had. There were signs indicating that they still hunted and cured the skins of the animals they killed. I thought to myself, *these are skills that any child should be proud to learn and use in their lifetime.*

After visiting the third camp, we were heading through some rocky terrain. I was focused on watching for a possible Apache attack. I took a glance at Jose, and he was looking as if he was thinking about something, so I asked him if he was. Jose said he was curious about how the Apaches greeted me. He said that he felt that they saw me as some sort of holy man. Maybe not as great as their medicine men, but higher than any brave or chief.

It was then that I realized that Jose wasn't aware of the details in my reports to the general, so he was not aware of the many things, some good and some not so good, that I had done over the past years.

We were in an open area that gave me a clear view all around us, so we stopped to rest the horses so that I could answer him.

I told him, "It is part of the Apache culture to respect their enemies. So, when each chief referred to me as "the Buffalo Scout," the tribal members whispered to each other because they considered it an honor to be in the presence of a great warrior. At the same time, the greatest of the braves had to swallow their pride and not attempt to fight me since I was a guest of the chief. The kids were curious because they hadn't seen a black man before, so they wanted to touch me." Jose just nodded so I went on to say, "Since the braves could not fight me, they showed their best prideful face. The squaws were not to look directly into the eyes of strangers, so they just stood still, seeming to be interested in something on the ground to keep from making the braves or chief upset with them. When you paint the whole picture, it could appear as if they saw me as a holy man of some sort."

Jose nodded to indicate that he understood and said, "I see that there is a side of you that I never knew." I wasn't ready to share too much about my adventures, so I just smiled and said, "Let's ride". I took a look around us while pretending that I was just stretching and yawning, to make sure we were not in danger. Then we mounted up and continued to ride to the next Apache camp.

As we rode, I told Jose some of the many tales about me that were circulating throughout the West. He had to laugh at some of them, gave me that "I don't believe that" look about some, and just stared in silence at the ones about me narrowly escaping death. After a while, he started teasing me about being my sidekick. We had a good laugh about that as we rode on to the next Apache camp. I told him that Indians knew I was a great warrior by the stories their people had told for years. I used how they thought of me as a means to show how humble I could be. Jose looked a little confused, so I said, "I always smile and touch the children, and I treated the squaws with as much respect as I do the braves. I always look the chiefs in the eyes and show no signs of weakness in my speech or body language. I always come fully armed and ready to protect myself, for in the past, some braves tried me, and I ended their aggression and kept communicating with the chiefs, showing no fear, hate, or aggression. Each chief knows my words are spoken with iron and cannot be blown away by the wind."

Jose said, "I have heard that statement before my friend, so if that is how they know you to be, I'm proud to be your friend." I told Jose that the army officers knew the same thing, so they never tried to put me in a bad situation. I reminded Jose that I had been a warrior since I was about sixteen and planned to be a warrior until I wasn't needed anymore or died in battle.

Jose just listened to me without interrupting to ask questions. His look showed admiration, and that was the greatest compliment that I could have gotten from anyone. I knew he was learning about that dark side of me that I left out on the battlefield. I wanted to share all of that with Jose, so that was why I wanted him to come on this mission with me.

He smiled and told me, "I understand why you keep your adventures to yourself and I promise to never say anything to Maria or Sophie." I just nodded to show my appreciation for that promise. We truly bonded professionally that day, and I saw that as a great time to have a little sip of whiskey, so we did.

When we finished at the last tribal camp a couple of days later, it was time to head back to the fort. Jose didn't know this area as well as I did, but he had a good sense of direction. So when I headed toward the hills of the secret canyon, he questioned the route I had chosen to get back to the fort. I told him to trust me because I had a surprise for him and said that we would be back at the fort a half day sooner than he expected. He shook his head in disbelief and told me he would have to see that to believe it based on the direction we were heading. I just smiled and kept riding and humming alone.

We did some talking to pass the time, but it was my way of covering up what I was actually doing. Jose was not a battle-tested soldier, so I knew I had to keep both of us safe. My eyes were constantly scanning the surrounding landscape for any signs of danger. We were still in Apache territory and being careless could be the last thing that one did in his life when Apaches were around. Renegade Apaches didn't care that their chiefs had signed a peace treaty. They would prey on small groups of people and kill at will, mostly just to practice their torturing skills.

After about an hour of riding, we were approaching the entrance to the secret canyon, so I asked Jose what he saw just ahead of us. He knew I was expecting him to see something that looked out of place, so he looked, scanning the rocks just ahead of us. He gave me a questioning look, and then he looked again and said he only saw rocks, some cacti, and a whole lot of desert dirt and tumbleweeds.

Smiling, I asked him if he thought there was anything special within those rocks, especially the big ole rock. He leaned forward in the saddle, looked left, then right, and told me that he didn't believe there was anything near this area that could surprise him. I told him that he was about to see a secret canyon within that big rock that was known only to one living man, me. I told him that Tall Knives had found it and showed it to me when he and I were needing to hide from some Apaches a few years back.

With Tall Knives' passing a year or so back, only his squaw and I knew of it, and she had sworn to Tall Knives and me to never tell anyone of it and never bring anyone to it. Jose looked at the rocks again and said, "You really expect me to believe there is a canyon in that big rock?" I said "Yes," and he said, "I have to see it to believe it."

I just laughed as I started riding to the entrance with him at my side. I had a big grin on my face, and he kept questioning the existence of such a canyon in the rocks.

I was humming the tune "Yellow Rose of Texas" and Jose was looking at me like he thought I was crazy as I guided him around some of the smaller rocks and into the entrance to the secret canyon. I pointed out the landmarks that one had to know and use to navigate the rocks to find the entrance to the canyon as we rode. I stressed that he had to learn and remember them because we were not leaving any markers as reminders in case others stumbled upon them and found their way into the canyon.

I told him that I would also point out the key landmarks on the trail to the fort when we headed back there. I had committed all the landmarks to memory as Tall Knives had instructed, and Jose would have to do the same. It was easy to get lost going in, and equally easy to get lost trying to find the way out of the canyon.

As we approached the final turn of the path into the canyon, I had Jose close his eyes before skirting around it to enter the opening. We had to advance only about twenty feet to get in position for him to see, so I took his horse's reins and led him in. Once there, I took in the beauty for a split second and then I had Jose open his eyes to see the canyon. I was watching as his jaw dropped and his eyes bucked wide open. He was speechless. As we sat in silence, I spoke the same words that I did every time I entered the canyon. "What a view. An absolutely breathtaking view."

He said, "I can't believe that I am seeing this." He looked up, behind us, left and then right before he looked at me and said, "So, you been keeping this a secret from your friend Jose?" We had a laugh and I told him that I felt the same way the first time that I saw it, and every time since, so we proceeded on in.

The secret canyon had rock walls that were more than two hundred feet straight up. The outside face was equally steep and tall, with many big rocks lying at the base of them. It looked as if God had come down from heaven and placed them to prevent anyone from attempting to climb that rock face. I certainly couldn't see no way to do it. The canyon was about two hundred yards deep and about one hundred yards wide.

A trickle of crystal-clear water originated out of the back rock wall, bringing water into a low area to create a pool that never filled, yet I could never find where the water escaped to.

There were never any fish or other critters in the water, so I guessed that was why you could see the bottom of the pool a little more than the length of my arm from the surface. To me, this was an oasis. Nothing grew in the canyon, so not even animals seemed to have migrated into it. We just sat there on the horses, for what else could one do when looking at such beauty?

We rode to the camping area and dismounted to find a good spot to talk. I said, "Jose, I want you to be my business partner for the rest of our lives." He looked a bit confused, so I continued, "I'm planning to homestead out here and I want you to be my business partner for a horse ranch."

He grinned and said, "I would love to do that with you, my friend." So for the next few hours we went over the plans for the horse ranch and settlement. Jose liked the plan and helped me with some of the key details for buildings and other structures we would need.

He was still concerned about how far he felt this place was from the fort, so I told him that we were not as far from the fort as he thought. He said, "Oh yeah, you know a shortcut! I'm still waiting to believe it when I see it." I just laughed and continued discussing the plans. We worked well together, and that confirmed that I had chosen the right person to be my partner.

We knew new settlers were coming into the area every month, and we saw no reason why we couldn't set up a trading post just outside of this secret canyon to provide goods for local settlers that we could convince to live near here.

There was a river less than a mile from the canyon, and during my many years of traveling through this part of the country, it had never been dry. With a little irrigation of the land close to the river, the farmers' crops would produce, and livestock could survive on the native grasses as long as there was grain and some hay during the winter months, all of which we could bring in as needed.

Jose liked the plan and the idea of other settlers and maybe even a little town. I told him he was about to see the best part of the plan when we headed back to the fort. He just nodded and said that he wanted to spend some more time in the canyon, and that was all right with me because the general wasn't expecting us back for another week, and we were only about a half day's ride from the fort.

As I looked toward the sky at the height of the canyon walls, I thought, as I often had, that if there was a way to scale those walls, we probably could have seen the chimney smoke from the fort. But Jose wasn't talking or listening to me anymore. He was just exploring the canyon and assessing how we could use it once we moved out this way.

About an hour before the sun disappeared behind the canyon wall, we started a fire and settled down, telling some ole tales and bragging about things we had done in the past. We had a little whiskey, and the stories got to be bigger lies.

As I poured more whiskey in Jose's cup, I was careful to not let us drink it all. I always carried whiskey for medical emergencies, so I needed to have some left, just in case. With all the rattlesnakes, scorpions, and other desert creatures, there was no telling when you would have a medical emergency and need whiskey to ward off an infection.

It wasn't totally dark yet, so we decided to explore the perimeter of the canyon walls to assess how stable they were. The walls were solid, as we expected, except for the one area where the water seemed to be coming through the face of the rocks. I didn't think much about it, but Jose thought he saw something that apparently excited him.

We stopped, and he rubbed his hand along the face of the wall just below where the water was coming through. When he held up his hand, there was something sparkling between his fingers. He played with it a little while and then attempted to bite it. I didn't understand what he was doing, but he seemed to be getting more excited about it, so I paid more and more attention to him. He looked at me with more excitement in his eyes than I had ever seen. I was wondering why, and then he said, "This is gold!"

I repeated it in a way that confused him, so he said it again. "Raymond, it's gold. Like what everybody is rushing to California to find." He said, "I think you are rich, my friend."

That was when my smile transformed into the biggest grin I had ever had. I had heard of gold but knew little about it. I was suddenly reminded of what Tall Knives told me on several occasions. I snapped my fingers, so Jose looked at me. I told him of Tall Knives telling me that this canyon held a secret that would allow me to have everything that I wanted.

He just smiled and said, "I think Tall Knives was right. There is a trail of gold dust from the place where the water is coming in through the canyon wall, extending down into the water in the pool."

Jose took off his vest and hat and reached down to the bottom of the pool, scooping up a handful of what we thought was dirt. The closer the handful of dirt got to the surface, the more it sparkled. When his hand broke the surface of the water, we could see that he had a handful of a mixture of pure gold and sand. There appeared to be a lot more gold than sand, and Jose said that it weighed more than sand should.

I just sat there, thinking about what I had experienced so far in my life. So much had been so painful. Now, with this discovery, I could have all the things that I'd never had before, and I could provide for Sophie. I couldn't wait to get back home and tell her the news.

For the first time in a while, I thought of my family in Africa. If I only knew where they were, I could also provide for them. Jose's voice brought me back by asking me what I was going to do with all the gold. I didn't know much about such matters, but Jose did. I quickly corrected him and said, "You mean what are we going to do with all of the gold?" He gave me a look of surprise, and I explained that had he not pointed out the gold to me, I probably would not have realized it was gold for many years to come. We shook on it and became lifelong business partners.

He knew that we needed to file a homestead claim first. More importantly, we needed to keep the gold a secret until the claim was filed and recognized by the government. We made plans for filing the claim and since we were so excited, we left then instead of waiting for morning. We were laughing and as excited as little boys that had just gotten more candy than they could eat for months.

The trail to the fort was easy to follow once we were away from that "Big Ole Rock" as it was labeled on the army maps. The moon was shining bright, and we were some happy men, so we made good time and were back at the fort before daybreak.

Several of the junior officers asked how we had completed the task so quickly. I told them that we were lucky; some of the chiefs had moved their camps closer together, making it easier for us to get to all of them faster. I didn't let on about the day we saved by using the secret trail.

I made my report for the general, and he was happy to know that all the chiefs were doing well, as were their tribal members. I had given them the gifts he sent, and I now delivered their gifts to him.

With all the army business completed, I called Jose in, and we told the general of our plan to build homesteads around the "Big Ole Rock". He wanted to know why, so we told him that it was a good location for a small town due to the nearby river. He liked how we were thinking so he didn't ask any more questions. Jose and I asked if we could file a claim for our planned ranch and homestead, and he confirmed how Jose and I could do so. He was so happy to hear that we wanted to do something else in our lifetimes. He told me how happy he was that I had lived through so much adversity and come through it a better man than I probably would have been had I not done so.

He encouraged me to see my life so far as a great adventure. Something that so many would never have in their lifetime. So many peoples' lives were basically programmed by others, causing them to just live to get through. He told me, "You have more courage than any man I know, including myself. You must think about all of that as you plan your future." I thanked him, holding back tears, and got out of there before I broke down.

As Jose and I were leaving, I thought about how he spoke about the Indian troubles being behind us and the government taking the lead in managing areas of the West more and more as territories would eventually become states and crossroads would become towns or cities. I felt that was why he had given that speech. By doing so with Jose there, I felt that he was telling him the same thing.

It was true that the gold rush out in California and Nevada was the current big concern for the U.S. government. More and more soldiers were being transferred out that way, but the general would not transfer me. He didn't say it, but I got the feeling that this fort's days might be numbered. If that were true, the timing of our find at the secret canyon couldn't have been any better.

The general was so wise and was such a great man. It was easy to understand why he was so respected by the officers and those in Washington. The men here at the fort, especially me, would do anything that he asked of us. I truly hoped that we would be friends for a very long time.

The process for filing for a homestead was simple. We had to do some convincing to get the land office to understand why we wanted that "Big Ole Rock" as part of our homestead. No one else wanted it or any of the land within miles of it, so we got the "Big Ole Rock" and about twelve hundred acres surrounding it.

That "Big Ole Rock" was technically wasteland according to the U.S. government. We knew better, but that was our secret for now.

Jose and I had totted back some of that gold and, during the following months, we managed to turn it into cash. That was part of our plan for paying for land improvements. We would take trips to areas where miners were finding gold to trade gold for cash. No one at the fort knew we were doing that, and since we never did the exchange in the same mining camp, we never attracted much attention. Thank goodness for the railroads that allowed us to travel so quickly.

Once the land was legally ours and we had told the women of our good fortunes, we would exchange larger amounts of gold for cash to pay for goods and services to build the ranch houses, barns, and other structures. For now, only Jose and I needed to know why we took those trips and never came back with any horses.

We were landowners within six months and could not have been any happier. Jose and I drafted a partnership agreement and signed it. He was surprised that I could read and write, so I had to tell him the story of how that came to be.

He made the sign of the cross on his chest, shook his head, and said that I was one hell of a lucky man. Once we had that all done legally, we were ready to put the full plan into action.

We would get the homestead started as the government required to establish ownership. Then we would start rounding up the livestock we wanted and hire some workers to live there full-time while Jose completed his tour of duty with the army. I only worked as a scout as the army needed me, so I would spend most of my time on the homestead.

A good drink of whiskey was the best way to seal such a deal, so we went to the house to celebrate for a while. We also had to make some more plans and decide how to tell the women. We had purposely not told them or any of the soldiers or army folks about the gold because it wasn't smart to let too many people know your business. Especially when a lot of money was involved.

That thought took me back to my youth. One of the primary warrior creeds was understanding the need for secrecy. Once again, I thanked the Great Spirit Warrior for protecting me and I was thankful for my good fortune.

CHAPTER 13: THE GREATEST BATTLE I FOUGHT

Jose and I gathered our ladies together to tell them about the rest of our good fortunes and how we would share the gold and build the homestead. They were both in shock at first, but then so happy to hear the news that we had to interrupt their planning for buying everything that they could think about.

We explained that we couldn't just appear to be rich overnight for fear that the whites would find a way to steal or legally take our claim. They had to agree that we could live better now but living like rich folks would have to wait a few years. We had to do everything that the law required and meet all the government requirements to get the clear deed for the land. It was important that no unforeseen technicalities would be introduced by someone wanting to take the land, but mainly the gold, from us. They understood and would do what we felt was best.

With the women in the know, there was no stopping our progress now. The American dream that we heard the whites talk of so often was going to be realized by us, two minority families. Yes, this America was the land of opportunity. And with lady luck on our side, we would own our portion of the American West.

Later that day, I took a short ride because I needed some quiet time. As I rode, I thought about all of this more. Time had a way of teaching you the greatest lessons. You just needed to survive the battles and grow stronger because of them. We all faced our separate unknowns each day. We all had to be ready and willing to work for and even fight for what we wanted most. If you took a journey back through your life, you realized that how you lived was what defined who you eventually became. So many people paid very little attention to such thoughts; they just settled for trying to have fun. In the end, fun was all that they ended up with, and that didn't bring you much comfort when you wanted to kick your own ass for passing up all those opportunities for adventures and bettering yourself.

The homestead was built during the following years as the government required. Jose and I caught about fifty wild horses and started breeding the mustang mares with Gvnige and Ole Lightning. After a couple of years, most of the mares had dropped foals, and we had a good start on a fine herd of horses. We kept some of the mustang mares separated to continue breeding them with the wild stallions, because we wanted to preserve those magnificent horses. We had bought some cows and bulls as well, and that herd was starting to grow too.

Jose had gotten his discharge from the army, so he and his wife had moved out to the homestead. I had built a fine house for Sophie and our family in the spot Sophie had picked out. She loved the homestead and had been going out there on the weekends to help me with the house.

A couple of new families settled out near us, and several of the families living adjacent to the fort settlement were in the process of moving out that way.

The hired workers, mostly Mexicans, had done a good job building everything and had started on the walls that Jose and I wanted around the houses, just in case we had to defend our homestead.

I had just one last thing to do: marry Sophie. That was weighing heavy on my mind more and more as the wedding day approached. I didn't understand why, but something was trying to make it to the front of my mind. I went back through the recent months and just couldn't figure out what was troubling me. So, I stopped doing everything and just thought.

The wedding plans were finalized, and it was a couple days before the date we set. My nerves were about worn out, but why? Sophie was so happy, and that was what mattered the most to me. She wasn't as happy about the fortune as she was about us being a family and living the rest of our days together, caring for each other and comforting ourselves through all of life's storms. Her early life wasn't as tragic as mine, but she had endured hardships. I loved her more than anything, and I liked her more than I loved her. She was my world and my inspiration for living, yet I felt something wasn't right in my heart.

I knew that she accepted who and what I was, and I knew she welcomed the new life that we would live. I knew she loved me as much as I loved her. No, the issue was not Sophie; I realized that the issue was within me. I still had this emptiness that I had not been able to get rid of.

I thought, *was it the shame that I felt for being captured at sixteen and not making sure that my family was safe? Was it the haunting memories of being in the belly of that damn ship, a slave or a runaway? Was it the knowledge that I had killed for vengeance after Sleeping Bird was murdered? Was it all of the killing that I had done for the army? Was it all the nights that I spent alone, wondering if I would live, if I would be thought of as a great warrior by the Great Spirit Warrior?*

Those and other questions kept clouding my thinking and tearing at my soul. I had to know that I was free of it all to assume the role of husband for such a fine woman as my Sophie. I needed to think. I needed to get rid of that emptiness. I needed to be whole to be what Sophie expected of me, to be what Sophie deserved.

I thought of the secret canyon, so I decided to head there to see if I could fix myself. I was always at peace there, so maybe it had some mystical power that would help me sort things out.

I had no assignment to do, so I saddled Ole Lightning, loaded all my weapons, and headed for the hills. I always got inspired as I looked at the big sky, the hills, and the wide-open country. I enjoyed the ride, but I never stopped thinking about what was troubling me. When I got to the secret canyon, the answer had still not been revealed to me. I kept riding the winding path into its depths and thinking. And as Sophie always encouraged me to do, I was praying, too, because I needed the answer to have joy in my heart.

As I approached the inner wall to the secret canyon, I was still looking for my answers. I took in that great view for a moment and went to the pool to water Ole Lightning. As he drank, I dismounted and looked up toward heaven.

I didn't have a lot of experience praying, but I got down on my knees and I tried anyway. My message was simple: "Lord, help me to understand what to do. I have been fighting since I was a child. It is all that I have ever known and, in a way, all that I have wanted to do. I need to find peace in my heart. Please help me understand what I must do."

I didn't hear any voices or see no burning bush. I didn't float in the air or feel the earth trembling, but I believed that if there was an answer, it was here in the secret canyon.

I was looking for a sign, something that would help me understand, so I just knelt there in silence, hoping. I didn't know if I was there minutes or hours because time didn't really matter if I couldn't find the answer. What mattered was that I wasn't leaving until I had a clear understanding of what was wrong with me. I couldn't be the man Sophie deserved until I knew. No, I was staying until I knew the answer.

I was about to stand up to get mounted and head to the camping area when I heard this soft sound that echoed around the canyon walls. I knew that I was the only person there, for Ole Lightning would have warned me if there was anyone else there.

As I turned, trying to locate the source of the soft sound, I was standing face-to-face with Tall Knives' widow. It was as if she had been watching and listening to me. She didn't say anything; she just reached up and touched my cheek with her small hand and smiled at me.

That touch felt just like that of my mother. The sparkling in her eyes was like the sparkles I remembered seeing in Sleeping Bird's eyes. She pointed to her heart, and I knew there was a message in that gesture, so I closed my eyes to make sure that I was seeing what my mind was telling me was there.

When I opened my eyes, she wasn't there no more. I blinked my eyes, looking around to be comforted by her again, but she was gone. I couldn't even tell that she had ever been there at all.

I was confused, as if the enemy was overpowering me in battle. I called on the Great Spirit Warrior to help me understand how to win this battle. It was then that a vision of my family and all of my village elders came to me. They were gathered around my American friends; Winter Wind, Fighting Bear, Chief Buffalo Killer, Tall Knives, the general, Jose, Maria and Sophie. That was when I got it.

Reliving my life was meant to cleanse my soul of those troubling times. I realized why I couldn't find the answer. I kept looking for the enemy around me, but the enemy was within me. Shame and hate had been driving me all these years. They were the enemy, not things outside myself. My dreams after my injuries, the weeks I spent thinking in my house, drifting in and out of consciousness, all of it was to help me find this enemy that was eating at me from the inside.

For the first time since arriving in America, I realized that I was fighting a battle with an enemy that was within me. I needed to let my great memories comfort my tormented soul. They would be my new weapons of war. In time they would conquer the enemy within me and allow me to live peacefully.

The clouds seemed to have been rolled away in my conscience, and I could see the bright sunny sky. The weight of burdens I had been carrying would be carried by the great memories that Sophie and I would make together from now on. Her love would bring me peace and joy, and that would comfort my soul.

I realized at that moment that I didn't need to fight being in America; I needed to embrace it, enjoy it, and achieve all of the American dream. How I got here was not the issue; how I lived tomorrow and the day after that and so forth would continue to define me.

America wasn't my birth home, but it was my home now. Was Africa the same as when I left, better, or had it fallen further behind? Did it matter or not? In America, I suffered, yet I had made myself an American warrior by gaining my freedom and coming west to fulfill what I thought was my purpose in life.

I had made myself an American pioneer by helping to settle the West. I had made myself an American hero by helping to make the West a safe place to live. I knew now that I must realize that I became a greater warrior here than I ever could have been in Africa.

The Great Spirit Warrior corrected the wrongs I had suffered in my life, and I owed it to him and myself to never do wrong just because I could. From this day forward, I had to let someone else do that while I developed a greater peace within myself.

I had to get my ass back to the fort and marry my Sophie and live to grow old together. I had to protect my new life and my new family just as my father died trying to do back in Africa.

I was already feeling different, for I was crying for the first time since Sophie agreed to marry me. I stood up, looked up toward the heavens, and thanked the Great Spirit Warrior for all that he had done for me. I knew I would never need to call on the Great Spirit Warrior again, so I wiped the remaining tears off my cheeks and mounted Ole Lightning.

He nickered as if he understood all I had just gone through. And, without me urging him, he set a fast pace, heading back to the fort. I saw more beauty on that trail home than I had ever noticed before, for my heart was no longer hurting; it was loving.

I was feeling better than I remembered feeling in my whole life. I no longer needed the Great Spirit Warrior, for I had fought my greatest battle today and won. I had lived the American dream, and I would continue living the American dream as a new man.

Tall Knives was right about the secret canyon. Being rich was a benefit, but in the secret canyon, I found myself. Yes, I, the one and only Buffalo Scout, legally named Mr. Raymond Dean Jackson, was an American hero, riding home to marry Sophie, the best woman in this world.

CHAPTER 14: THE BUFFALO SCOUT, LARGER THAN LIFE

The next day, Sophie and I had a small wedding at the fort. Neither of us had any family that we knew of, so the people that we worked with were the only ones there. She looked so lovely in that new dress that we ordered from one of those eastern city stores. I even dressed up in a suit. It was the first time that I had worn a suit. Even though I was looking fine, if I had to say so myself, I just couldn't understand why people dressed like that.

Jose and his wife stood with us at the altar, just as great friends should. We had a great party afterward in my barn. Jose and his wife had decorated it. Ole Lightning was wearing a fancy saddle; a wedding gift from the general. A few of the soldiers played music and sang to entertain us. I knew that it was the greatest day of my life as I watched Sophie show happiness that I had never seen before.

She moved in with me at the house I still had close to the fort. We had a very happy temporary home there until we moved out to the homestead for good about a month later. She made that little house look like a home in just a few days.

There were a lot of old things that I thought I wanted but got rid of just because she asked me why I had them. When I couldn't give a good answer, she would point to the door, and I got rid of them. It is amazing what a man in love will do to keep his woman happy.

Jose and I had retired earlier, so we had enough time to complete the houses and barns with corrals on our homestead. The workers were almost finished with building the protective walls around the houses, barns, and corrals, and we moved out there permanently. We would build a big storehouse as well to keep supplies in and to hide our gold until it was ready to be transported to the mint.

We had already collected enough gold and taken it to several out-of-state mints to get enough money to buy all that we needed to build on our homestead. No one looked at you twice if you brought in about $500 of gold dust in a gold camp area.

We had already exchanged about $8,000 worth of gold, and you could not tell that we had even disturbed the bottom of our oasis pool in the secret canyon. Life for us had gotten pretty damn good, and we appreciated it.

I was retired, but still did some work for the army from time to time. As I traveled throughout the state and into surrounding states, I would hear tales about the buffalo soldier known as the Buffalo Scout. It made me proud to be talked about, but I didn't want to be seen as some superhuman person.

But, apparently, the adventures of the buffalo soldiers were an interesting part of the American western life to those back in the eastern states. So much so that there were books, statues, paintings, and photographs selling like hotcakes about them.

I wasn't interested in any of that because it reminded me of a time in my life that I fought my greatest battle to escape. I was past fighting for vengeance and killing for my country. I had Sophie, and we were living a very happy life. Living happily until I died was my only goal these days.

We had been out on the homestead for about a year, and everything was going just as Jose and I had planned it. There were a couple more homesteaders near our place, and they were the farmers that our settlement needed.

Once the general knew of the shortcut we all now used to get to the fort, he sent out small patrols a couple of times a week on training missions. They always made their way to our homestead, and I knew that was the general's way of providing us some additional protection and finding out how me and Jose were doing. We appreciated it and always served the soldiers a meal or coffee and cake if they were in a hurry. They didn't have much fighting to do anymore, so the men did a whole lot of training. I certainly hoped that they would not have to go into battle any time soon since I had gotten to know many of the soldiers and would hate for any of them to get hurt or die.

Late one afternoon, a soldier galloped up to the house to tell me that the general wanted to see me at the fort. I asked if all was okay, and he said that it was. I read the general's message while he waited for an answer. There was some official government business that needed to be addressed, and I needed to attend a meeting with the general and some gentlemen from the War Department in Washington.

I told Sophie and asked if she wanted to go with me, but she told me she had too much to do to take a day off. As I thought about her response, I realized that we had been out on the homestead for about a year, and she had become one fine horsewoman, gardener, and ranch boss lady in addition to being a great wife.

I thought about how the Mexican cowboys called her "gran jefa," so I just smiled and told the soldier that I would return with him.

The soldier spent the night after protesting like hell since we needed to be at the fort by noon the next day. He protested, saying that it had taken him most of a day to get out here. He was a new recruit, and apparently one of the junior officers had played a trick on him and sent him on the long route. I told him to relax because we would leave before daybreak and be there early.

He was not happy, but he knew about me and knew he could trust my judgment. We left the next morning, as planned, and he kept riding and saying that the route we were taking wasn't on the map that he had.

I told him he was right, and it was going to stay that way for now, but the army knew of it and used it weekly. He looked puzzled, so I told him that someone had played a trick on him.

He nodded, cracked a smile, stopped protesting and rode like hell to keep up with Ole Lightning. Taking the shorter route, we made it to the meeting by 11 a.m., leaving an hour to spare.

The men from the War Department had other business they had already completed, so they were waiting to meet the one and only Buffalo Scout. I greeted the general, and after the introductions were done, the man in charge asked me to stand up and meet him in a corner of the room.

I looked at the general, and he gave me the okay, so I moved to the corner to meet the man. He spoke to me quickly and quietly, but he had a hard time looking me in the eye. I was used to whites acting that way, so I just ignored it. He was the main assistant for the secretary of state and had come out here to recognize me for bravery and my fifteen years of service to the U.S. government. He did his best to be nice and official, but I could tell that he didn't really want to be here. He told me that the president and the secretary of defense, along with the secretary of state, wanted to recognize me for my accomplishment and bravery.

He handed me a small case with several metals. He told me that they were reserved for military personnel only, but I qualified to receive them due to my service for the army. He also gave me a box containing a gold watch. I accepted them with thanks, placed them in my pockets as instructed, and took my seat again.

I had witnessed this type of ceremony a couple times before when white officers or soldiers were given similar medals of honor. The army always made a big to-do about it. There were dinners, a platform filled with high-ranking army personnel, and a parade ground full of soldiers standing at attention. Inside, I was steaming because I was receiving mine in the corner of the general's office in secret.

I knew what was going on, but I had so much respect for the general and did not want to do anything that could affect his career, so I took it like the man I had become. After all, I was an American hero, and my army career was over. Sophie was all that I really needed. As he walked away, I turned around and smiled at the general to let him know how much I appreciated him.

The next man spoke up, and some other men in suits came into the room. They were reporters and writers. They already knew about my missions and accomplishments since all of that was in the government records. They were here to get my personal statement and opinion about issues the western states were dealing with.

I answered them as best as I could, and the meeting was about to conclude. Then the general spoke up and made it very clear that he represented me still, as he always had since I came to the fort. He made the writers agree to royalty payments to me for any books written about my adventures in western America. Then he smiled and excused them. They left him the information necessary to find them back east, and after they left, he gave it to me.

We talked for about an hour afterward, and he explained how all that book writing worked. He told me that if my story was a good enough book to sell, I would get paid a lot of money. I just smiled and felt that the time had come to share some things with the general, my friend and protector. I didn't keep very many secrets from him, and I knew that I could trust him with my life.

I told him about the gold in the secret canyon and told him it was okay to show the shortcut trail to get to our homestead on the army maps for everyone else to use. I asked him to keep the gold secret until Jose and I had the official deed for the land. He said, "Your secret is safe with me, you sneaky old fox." We laughed about it and shook hands. We talked more and had some laughs about all the great times that we had shared. It was a great time for a drink, so the general produced a bottle, and we had ourselves a couple good ones.

As we drank that good whiskey, I leaned forward in my chair, pulled out the document I had in my coat pocket, and smiled at the general as I held out my hand toward him. That caused him to lean forward in his chair, giving me that "what is this" look. As I pushed the document toward him, I told him that Jose and I would need some management assistance when we publicized that we had found gold.

He was opening the document, so he raised his head, appearing to be wondering why, I said, "You know how it is to try making deals when you are a black man." He shook his head, indicating his dislike and said that he did understand that.

I told him that Jose and I had planned for this and agreed to a fee of ten percent for his assistance. Smiling, the general said that he thought it was a great deal and indicated that it also was a timely offer since he had planned to get out of the army at the end of the year. We shook hands and had some whiskey to seal the deal.

Several months later, it was hard to pick up a newspaper from one of the eastern cities and not find an article or two about the buffalo soldiers in the western states. I just wondered if any of them would invite any of us buffalo soldiers to dine with them in their big, fine homes.

Then I thought, *oh well, being a legend isn't one of the important things in my life*. Because, while kneeling in the silence of the secret canyon, I had learned that finding peace of mind was all the recognition I truly needed.

Sophie and the homestead with Jose were my peace of mind. With a little luck, the voices of children would be heard in that homestead soon, making it the home that I so desired.

Several months later, I went to Washington, D.C. with the general to meet some of the top government officials. I appeared before Congress to receive some shiny metals along with some of the other famous buffalo soldiers.

The general also took me to visit some of the book publishers that had been sending me royalty checks for books written about me. They were all as excited as kids getting a new puppy, and I was just thinking about my Sophie and wanting to get home.

The president even invited us buffalo soldiers to come to the White House, but we still had to enter through the servants' entrance. He took some pictures with us, but we were not invited to have dinner with him. He did assign the top military officers to hold a dinner in our honor. We felt proud, but we knew that had we been white, we would have had dinner with the president.

Oh, what a tale we could have told our children and grandchildren had we gotten to eat with the president in the White House. As I thought about it, we still had a mighty nice story to tell. We were western heroes, decorated soldiers, and some of the famous peacekeepers of the West.

That made me think of home, so I was glad we were catching the midnight train known as the Western Flyer. We would take it to Denver, stop to talk to the managers of the Denver Mint, and then head south to New Mexico Territory: home sweet home.

CHAPTER 15: FAMILY LIVING

The homestead was doing great after about five years of hard work and we had our deeds in hand. We had a good herd of horses and cattle, and the market for both was thriving. New Mexico Territory was much closer to California and the rest of the West Coast states and territories than most cattle and horse ranches, so shipping the livestock by train made it much easier for us to deliver to them.

The neighboring settlers were making good crops along the river, thanks to the engineered irrigation levees and dams. It was great land once you did the hard work to make it productive.

More and more settlers were requesting homesteads in the area, and there was talk of starting a real town around the general store. Jose and I had the only gold mine in the area, but others were crawling throughout the hills in search of some after we went public about the gold we found.

Once there was a town, Jose and I would start our own bank. The name would be the Lightning Miner's Bank. The settlers had agreed to name the town Secret Canyon, thanks to the efforts of Sophie and Maria.

The general had started working with Jose and me on the mining business, and he established a small homestead near ours. He had liked our grand plan to start a town and was helping us and the settlers with the legal paperwork. That meant Jose and I didn't have to bother with trying to do that, so we concentrated on our gold mining and raising livestock.

With the general's help, we recruited workers to do the mining, and he insisted that some of the discharged buffalo soldiers got the first chances to fill the jobs. He was a real man and a great friend, so not much of what he did surprised me.

Jose had hired some of his Mexican family members that were good with horses and cattle, so they were our cowboys. Yes, we had become some important American minorities, and we were doing our best to help other minorities get their piece of the American dream.

I didn't know much about ranching, but it didn't take the Mexicans long to teach me. Before long, I could rope and brand with the best of them. Being almost forty, I let the youngsters do all the bronc busting because I still had good sense. I didn't want any broken bones at my age. I had enough nagging injuries from years gone by.

Besides, Sophie had sworn to kill me if she caught me doing anything foolish, and I could tell she meant it because she had her hands on her hips and that stern look in her eyes. There was a hint of a smile that said, "Try me, and you will regret it," so I knew I needed to be a good husband and obey.

We were isolated, so every employee had to be able to help us defend our property. We purchased the latest and best firearms that money could buy and taught the workers army tactics. The general came in real handy for that, and judging by the pep in his step, he was enjoying drilling the workers.

We even had cannons on the walls around the two homes. Some said that our homestead looked like a fort. That was just about right, and that was what Jose and I wanted everybody to think and believe.

Basically, we ran it like it was a fort. The entrance to the secret canyon was behind the walls of my homestead, so we had extra artillery in guardhouses near its entrance.

Those two Gatling guns would hold off an army of raiders. The discharged soldiers that we employed got a share of the profits, so they would defend the homesteads with their lives.

With the ranching in good hands, we had started mining into the face of the canyon wall and discovered that there was a large vein of almost solid gold. As we dug into the rock, more and more water flowed into the oasis pond, carrying more gold pebbles with it. Even with the greater flow of water, the pool level didn't rise enough to really notice.

The mining engineer that we hired had already engineered a sieve system to catch the larger gold pebbles, and each night we used tools to dredge the pool bottom to collect the smaller gold specks.

Tall Knives knew what he was talking about relative to his revelation of the secret canyon. I thanked God daily that he had no interest in being rich. I figured that he, as I, valued other things much more than the gold. He liked the open sky, the mountains, trapping and fishing, and living off the land. He had told me that he ran away from civilization and wanted nothing to do with it. I couldn't do that, but within the walls of the secret canyon, I did learn the secret to dealing with it.

After my revelation, I fully understood why he didn't give a damn about gold. For once you discover your purpose, there is not much that you will allow to disrupt your peace and joy.

The general had worked out a deal with Wells Fargo to transport the gold shipments and have them escorted by several heavily armed guards. Thank God we had not lost a shipment yet.

I understood that we were blessed, so I kept planning with the general to have alternate means of transporting the gold shipments. Hopefully, the railroads would add the spur that we had requested once the town was recognized as such.

With Mexican workers and the farmers supplying the produce we needed, Sophie stayed in the house much more. We had our first child the second year after moving to the homestead and the next one two years after that. Number three was on the way, and she was already talking about another one.

I had hoped to change her mind about all that because I married her to love her, not to have her birthing a baby every other year. Problem was, she was in charge of having babies, and she wanted more.

I had started to understand why there were times that my father just wanted to be gone for a while. I certainly wanted to, but like my father, I knew the wife was not going to stand for it. It was best to act like a fully grown child and do what Mother said.

I was about forty, and I wanted to be able to watch my children grow up to be adults. My father never saw that, and I fought my greatest battle to ensure that the same thing didn't happen to me.

The sun was getting low in the western sky and I still had work I needed to get busy doing, so I did. Sophie had her mind made up, and we could afford to have lots of children, so why not? I smiled at that thought and got busy doing my chores because she was standing in the door with one hand on a hip and the other one holding our beautiful little girl's arm. Smiling, I waved at them and got to work.

After that third child was born, I thought how amazing it was that with time, everything in your life seemed to make a full circle. You went from being a child to being a man. Then you had children and watched them go from being children to being adults. One could feel like that cat chasing its tail and seeming to accomplish nothing. Yet if you really studied your life, you would remember all the great memories, accomplishments, and joyful moments. They would overshadow the hurts and pain that you suffered and always bring you back to your purpose for living.

I walked outside to watch the sun set in the western sky. After enjoying that view for a minute or two, I looked over my shoulder, toward the east. I hadn't told anyone yet, but I had one big mission left to do when the children were older. I would return to Africa to find the village that was my home. Hopefully, some of the villagers, and maybe some of my family, would still be there.

I was going to make that voyage back across the Atlantic. But this time, I wouldn't be traveling in no slave ship named "Swamp Devil". I would be traveling in style as a man, as a father, as a husband, and as an American hero.

With the blessing of God, I would find some of my family and bring them to the American home that I paid for with the suffering I endured from the time that I was betrayed, captured, enslaved, and stripped of my dignity and pride in my homeland. That was until I, the warrior, escaped all of that to become an American hero. The same American hero who had fought and won the greatest battle of his life and became the husband and father that God meant for him to be. The father who would return to his native home with the hope of finding the treasure that he left behind so many years ago.

The end

ABOUT THE AUTHOR

Stephen McDonald was born in the 1950s to great parents. He is a graduate of Texas A&M University and had a successful thirty-eight-year career in the construction industry. Writing is a hobby for him, for it allows him to share his thoughts and experiences with others. Keep in touch with Stephen on his website: discoveringyourtreasures.com.

www.ingramcontent.com/pod-product-compliance
Lightning Source LLC
Chambersburg PA
CBHW061444030726
47503CB00005B/1561